I0727374

DEADRAGE

ANTHONY GIANGREGORIO

OTHER LIVING DEAD PRESS BOOKS
BLOOD RAGE, DEAD END: A ZOMBIE NOVEL
BOOK OF THE DEAD: A ZOMBIE ANTHOLOGY
BOOK OF THE DEAD 2: NOT DEAD YET
BOOK OF THE DEAD 3: DEAD AND ROTTING
END OF DAYS: AN APOCALYPTIC ANTHOLOGY VOLUME 1 & 2
DEAD HOUSE: A ZOMBIE GHOST STORY
THE ZOMBIE IN THE BASEMENT (FOR ALL AGES)
THE LAZARUS CULTURE: A ZOMBIE NOVEL
DEAD WORLDS: UNDEAD STORIES VOLUMES 1, 2, 3 & 4
FAMILY OF THE DEAD, REVOLUTION OF THE DEAD
RANDY AND WALTER: PORTRAIT OF TWO KILLERS
KINGDOM OF THE DEAD
THE MONSTER UNDER THE BED
DEAD TALES: SHORT STORIES TO DIE FOR
ROAD KILL: A ZOMBIE TALE
DEADFREEZE, DEADFALL
SOUL EATER, THE DARK,
RISE OF THE DEAD,
DARK PLACES
VISIONS OF THE DEAD
THE DEADWATER SERIES
DEADWATER
DEADWATER: Expanded Edition
DEADRAIN, DEADCITY
DEADWAVE, DEAD HARVEST
DEAD UNION, DEAD VALLEY
DEAD TOWN, DEAD SALVATION
DEAD ARMY (coming soon)
COMING SOON
DEAD HISTORY: A ZOMBIE ANTHOLOGY
THE WAR AGAINST THEM: A ZOMBIE NOVEL by Jose Vazquez
DEAD WORLDS: UNDEAD STORIES VOLUME 5
THE CHRONICLES OF JACK PRIMUS by Michael D. Griffiths

DEAD RAGE

Copyright © 2009 by Anthony Giangregorio
ISBN   Softcover ISBN 13: 978-1-935458-41-8   ISBN 10: 1-935458-41-8
All rights reserved. No part of this book may be reproduced or transmitted in any form or by any means, electronic or mechanical, including photocopying, recording, or by any information storage and retrieval system, without permission in writing from the copyright owner.
This is a work of fiction. Names, characters, places and incidents either are the product of the author's imagination or are used fictitiously, and any resemblance to any actual persons, living or dead, events, or locales is entirely coincidental. This book was printed in the United States of America. For more info on obtaining additional copies of this book, contact:
www.livingdeadpress.com

FOREWORD

Welcome again to yet another chapter in my ruminations.

If you've been reading my work, then you know I love zombies and what they represent.

But to me a zombie doesn't necessarily have to be a walking corpse. To me, a zombie is anytime a person is not themselves. Whether the soul is gone from the body or if the person is just acting contrary to their normal behavior, to me that signifies what a zombie is.

I'm sure most of you have heard someone refer to a friend who has worked way to many hours or a mother who has just had a new baby and hasn't slept in a week, and they'll comment on how they look like a zombie.

Well, that's the same thing.

In the book you hold in your hands, while the people aren't dead, they have been overtaken by a virus that sends them into a murderous rage, wanting to kill all who stand in their way.

They've been altered.

While this book is a work of fiction perhaps, one day it might be a window into our future. With the threat of biological attack from Middle Eastern countries seeming to be always looming over all our heads and the threat of invisible terrorists jumping out and trying to kill us every five minutes, these kinds of stories become closer to reality than we might want to admit to ourselves.

Now no, I don't want to wake up one morning and find that civilization has collapsed, and no, I wouldn't want to have to spend every waking second just trying to survive.

But what if it did happen? Could you, the reader, be able to survive in a world turned upside down? Or would you be one of the first killed as the rampaging horde flooded through your town.

Frankly I'd rather not find out.

Better not to think about it, after all, it's only a book and tomorrow is another day.

I hope.

CHAPTER 1

"HURRY UP, THEY'RE gaining on us!" Bill Thompson yelled while running down the school hallway, the slap of dozens of heavy footsteps following him with murderous glee. There was something else behind those footsteps.

Was it growling?

Yes, it was. A low, guttural rumble that turned his blood to ice, sounding like a hundred snarling wolves were in pursuit.

As he ran, pictures of school photos and paintings from the second grade elementary brushed by his vision, fluttering on the hallway walls. It was a reminder to how things had been, how normal the world had been only a few short days ago.

Behind him were four other survivors, each looking as bad as he felt. Elizabeth was in the lead, followed by Janice. Behind the two women was an old man in his late seventies. His name was Walter, if Bill remembered right. Behind Walter was another woman, Kathy Myers. Bill remembered someone mentioning her name when he'd been introduced to the entire group.

That had been three days ago.

That had been before people starting acting crazy and your neighbor tried to kill you if you looked at him the wrong way.

Bill put on another burst of speed as he rounded the hallway corner. His shoes slipped on the ceramic tile and he almost crashed to the floor, but only a sheer miracle kept him upright.

He just had to make it to the end of the hall. The ladder leading to the roof access was only a few yards away and he knew he would make it the moment he turned the corner. He glanced over his shoulder to see the others behind him, Walter not moving as fast due to his age and Kathy was helping him along.

But it was when Bill looked over their shoulders, behind them, that he really felt a cold shiver of dread slide down his back. Behind the running couple were more than twenty crazed people charging down the hallway. Bill saw the faces of the first few when they ran under one of the fluorescent ceiling lights that still worked. Their faces were set in feral countenances, their tongues hanging out like wild animals as they ran. But it was the eyes that were the most unsettling thing to behold. Their eyes were wild and mad, as if whoever lived there had moved out and wouldn't be back for a few days; or maybe never, and the only thing still home was rage.

Pure unadulterated rage.

When he was only a few feet from the ladder, he slowed and stopped. Both Elizabeth and Janice ran by him, then quickly scurried up the metal rungs. Bill watched the crazies slowly gain on Walter and Kathy.

"Come on, they're going to catch you!" He screamed to them, hoping by some miracle of God they would manage to outrun the blood thirsty horde.

Kathy started running faster, dragging Walter behind her and it looked like both of them would reach the ladder in time until Kathy broke a heel on her high-priced shoes. The two inch heel gave out and slid away from her, and her leg buckled, not expecting the shift in weight.

She fell heavily to the floor, dragging Walter down with her. Both screamed in surprise and Bill heard the distinctive sound of bone breaking the moment Walter's hip struck the tile floor.

Bill hesitated for only a moment, weighing his options. The S&W .38 revolver in his hand would certainly deter a few of the crazies, but the others in the crowd wouldn't care. He decided he had no choice but to leave them where they'd fallen; despite the fact he was sentencing them to death. A small voice screamed at him to go help them, that he was a monster no worse than the crazies trying to kill them if he left them to be torn apart and murdered, but he forced the voice down, his own fear, his own survival instinct taking control of his mind.

"I'm sorry, but there's just too damn many," he called to them, then turned and sprinted towards the ladder. The others ahead of him were already gone, having climbed back to the roof.

Bill reached the ladder, placed his feet on the bottom two rungs and turned to look over his shoulder one last time. He could only watch as both Walter and Kathy were buried in an avalanche of snarling bodies. Kathy's yellow dress could be seen for a few brief seconds, until it was smothered under body after body. Their screams filled the hallway, bouncing off the metal lockers to be lost amidst the guttural growls of their attackers.

For one instant there was a window between the bodies and Bill saw Kathy pull a pencil from somewhere on her person and jam it into the eye of a crazed man. The man barely slowed, but instead jumped on top of her to continue ripping her apart, his eye now dripping white and pinkish ooze down his cheek until he would flick his head, sending the pudding like ichor flying away to land on another ravenous soul.

Bill looked away, nor able to witness the carnage any longer, and scurried up the ladder just as the first crazy reached the bottom of the ladder. Bill climbed onto the roof, rolling away from the hatch just as another man slammed the metal hatch down, sliding a jury-rigged metal bar through the latch to prevent it from being opened from the inside. The sounds of banging could be heard below the hatch while Bill's attackers tried fruitlessly to gain access to the roof. The hatch repeatedly jumped with each punch and the unmistakable sound of bare flesh on metal floated through the metal.

Bill lay on his back, barely feeling the loose gravel digging into his skin through his shirt. His breathing came in heavy gasps and for a second he wondered if this would finally be the time he had a heart attack. He remembered his last visit to the doctor's office. When his blood test had come back and he'd found out his cholesterol was way too high, as was his blood pressure. It wasn't much of a surprise, of course. Just like more than seventy percent of America, he indulged in fast food and even faster snacks, chomping on pork rinds and potato chips till the cows came home.

His doctor had advised him to watch his diet and start exercising before he ended up having a heart attack or a stroke.

A smile creased his lips as he lay there panting and looking up at the few stars visible through the low cloud cover, and he started to chuckle. Realizing he would be dead long before his heart gave out.

"What are you laughing at? What the hell could possibly be so funny?" A blond-haired man in his late twenties asked. "Where are Kathy and the old man?"

Bill turned his eyes from the night sky to look up at the scowling countenance of Mike Fogarty. The man's eyes were wide open and his mouth was set in a tight grimace as he stared down at Bill's supine body.

"Nothing's funny, Mike, not a damn thing; as for Kathy and Walter…they didn't make it."

Another woman came over to Bill and looked down at him. Her red hair blew across her face from the light breeze coming in from the north and she casually brushed it away so she could see.

"What are you talking about? She has to be with you. Come on, Bill, where's Kathy and the old man?"

Bill frowned long and deep, and with a moan of his own from aching muscles, he climbed to his feet. He was almost fifty and right now, at this precise moment in time, he felt every year bearing down on him.

He placed his hands on her shoulders and let out another deep sigh, this one with an underlay of loss.

"I'm really sorry, Melissa, but her shoe broke and she fell. Before she could get back to her feet, the bastards were on top of her. She never had a chance, Walter either."

Melissa's face froze in shock, her eyes barely moving. Then she turned away and started to cry. Kathy had been her best friend for more than half her life and the shock of her death was hitting her pretty hard.

Mike pushed into Bill with a sharp finger, the swung his arm and pointed at the roof access. "Okay fine, that explains Kathy, but where's Walter. Did his shoe break, too?"

Bill pushed the man away from him and put his hand in front of him to keep it that way. "No, his damn shoe didn't break. He was old, for Christ's sake, and he couldn't outrun the bastards. Kathy tried to help him and it cost her, her life. I told you the man was too damn old to help, but would you listen to me? Hell no!" Bill was now screaming at Mike, letting out the guilt and frustration he felt for leaving two of his team behind.

Mike wasn't about to give in until an older woman stepped between them. Her name was Marie Connelly and she had arrived at the school with Walter. They'd been friends and if anyone should be upset that the older man was dead, then it should be her.

Marie's gray hair never moved from the stiff breeze on the roof, all the hairspray she had applied before arriving doing its job well. Two small intelligent eyes peeked out from behind a pair of large eyeglasses. Her smile was enough to make any man or woman think of their grandmother and she used everything she had to calm the two men down.

"All right, you two, that's enough." She looked to Mike. "Now, Mike, Walter wanted to go with them and he was too stubborn to listen to anyone. It's just a shame that Kathy had to go down with the old fool," she said soothingly with a touch of loss.

Mike wasn't about to give in that easily. Since he'd arrived a day after Bill, he had been gunning for lead man in their little survival group. Though most of the others leaned toward Bill for the role as leader, Mike felt he could do a better job and tried to undermine Bill at every opportunity.

The deaths of both Kathy and Walter were just another excuse for Mike to try and grab the reigns of power, as far as Bill was concerned. As long as Mike didn't make him do anything that would risk his own life, Bill could care less who was actually in charge, but if the others wanted him to lead, then he was happy to go along with it.

Mike pointed to the gun in Bill's hand. "Fine, Marie, if you want to stick up for him then you know I can't stop you, but what about the gun? Why didn't he use it to save them?"

Bill spit onto the roof and took a step forward again. "Because there were too damn many of them, you dumb shit! Even if I'd tried, after the first few shots they would have overwhelmed me, too. The crazy bastards aren't scared of anything, you know that!"

Marie turned to Mike and stepped closer to the young man. "He's got a point, Mike, and as soon as you calm down you'll realize he was right to leave them, distasteful as that had to be."

Mike was about to argue some more when his girlfriend, Becky, walked up to him and grabbed his hand. "Come on, honey, that's enough for now. You can talk about it more later, I'm lonely." Becky was a young woman in her early twenties with a figure that would make any man drool. Her long blonde hair reached down her back and caressed the top of her buttocks. Her blue eyes would make any male melt and she knew it. She used those same eyes now to pull Mike away from the others.

She bit her lower lip and cooed softy. "Please, baby, come keep me company, I'm cold and I need you to keep me warm."

Mike quickly gave in and began moving away with Becky like a small child being dragged by its mother when it eyes something pretty in a store window. She continued pulling him away from Marie and Bill, but then Mike slowed his retreat, turned, and stared Bill square in the face, pointing with his right index finger accusingly.

"This ain't over, old man, not by a long shot." Then he gave in and let his girlfriend pull him away.

Bill looked to Marie and grinned. "Thank you, Marie. I don't know what I'd do with out you."

She chuckled at that. "You don't? I would think the answer to that would be obvious. Either you or him would have to knock the other on his butt and settle the little feud you've both started."

Bill brought his hand to his chest and smiled sheepishly. "Me? I'm innocent in all of this and you know it."

She nodded, agreeably. "Perhaps, but you could still listen a little when the man talks. He may be young, but he has a good head on his shoulders. You shouldn't be so quick to dismiss him when he suggests something."

Bill turned away from her and looked out onto the street lining the front of the school.

"Please, that boy has some serious daddy issues to work out, and if you don't mind, I'd rather not be his surrogate. He's an arrogant bastard."

"Perhaps, Bill. But maybe he respects you more than you think and he's just too afraid to admit it. Have you ever thought of that?"

Bill frowned deeply. He hadn't actually. He resolved to take Marie's advice and try to listen more to Mike the next time they had a problem, and after the fiasco that downstairs in the school, it wouldn't be too much longer.

Bill thought back to how he and the others had found themselves being chased by a city full of ravenous killers.

After all of them had arrived at the school, as pairs or alone, everyone agreed they needed to close all the school's doors, then they could barricade themselves in until help arrived. Sooner or later the police or National Guard would straighten the mess of whatever was happening and haul all the crazies away.

Many of the lunatics had managed to infiltrate the school and so it had been agreed that until the school was locked down, the safest place to stay would be on the roof. And that was where they had stayed until lack of food and water became a concern. Down below was a cafeteria full of food and water, juice and milk.

After the first day the school had quieted down and Bill had snuck down the ladder to find the hallways almost completely deserted. After reporting his findings to the others, they had all agreed now was the time to close the school doors for good.

Walter had wanted to help, as did the three women. Bill had agreed. He wasn't in charge of anyone and if they wanted to help, then that was great, the more the merrier.

What he or the others didn't know was that the north side of the building was slowly filling up with more and more crazies, and the small group didn't find this out until after they'd cut through the gym. They'd been stopped in their tracks by more than a score of people with murder in their eyes. Behind them, more were entering the building with each tick of the clock.

Bill had called for a retreat and the group of five ran back the way they'd come, their only hope to make it back to the ladder and the relative safety of the roof. Bill had shot a few of the more adventurous of the crazies, but only when they came dangerously close to the groups retreating backs.

The wounded men and women dropped to the floor and were immediately trampled by their brethren.

After that, Bill had saved his bullets, realizing they were useless. The mob didn't care if one of their numbers was brought down; all they had were rage filled eyes for the five people trying to escape.

They'd almost made it, too, but for a pair of defective footwear.

With a sigh, Bill walked over to the rest of the survivors huddling around the gravel roof. There were a few others on the roof with him, but he couldn't remember all their names. A teenage boy, maybe twelve or thirteen sat quietly against an air conditioning unit. His younger brother was leaning against him, no more than four or five. The teen had told Marie how he'd witnessed his father kill his mother and then the raving father had turned his sights on the two boys. The teen had managed to lock both him and his brother in their bedroom and, then both had crawled out the window to the front lawn.

From there the teen had protected his brother until he'd seen the school. Not knowing where else to go, he'd taken a chance and had been lucky enough to find the rest of their small band of survivors. As Bill looked down at the two boys, their names finally came back to him. The older boy was Roger and the younger boy was Phillip.

Next to him was another man. He was about thirty or so and his eyes stared out over the roof. He had lost his wife before finally making it to the school and the man was still in shock. He hadn't uttered a single word since arriving, but just followed orders and sat quietly when not needed. Bill could only imagine what the man had seen. The only reason he knew about the man's wife was because of the bloody picture he'd held in his bloody hand when he arrived. It had been pretty easy after that to figure out what must have happened.

There were a few others, both men and women he didn't know. There really hadn't been much time for socializing.

It was mid summer and a cool, comfortable breeze blew over the roof. He wasn't looking forward to tomorrow when the sun would bake their heads with its rays. And the gravel on the roof would only help to amplify the heat. He decided to worry about tomorrow when it came.

He sat down next to Janice and Elizabeth. Both women were solemn after losing Kathy. He knew what they felt. Kathy had been a fun woman, full of smiles and always positive, despite everything she'd experienced before reaching the safety of the school.

And now she was dead, just another casualty in whatever was going on in the city and surrounding suburbs.

Screams and yells caused him to stand up and walk over to the edge of the roof.

Looking down, he saw the front lawn of the school was filled with people from all walks of life. Janitors stood next to lawyers and housewives next to mechanics. Some of their professions were easy to identify, some wore torn, ripped and sometimes bloody clothes, their identities a mystery other than whether they were male or female. They staggered around, jumping and pushing each other.

"There's more of them," he said to no one in particular.

Whatever was happening to people had happened to the crowd down below.

It had happened so gradually, at first no one had realized what was truly happening. In the beginning, the police had chalked it up to a few psychotics, a few unstable people that had finally lost what little sanity they'd been grasping on to. But then it continued to grow until the police couldn't contain all the outbreaks.

The news could only hypothesize about the origin of the psychosis. The words terrorist and biological warfare were tossed around until they meant nothing. But in the end all anyone had was guesses. The truth was no one knew what was happening. Outbreaks began appearing all over the world and flights were canceled, all planes grounded. Countries closed their borders quickly, but it was all a day late and a dollar short.

Whatever the virus was, it had reached every corner of the world and was consuming people at an astounding rate.

Before Bill had abandoned his home, the percentage figures on the local news estimated by the same time next week, the entire world would be infected.

But what the eggheads in Washington and across the world didn't realize was that a small portion of the population was immune to whatever was attacking humanity like rust on a Ford Chevy.

And though Bill had never won anything his entire life and frankly considered himself to be rather unlucky. It seems he'd won the most important lottery to ever be played by a human being.

Bill and all the others on the roof with him were somehow immune to the virus. And though that may sound like a good thing, and deep inside himself, Bill was glad he wasn't a raving lunatic, he also wondered if the ones below him, yelling and screaming like wild animals, were the lucky ones, and he and his fellow refugees were the unfortunates.

He looked across the treetops, where the skyline of Chicago could be seen a few miles away. It wasn't the same as before. Where once tall buildings glittered with the lights of a thousand windows, now it was dark, blending in with the night sky. Fires burned from some of the taller buildings, the smoke lost in the night sky. Off to his right, the Sears Tower burned like a beacon for approaching ships, the molten metal from the steel girders glowing white hot from the inferno slowly consuming it floor by floor.

He sighed heavily. He had no idea how they were supposed to survive what was happening to them, but he knew for a fact he wouldn't go down without a fight.

For now he decided to just rest. He'd earned it.

Sitting down next to Janice again, the woman flashed him a dull smile. He returned it, and with the sounds of the mad calling to him from below, he tried to relax, and for just a little while, close his eyes and forget what was becoming of the world and the people who dwelt on its surface.

Chapter 2

BILL OPENED HIS eyes and gazed around the roof, pulled from sleep at the sound of raised voices.

On the opposite side of the roof, both Becky and Mike were arguing.

He didn't know what the argument was about, but by the way Mike was waving his arms around, it looked like it might come to blows at any second.

Some of the others were also watching the couple, curious. Others could have cared less, only thinking of their problems and what they were going to do about them.

Bill rose to his feet, crossing the half dozen yards separating him from the arguing couple. Marie came up to his side and nodded in the direction of Mike and Becky.

"They're having quite the disagreement, aren't they?" She asked and stated to Bill with a wry smile.

"Seems so. As long as it's just words, I reckon it's none of our affair, but if it becomes physical…well, that's where I draw the line."

Marie nodded. "Nothing to do but wait then."

"Guess so," Bill said.

They stood together watching Mike and Becky, the two arguing like a married couple who'd spent far too many years together. Bill had to admit the little spitfire gave as well as she got. Bill watched Mike's face slowly growing more enraged. If he was going to pop, it would happen soon.

Becky took a step closer to Mike, so close she could probably smell his breath. That's when Mike pushed her away. The smaller woman fell back and landed on her butt, the gravel cushioning her fall, her hands digging divots in the small pebbles.

Mike advance on her and that was when Bill decided he needed to step in.

"Good luck," Marie said to his back as he walked away from her.

"Thanks, I think I'll need it," he answered over his shoulder.

Becky was just climbing to her feet again and sent a few choice imprecations at Mike. The man responded by raising his hand, preparing to strike her.

Bill closed the gap quickly and managed to reach Mike just as the blonde-haired man's hand was coming down to slap Becky. Bill wrapped his hand around the arm, halting the motion.

Mike turned to stare at Bill in shock, not quite believing the older man had the stones to try and stop him.

"Why, you old bastard. Finally decided to try and get a piece of me. Well, if you want some so bad, here!" Mike yelled and spun, sending his other fist towards Bill's jaw.

The punch was sloppy, but Mike was a strong man and Bill still saw stars for a few seconds. He backed away from the blow, shaking his head to clear it and rubbing his bruised jaw.

What Mike didn't know, couldn't know, was that Bill had been quite an accomplished boxer in college, though he tended to keep it to himself. And though many years had gone by since he'd left the academic walls of learning, he still knew how to handle himself.

Still shaking off the clumsy blow from Mike, Bill almost didn't see the next punch. Reflexes took over and Bill stepped to the side, Mike's punch going wide.

Gritting his teeth in anger, Bill decided the time for talk was definitely over.

Like Marie had said earlier, if the two men were ever going to co-exist together, one of them would have to knock some sense into the other.

Bill brought hands up in the classic boxer's stance and Mike started to laugh.

"What the hell is this?"

Bill said nothing, but answered by sending his first punch into Mike's side. The man doubled over from the blow, hardly believing it.

Sucking in gasps of air, he stood straight up and flexed his hands as they prepared to grasp Bill and tear him apart.

"That was a big mistake, old man," Mike wheezed.

Marie was closer now and she yelled out, trying to get them to stop, realizing someone could get hurt. "Both of you stop fighting this instant. We need to work together or all is lost."

Mike glanced at her fleetingly, his eyes never looking away from Bill.

"Screw that, old woman, he's had this coming ever since he got here, it's time to decide who's in charge once and for all." Then he lunged for Bill, arms wide to wrap around his opponent.

Mike's hands locked around Bill's waist, squeezing as he picked him off the roof. Bill felt his breath forced from his lungs, the bear hug devastating powerful, and he desperately tried to suck in one more breath of rapidly thinning air.

Bill was actually looking down on Mike's face as the younger man added yet more pressure. Mike's arms were powerful from years of weightlifting and Bill quickly realized he would never win a close quarter's brawl with the younger man.

Bill brought up both his arms, and with palms spread wide slapped them against Mike's ears like he was clapping a set of cymbals. Mike howled in rage, dropping Bill as he reached up to cup his sore ears. He now had a soft ringing in his head he couldn't seem to shake.

Bill stepped away from him, sucking in great lungfuls of air. He was light-headed, but with each breath of oxygen that entered his lungs, his head began to clear. By now all the other survivors had gathered around the two men. Some cheered for Bill while others seemed to want Mike to be the victor.

Mike brought his hands away from his ears and spit a wad of phlegm onto the roof.

"Not bad, old man, but I promise you that will be your last shot," Mike snarled.

Bill brought his hands in front of him again, this time determined to stay out of reach of Mike's massive arms. He cupped his hand, gesturing Mike to have at it.

With a deeper snarl, Mike charged forward and Bill danced skillfully aside. When Mike passed him, Bill sent a roundhouse blow into the back of Mike's neck, directly over his spine.

The blow sent Mike forward to land on the gravel of the roof like he was a baseball player sliding into first base after sending a ground ball to shortstop.

Rolling onto his back, Mike quickly climbed to his feet, although a little woozier than before he'd gone down.

Bill decided it was time to end this.

Not waiting for the younger man to regain his balance, he stepped close to him and sent not one, but two, shots into the prone man's midsection. Mike bent over from the blows and Bill sent an uppercut straight under his chin.

Mike's head flew back like the man had been shot and he dropped back to the roof. He was still moving, but not fast enough to defend himself if Bill wanted to continue the brawl.

Bill crossed the few steps separating them slowly, not knowing what to expect next. He leaned down on one knee and whispered into Mike's ear.

"As far as I'm concerned, we're done, unless you want to keep going."

Mike's eyes were glazed with pain and he shook his head no.

Bill stood up and wiped bits of gravel from his knee.

"Okay then, I guess this discussion is closed." He walked over to Becky, the woman looked into his eyes and it appeared she would start crying at any moment.

"You okay?" Bill asked while Marie came up next to him.

She nodded and looked down at her feet.

"What were you two arguing about, dear?" Marie asked sweetly.

Becky looked past the two of them to check on Mike. He was now sitting up, and though he had a few bruises, seemed to be recovering nicely.

She shrugged. "Nothing really. Mike just said we should get out of here. You know, leave the school, maybe find a better place to go."

Bill's eyebrows went up in surprise. "Better? And just where would that be? Hell, if he knows something I don't, I'd be happy to go, too."

Becky shook her head, her hair falling in front of her face. "That's just it, he doesn't know where to go, he just wants to leave. I said I wanted to stay here with you guys." Her voice grew soft. "That's when he pushed me and started to really get angry. It's my fault, though; I shouldn't have disagreed with him."

Both Marie and Bill looked at each other, each having the same thoughts.

"Becky, did Mike ever hit you before all this craziness started to happen to the city?" Marie asked softly.

Becky shrugged again. "No, not really, I mean, sometimes I do things to upset him, it's my fault really."

Bill placed a hand gently on her shoulder. "That's a load of bull, Becky, and you know it. No one should ever be hitting you, especially your boyfriend."

Mike had regained his footing and called out to Becky.

"Hey, baby, I'm sorry about that, I was wrong." He held out his right hand to her, gesturing for her to come to him.

Becky looked at Bill's face and then Marie's.

"He said he was sorry, look, he's all I've got." She slid between them and walked over to Mike. Mike took her hand and started moving away with her across the roof. His arm went around her waist, holding her from moving away from him.

Bill watched them go and sighed.

"Christ, with everything that's happening and we've got a wife beater on our hands," Bill said to Marie.

"Well, technically he's not one. After all, they're not married," she jibed back.

Bill turned to her and frowned.

"Jesus, Marie, he beats her like a sack of potatoes and you give me semantics?"

She smiled. "What else should I do? No matter how much we dislike the situation, it's still her choice. If she wants to stay with him, then good luck to her."

Bill threw up his hands in surrender. "The whole damn world is going nuts and I'm stuck with you and your damn rationalizations."

She patted his back and chuckled, and the two of them went to rejoin the others and fill them in on what the argument and following fight had been about.

Mike took Becky and stopped at the other end of the roof. He sat down on the edge; his legs swinging off the side, Becky plopped down next to him, staying silent until she was spoken to.

Mike closed his eyes; trying to let the anger and frustration he was feeling flow through him. The cool breeze calmed him and dried the perspiration covering his face and arms. He looked over his shoulder at Bill, cold hatred in his eyes. Before he'd just disliked the man, but now he wanted him dead; especially after humiliating him in front of Becky and the other survivors.

The old man had fought pretty well, much better than Mike would have expected. But if Bill thought their feud was over, he was very, very, wrong.

Dead wrong, in fact.

CHAPTER 3

Bɪʟʟ ᴘʟᴏᴘᴘᴇᴅ ᴅᴏᴡɴ onto the roof, his body sore in places that had been just fine before the fight. His legs dangled over the edge, far above the screaming mob. He chuckled to himself. No matter how hard he tried to fight it, old Father Time would always remind him he wasn't twenty anymore.

He thought of his wife then, her beautiful face and long, brown hair. That was how he tried to remember her, full of life and beauty, not the withered husk of a dying woman who had fought a heroic battle with cancer and lost.

She had fought valiantly, for many years, but once the chemotherapy hadn't worked, she knew it was the end.

Bill still remembered his last moments with her; sitting on the edge of the bed they had made love in countless time. When he'd looked into her eyes, it was like she knew her time was up. She had smiled wanly at him; even in the end she was stronger than him. He would have given anything to take her place, to let her go on living for many years to come, but God or whatever force that made the rules had deemed to take her instead.

After years of fighting a losing battle she had finally succumbed to an overwhelming force and had closed her eyes and breathed her last breath. Before she'd died, she had whispered her last words to him. She told him to not give up on life, and though she would be gone, he needed to keep on living for the both of them. She had made him promise.

He had promised, but since her passing, he'd been loathe to meet another woman, instead keeping to himself, not wanting to desecrate her memory.

But now, as he sat on the edge of the roof and watched all the people wandering around below him, he realized if he made it through this, whatever *this* was, then he would follow through on his promise and start living again.

But before he could do that, he needed to just survive. Survive first, then live, in that order.

Marie finished filling the others in about the fight and then walked over to Bill. She stood over him, gazing down on his head, a smile creasing her thin lips, and he gestured for her to sit down next to him. With a groan of old muscles, she plopped down and chuckled.

Bill smiled wanly, not in a jovial mood, but whenever he was around Marie he always found his mood lightening. She was just a natural at bringing out the good in people.

She noticed his smile and shot one back of her own, only three times as large as before. "What, do I amuse you?" She asked lightly.

He nodded. "As a matter of fact, you do. Muscles a little sore?"

Her lips became a thin line while she thought over his question. "Afraid so; arthritis. How 'bout you?"

Bill shook his head. "No, I've been lucky so far. A few aches and pains in the morning, but nothing that slows me down."

"I saw, you handled yourself pretty well against Mike, and that boy must be half your age."

Bill shrugged. "Did some boxing when I was younger. Guess it's like riding a bike."

One of the crazies below threw a glass bottle at the school, trying to reach Bill and Marie. The bottle made it to the second floor of the school before smashing against the red brickwork. Shards of glass rained back down on the crowd, many turning their faces away to avoid being struck by debris. More howls of pain and madness filled the night.

Marie watched with mild interest. "You know they are us and we are them."

Bill watched her face to see if she was going to elaborate some more, but when she didn't, he spoke up.

"You think? Can't say I agree with you on that one, Marie. Whatever the hell has happened to those people, I just thank God it hasn't happened to me." He looked down below his feet at the crowd. Even in the darkness their faces could be seen, eyes and teeth reflecting whatever ambient light was around them. The power was still on in the neighborhood and the streetlamps cast circles of light about the street.

"There are some things worse than death," he said softly.

She looked away from the crowd and turned to gaze at him. Bill's face was nothing but a shadow mixed in with the night. "Like what?" She asked.

He shrugged, the gesture going unnoticed. "Like losing your own sense of identity for one. Those people down there and the rest are changed now. Whatever they once were, teachers, doctors, truck drivers, is gone now. Now all that's left is the instinct to hunt and kill. Their personalities--who they once were-- are gone now and without that, we're nothing more than meat and tissue. Now maybe some scientist somewhere will figure out a way to reverse what's happened, but until they do, we are most definitely on our own."

"Okay, and what does all that mean for the rest of us?" She asked.

Bill turned to look at her and his face was set in a hard grimace. "Well, for one thing, we need to get off this roof or we're going to die up here."

As if to illustrate his statement, a pack of crazies hollered up to them, their hands opening and closing as they imagined themselves pulling Bill and Marie from their perch into their waiting arms.

Marie felt a chill, like someone had just walked over her grave, and as she sat next to Bill, she hoped that chill was in no way some form of premonition.

The rest of the night was uneventful and despite the yelling, shouting crowd of people surrounding the school, Bill finally managed to grab a few hours of rest. Though he slept, it was far from restful. Constant visions of raging lunatics filled his dreams as he ran screaming from them. Sometimes he escaped, and other times he went down under an avalanche of human bodies. Each time before he would start to feel his flesh become ripped from his body, he would wake up, usually with his heart pounding in his chest.

After the last nightmare, he decided he'd taken enough rest and would stay awake. The sun was just starting to rise, sending its warm rays across the neighborhood.

Off in the distance, Chicago continued to burn. He wished for the hundredth time since he had found his way to the school that someone had a radio with them or a cell phone. He would give almost anything to know what was happening beyond the street the school was on.

Since they had managed to make it to the roof the night before, none of them had seen another non-infected person, only snarling, screaming animals that still walked upright.

It was a chilling thought.

Could they be the only survivors for the entire Chicago area? Though it seemed implausible without any further information on the subject, it was hard to guess otherwise.

Bill thought back to his conversation with Marie the night before. After he had stated they needed to leave the roof, she'd argued they were safe from attack where they were and to venture off the roof would surely spell their doom.

He'd chuckled at that, her choice of words making their situation sound like a bad horror movie, but despite this, her words were apt.

He had explained to her that without food and water, and with the sun coming up on yet another hot day, if they didn't leave soon they would be far too weak to change their minds later.

Reluctantly, she had agreed and had stood up and walked away to share Bill's insight with the rest of the group. As for Mike, he chose to stay at the opposite end of the roof with Becky on his arm.

Bill and Mike locked eyes for a few moments after Marie left him and the young man's eyes had made Bill shiver. Not with fear, but with the simple fact that Mike's gaze was filled with venom, venom now directly aimed at him.

For whatever reason Bill had made himself an enemy and he knew when it was time to leave, he needed to keep Mike where he could always see him. Not because he was afraid of the man, mind you, but because he respected the danger the man represented.

He looked up when Melissa walked over to him and plopped down next to him. Her hair glowed like fire, the sun's rays reflecting off her scarlet mane. Shaking her head so the wind blew the hair from her face, she smiled at him.

"Hey," she said in way of greeting.

"Hey, yourself," Bill answered back. Though he was far from shy around women, he had to admit to feeling a little bit of an attraction to Melissa. He had no way of knowing if she felt the same, and with their current dire situation, he figured it wouldn't be the right time to ask.

"Marie filled us in…about your idea to leave," she said.

"Good, that's good. So, what do you think?"

She nodded. "I think you're right. We need to get out of here and fast, before more people show up down there. So far, they're all in the front of the school; it shouldn't be too hard to sneak away from here using the rear of the building. The only thing is…" She hesitated and Bill picked up on her thoughts.

"The only thing is where do we go once we leave here," he finished for her.

Her smile grew wider, her eyes glinting in the sunlight. "Exactly. Once we leave here, where the hell do we go?"

Bill frowned. "You know, I haven't thought that far ahead yet, but we need to decide quickly. Why don't you share with the others; see if anybody else has any ideas. Tell them to offer anything, no ideas too stupid; the more the better."

Her smile never wavered and she climbed back to her feet, wiping her butt free of gravel. "Okay, I'll do it now." Then she trotted off back to the others who were even now waking up. Without food it should be easy to motivate the rest of them, Bill was starving and wanted to get off the roof as soon as possible so he could get something to eat.

Deciding he needed to take a piss, he stood up and unzipped where he stood. Pulling out his penis, he emptied his bladder over the edge of the roof, the long stream of urine arcing through the air to strike the crowd below. Angry cries floated up to him as the mass separated to avoid his pee. He solved that by swinging to the left and right, his urine like a poor excuse for a waterfall. Below him, more aggravated cries floated up to him and only stopped when his bladder finally went dry.

Finishing, he zipped up his pants and turned away from the edge. When he turned around, he was surprised to see Marie standing behind him with arms crossed over her chest like a stern matron. She had on a frown that made her look just like his grandmother, and despite himself, he felt like a small child caught eating cookies before dinner.

"Was that really necessary?" She asked.

Bill shrugged. "Probably not, but it's not like they can get any more mad at us than they already are, I mean, as it is now they want to kill us, right? So I ask you, how exactly does my pissing on them make it any worse?"

She chuckled at him. "You know, that makes to much damn sense for me to argue with you." She changed the subject. "Listen, everybody's awake and wants to talk about leaving. Evidently you aren't the only one who wants to leave. We're all tired and hungry, so if you're ready, come join us." Then she walked away, back to the others.

Bill's stomach rumbled; reminding him it needed to be fed on a daily basis. Then he, too, followed her over the rooftop to join the others.

Though he hadn't come up with anything remotely resembling a plan to leave the roof, he hoped with the others involved, they could all make it happen.

With the shouts of anger and frustration from the murderous crowd below, Bill followed her footsteps on the quickly warming rooftop, while the sun continued to rise overhead in the clear, blue sky.

Upon reaching the small circle of people, Elizabeth took him aside; the concern clearly visible on her face. "There's a problem, Bill, some of the others don't want to wait for a plan; they want to leave now."

"Now? But how?"

Elizabeth pointed to the roof hatch. "They think they can sneak back into the school and go out the back door."

Bill shook his head back and forth. "That's crazy. The moment they step foot off the ladder they'll probably be overrun. Look, let me talk to them."

"Okay, they're over there, the bald guy and the four others with him," Elizabeth said, gesturing with her chin at the small knot of people huddling together like street bums around a fire barrel in the middle of winter.

Marie heard the conversation and joined him. Bill nodded his thanks and walked over to the small group.

The man who was taking charge of the small group was around forty or so, with no hair and a high forehead. His stomach had grown with the classic male, beer belly and his dirty-white, too short t-shirt didn't help the look of the stereotypical representation of trailer trash.

Bill barely glanced at the others, knowing the man in charge would make the decisions.

"So, I hear you want to leave?" Bill stated calmly. "You should know the moment you step off that ladder you'll probably be torn to pieces."

Baldie shrugged. "That's not the way I see it. There hasn't been any banging on that hatch for hours. Way I see it; they all left for better pickings."

Bill nodded. "Perhaps. Or maybe they're just waiting patiently for someone stupid enough to try to go back down there."

Baldie laughed at that. "That's ridiculous and you know it, they're nothing but animals, they can't reason like you and me. Anyone with a brain can see that just by watching them for a few minutes."

"Well, they can't reason like me, anyway," Bill muttered as he turned to look at Marie. She grinned, but wiped her face of it, not wanting to agitate the bald man or any of his compatriots.

Marie spoke up. "But why do you have to try now? Wait a while; give us a chance to come up with another form of escape. Surely, one of us will figure a way off the roof and to safety."

Baldie shook his head and crossed his arms over his man-breasts. "No deal, look, I've already decided and these people all agree with me, now unless you're going to try and stop us…" He let the rest trail off as he looked down at the .38 in Bill's waistband.

Bill saw where Baldie's gaze was directed and then looked back at the man. "No, I won't stop you. If you want to kill yourself and these deluded people want to follow you, then have at it."

The man's face softened a little and he turned to his followers for support. Their faces told him they were still behind him and he turned to back to Bill, then Marie.

"All right then, we'll be going now, before the sun's fully up. Figure we got at least another fifteen minutes."

Bill held out his hand to the bald man. "Listen, friend, I think you're making a big mistake, but good luck, just the same."

Baldie was a little surprised, but he took Bill's hand and the two men shook, then Bill looked at the others behind Baldie. "It's not too late to back out, you know. You don't have to go with him. We'll find a way out of here, a safe way, I promise."

Heads swayed back and forth and mouths became slits, the others behind Baldie all saying no.

"We think you're the crazy ones for staying up here. You'll die up here without food and water," a skinny man behind Baldie said.

Bill threw up his hands in surrender. "I give up, I'm done." And he walked away.

Marie smiled sweetly and looked at each of their faces one at a time, holding her gaze on each person for just a moment before moving on to the next. "Are you sure, now? Is there no way to change your minds?" No one answered her. "Okay then, good luck and God speed."

Baldie clapped his hands and got his small group together. Marie walked over to Bill and he glanced at her, his face set in stone. "They're going to their deaths, you know."

"Uh-huh, but it's their lives and what they do with them is still their business. Last time I checked, it was still a free country."

Bill only grunted as he watched the group move to the roof hatch.

Sighing, he decided if they were going, than he should at least help with the hatch, that way if there were any problems, he could shut it down before it got out of control.

Baldie was already pulling the metal bar from the top of the hatch, preparing to go down first. The man glanced at Bill, but Bill had nothing for him. He was done talking, if the damn fool wanted to die, then so be it.

Baldie opened the hatch slowly, the sweat already dripping off his large forehead. Nothing but silence greeted him. He flashed Bill a smile that said, "I told you so," and then he stepped into the hatch and disappeared down into the darkness.

For a few heartbeats, no one moved, waiting for the worst, but then Baldie called up, his voice echoing. "See, I told you it was safe, come on down and let's get out of here!"

One at a time, the four others went through the hatch, each saying bye to the others staying behind. When the last one was ready to disappear from sight, a young man in his early twenties, he stopped and looked up Bill

"Don't worry, once we find help we'll tell them about you, I promise." Then his head disappeared from view and Bill slammed the hatch closed, securing the metal bar once more.

Once finished, he turned to the others gathered around him and pointed to the hatch. "No one opens that, no matter what. They made their bed now they can lie in it, promise me."

"But what if they need to come back up? Like we did?" Janice asked.

"It's too late, they made their decision," Bill told her. "Now, does everybody agree or are we going to have to vote on it?" His eyes darted to Mike who only gazed back blank-faced. Good, he wasn't going to have to deal with Mike about the situation.

One at a time he received mumbled words of agreement, then everyone scattered to their favorite places on the roof. With no sounds coming from below, Bill wondered if maybe Baldie had been right and it was him and the others who were crazy for staying stranded on the roof.

Deciding it was too late for regrets; he went back and stretched out by a ventilation unit. He picked the side opposite the rising sun, hoping to steal a little shade. Closing his eyes, he sighed and tried to see if he could catch up on some of the sleep he'd lost the night before thanks to way too many nightmares.

Bill's eyes shot open by the shouts of the others. Checking his watch, he realized he had been asleep for a little more than half an hour. People were hovering over the hatch, and as Bill climbed to his feet, he saw that Mike was about to slide the bar off the hatch. Running towards them, he started to hear the sounds of banging and screams of terror coming through the metal hatch.

With his eyes still blurry from sleep, he staggered over to the others. "What the hell's going on?"

Melissa was closest and so filled him in on the situation. "It just started, screams from inside the school and then pounding. Someone's begging us to open the hatch!"

"What are we supposed to do? Let them die down there?" Elizabeth screamed, clearly upset.

"No, we're not, I'm opening the hatch," Mike stated, preparing to do just that. Bill whirled on the man and pulled the .38 from his waistband. "You'll do no such thing, unless you want a bullet in the chest. Look, Mike, this is nothing between us, but if you open that hatch those killers will get up here and I don't have enough bullets to stop them all, so for the love of God, back off!"

Mike's face went hard and he looked into Bill's eyes and then at the muzzle of the .38, like he was weighing his options. All the while the banging continued, screams of pain and pleadings for them to open the hatch continuing.

Bill's gun hand never wavered and he placed his finger on the trigger. "Don't test me, Mike, I don't want to, but I will if it means keeping the rest of us safe."

Becky scooted up to Mike and tried to pull him away. "Come on, honey, those people aren't worth it, they chose to go down there and they knew what would happen if they did."

Mike's face softened just a little, and if Bill had to guess, he was using Becky as his way out of the predicament he'd gotten himself into without losing face with the others. "All right, baby, I'll do it for you." He pointed to Bill. "You win this one, old man, but you've sentenced those people to death!"

Bill nodded, gun still up. "Won't be the first time, and God help me, it probably won't be the last. It's a different world now, Mike. Sometimes the decisions might seem cruel, but they have to be made. The sooner you realize that the better off you'll be."

Mike flipped him off and walked away, Becky following like a little puppy. Bill surveyed the others around him. "All right then, no one touches that hatch!"

No one said anything. The small group of survivors huddled around the hatch and listened to the sounds of carnage for another three minutes, then it stopped abruptly, like a door being slammed.

There was nothing below filtering through, no screams, no pleadings, only silence.

Bill lowered the .38. "Okay then; that ends that."

He waited for more than an hour and finally decided it should be clear inside the school, so he called Melissa over to him. "Will you help me? I want to see for myself what I already know to be true, but I think the others need to know, too. If everyone doubts me every time I make a decision, then what will happen the next time I make one?"

"What do you want me to do?" Melissa asked.

Bill kicked the hatch with his foot. I want you to open that for me. Don't worry, I'll have you covered in case there's any surprises, but I'm pretty sure it's safe now."

"Pretty sure? I don't know, Bill."

"Look, there's been nothing for more than an hour. Whatever was down there has moved on."

Sighing, she agreed. "Fine, but you better have me covered. I don't feel like dying today."

He chuckled at her and waved for her to open the hatch. Sliding the bar free, she set it down on the roof, the bar stationary thanks to the gravel. Then, with her heart in her throat, she opened it, slowly at first, but when no hands shot out to try and grab her, she soon relaxed and opened it all the way.

The sun was high overhead and shone its rays directly into the opening. Marie and Elizabeth had joined him, and as one group they looked into the opening, their heads blocking out most of the light. The first thing they saw was the underside of the hatch, before it had been painted a dull gray color, but now it was a maroon color, the partially dried blood coating the entire inside. Looking down the ladder, Bill saw bits of gristle and meat hanging from the ladder rungs and he quickly turned away, the onerous smell of death too much to take.

But before he did, he got a glimpse of the floor of the hallway, pools of blood covering the entire section the light illuminated.

"You can close it. I think I got my answer. Make sure you tell the others, too. They need to know. Hopefully, after this, no one will do anything too foolhardy."

Melissa let the hatch fall shut, sliding the bar back in place. Marie patted Bill's shoulder, and then, she too, walked away.

He'd been right all along and now five more of them were dead.

Looking out across the horizon, he wondered just how many more would lose their lives before their odyssey was finished.

CHAPTER 4

DEAN CARLSON WAS feeling pretty well about himself.

Although he was one of the *Changed*, he'd somehow managed to keep his intelligence intact. Why he, out of all the other infected, was the only one who still remembered who he once was, was a mystery to him.

And frankly, he didn't really care.

While he still felt the urge to hunt and kill any of the normals he came across; his will was able to keep the urges mostly in check. Of course, he still let the dog out of the house once in a while, to coin a phrase.

He grinned; thinking about his latest kill as he strolled down traffic jammed State Street in the heart of Chicago.

She had been a pretty little blonde thing. She'd been running from a large group of the Changed and when she saw Dean, she immediately crossed the street and had fallen into his arms. She had looked up at him then, her eyes filled with terror and fear. She'd whispered the words: "Help me, please," and had passed out from fatigue.

Dean had stopped the crowd of Changed when they caught up to her. He still hadn't figured it out yet, but for some unknown reason, the Changed listened to him when he gave them an order. He made them leave them both alone, the crowd moving off to find more prey.

He'd half-carried, half-dragged her down the street until coming upon an abandoned coffee shop. Dragging her inside, he'd set her down on a chair, her head falling to an unnatural angle as she slumped across the table, unconscious. Then he'd waited for her to revive.

So far, all he had used his new found gift for was to have a few of the Changed find food for him and clothes when he needed a fresh change of attire; anything grander than that was far beyond their limited thoughts.

Dean was what people would call uninspired, though in fact he was really quite bright. He'd barely managed to graduate high school before he'd gone to work full-time to survive on his own, so college would have been out of the question. Before Chicago had fallen apart from the inside out, he'd been a dish washer for a small bistro on the edge of town. He had no parents. He was an orphan from the age of five.

His parents had gone out one night for a night on the town and a drunk driver had jumped the medium and ended their lives in a blink of an eye. With no other close relatives, Dean found himself tossed into the foster care system where he had been placed in home after home until finally reaching the age of eighteen. Then he was given a pat on the back and a hearty good luck and sent out into the big, wide world.

He'd floated from job to menial job until landing the dish washing gig. It didn't pay much, but he got to eat all the leftovers he could stomach, and sometimes the owner would let him take some home to his small, one room apartment which was situated in what was not much more than a glorified boarding house.

Up until a few days ago, the best Dean had to look forward to were a couple of leftover steaks or an extra bowl of soup. But now it seemed, he'd been given a new destiny.

Unfortunately, he still didn't quite know what that destiny was just yet.

He sat in his chair, watching the pretty blonde across from him. His arms were folded on the table in front of him and his chin rested on one of his arms. He just sat there, watching her breathe, her ample cleavage rising and falling with each breath, though any normal sexual ideas were the farthest thing from his thoughts.

Her shirt had lost a few buttons and half of her left breast was trying to break free of her bra. Before he'd been changed, Dean believed he would have found the sight of the partially clad woman arousing, but now it did nothing for him. In fact, as he watched her, he noticed the pulsing vein on the side of her throat. That seemed to stimulate him. It beat with each pulse of her heart and while he watched it minute after minute, he found himself becoming more aroused with each passing second.

Suddenly, his pants felt too snug and he shifted position on his chair to accommodate the new situation. That was when the woman moaned and her eyes fluttered open as she regained consciousness.

"Oh, where am I?" She asked, her head snapping up and around as she tried to look every which way at once.

"We're in a coffee shop; you should be safe…for now," he said.

If she caught on to his hesitation, she didn't show it. Sitting up, she pulled her shirt closed and tried to compose herself better. The panic filled her eyes and she got ready to bolt out of the shop. Until Dean held up his hands for her to wait.

"I wouldn't do that if I were you," he said. "The second you run out that door they'll be on top of you, I guarantee it."

She blinked away the panic, but it was quickly replaced by confusion.

"How did you get us here safely? I was being chased by a dozen or more of those lunatics, why didn't they tear us apart?"

"We prefer to be called the Changed," Dean stated politely. "Or at least I do."

The woman blinked again, as if seeing Dean for the first time. Across from her, sitting casually was a rather non-descript man. He had brown hair and rough skin. If she had to guess, she would have figured he had an acne problem when he was younger that had played havoc with his skin. His slim frame was dressed in a button down shirt with long sleeves and a pair of tan Dockers.

All in all, nothing threatening about the man at all; in fact, it was this very man who had saved her from the lunatics.

So if all this was true, then why did she get the creeps every time she looked into his eyes?

"How come they didn't attack you and me when I ran into you? We should both be dead," she said hesitantly.

Dean shrugged. "That's easy; I told them to leave us alone."

"And they do what you tell them? But how, why?"

Dean leaned closer to her and grinned, his teeth flashing in the wan light of the coffee shop, his eyes squinting malevolently.

"It's really quite simple. I'm one of them. I don't know why, but they listen to me. Pretty cool, huh? I can tell them to do whatever I want. Though I haven't thought about what to do with them just yet."

The woman slid off her chair and started backing away from Dean. Her destination was the front door. For some reason Dean didn't so much as flinch, just sat in his chair, watching her move for the door, his grin never leaving his lips.

Her footsteps made crackling sounds as she stepped over the carpet of broken glass covering the floor. For the first time since waking, she realized the coffee shop was a shambles. It seemed not a single cup or dish had been spared. The coffee shop once had mirrors lining one side of it in hopes of making the small shop appear bigger than it actually was, but now every mirror was shattered, the silver pieces reflecting the dim illumination filtering in from the street.

Upon reaching the front door, she allowed herself a sigh of relief. Evidently, the man meant her no harm as he was still seated. Turning for the door, she stopped as if she'd walked into an invisible barrier. Outside in the street, amidst the abandoned cars and taxi cabs were dozens, if not hundreds, of the lunatics.

It was easy to spot them immediately as almost every one she could see was covered in red and scarlet. Though loathe to admit it, she knew it had to be blood.

But it was their eyes that were the most disconcerting. Despite the fact that the crowd moved like a pack of animals, their eyes had a glazed over look, as if they were staring at something far away for all of eternity. But then they would change and stare at you with hatred and rage.

When she stopped at the front door, every face turned to look at her. Mouths curved into feral grins and teeth flashed in the sunlight, more than a few having lips tinted red from fresh kills.

It was at that precise moment the woman realized she wouldn't be leaving that way anytime soon. She was about to turn around and move back to the table where Dean was waiting, when she heard the sound of footsteps behind her.

Spinning around, she was shocked to see Dean no more than a foot away from her. How he had managed to cross the distance between them so fast was unknown and she was about to ask him when he grabbed her by the throat and pushed her against the wall. She struggled to escape from Dean, not understanding how this skinny man with about the same amount of body weight as herself, could hold her so forcefully against the wall. In fact, she could almost feel her feet being lifted off the floor.

"Why?" She managed to croak out, before his hand squeezed tighter and made speaking impossible.

He laughed at her, his laughter filling the coffee shop. "Why? Because I can, that's why. You know, it's amazing what you can do when you realize there's no one to punish you for it."

Then he snapped her neck like a dry twig. Her head fell to the side and her eyes glazed over in death. He supposed he should have tortured her more, but he found he liked the dramatic, and snapping her neck had felt right.

Dragging the corpse to the front door, he tossed it out into the street. Immediately, the Changed surrounded her and started to rip the pretty blonde corpse to bloody pieces.

Dean looked away, not really interested.

So he hadn't tortured her; that was okay. He'd just make up for it on the next normal he came across.

While the Changed fed on the woman in the street outside the shattered coffee shop, Dean went back inside, his destination; behind the counter.

After smelling all the coffee beans, he realized he was dying for a cup of coffee.

Chapter 5

Bill gazed down at the murderous mass of humanity below him. The bodies seemed to shift like the tide, ebbing and flowing continually. Every so often two of the crazies would turn on one another, and a fight would break out. The fight wouldn't stop until one of the opponents was lying dead in the dirt, bleeding out onto the crushed grass that lined the front of the school.

Leaving the screams of the murderous crowd behind him, Bill walked across the roof, away from the edge. The others were all standing together in the center of the gravel strewn roof, talking amongst themselves, and looking as tired and scared as he felt.

When he was only a few feet away, Melissa moved closer to him, slowing him before he reached the others.

"We've been talking and we've all decided its time to get off this roof. We're all hungry and thirsty and with the sun now up it's only going to get worse."

Elizabeth was the closest to her and she stepped forward, nodding in agreement. "That's right, we all want to go."

Bill didn't know what to say, so he gazed at the faces of the others. Both Roger and Phillip were standing near the back of the group, not saying anything, their young faces almost blank. The two boys had been through a lot and if he was right, there would be more hell to come before they were safe,

Bill was fairly certain they would do whatever the adults decided. Janice was standing next to Elizabeth, her arms folded across her chest. The light wind caused her hair to blow in her face and she would quickly brush it away, only to have the wind repeat the process again and again.

As for Mike and Becky, they too were part of the group, although both were standing on the fringe of the circle of survivors. Before he said anything to the others, he felt himself looking towards Marie for advice. The woman had become a good sounding board for his conscience; whether it was because of a disagreement with another of the group or just someone to talk to. She was wise and he valued her wisdom.

He found he had a real attraction to the woman. Not sexual, but more of a brother to a sister. So, as he stood in front of the group, all of them looking to him for a way to escape, he found himself looking to Marie once more, hoping for her counsel.

Marie walked over to him, as if she could somehow sense his trepidation.

"All right now, just everyone calm down. Nothing has been decided yet. Before we leave here, we need to have a plan of action. We need to know where we're going once we leave or we won't get twenty feet before we're attacked by those people down there."

Janice spoke up then, causing the others to look at her. Though it made her uncomfortable to be the center of attention, she continued sharing her idea.

"You mean we need a distraction so we can get away from them, right?" She asked.

Bill nodded and grinned. "Exactly," he said, running with the idea. "We need a way to keep those bastards down there at the front of the school, and while they stay there, occupied, we can climb down the back and disappear into one of the back yards of those houses across the street."

Bill was referring to what appeared to be abandoned houses directly across from the school's front and back sides. The school was situated smack dab in the middle of more than a dozen suburban streets, all with neat rows of middle-class homes.

If they were lucky, they could run across the street, and after picking a house, they could run through the backyard and out to one of the other side streets. From there they could either find transportation or just hide out in one of the many houses they came across, maybe one of the basements or attics.

True, it might not have been the best plan, but so far it was all he had.

"How the hell are we gonna get down from here? It's not like you have a ladder up your ass that you can pull out for us to use."

Bill looked through a few bodies to see Mike looking at him. It was he who had spoken up, his voice cold and low.

Bill didn't know if the younger man was asking a real question or just trying to undermine his authority, such as it was. So he decided to treat it as a real question.

"That's true, Mike. I've been thinking about that, too. What about if we all take a piece of clothing off and tie it together to make a half-ass rope? I mean, if we make sure the knots are tight enough, we should be able to get down all right."

Faces turned to look at each other and voices rose as the group discussed the idea.

"Even if we did that and we all ran around in our underwear, that still doesn't explain how the heck we're going to be able to distract those nut jobs down there long enough to get away from here." Melissa stated.

That started more voices and arguments as they all argued about the situation. Marie stood next to Bill, watching the group with a sly grin on her face. Bill noticed this and leaned in close so only she could hear him.

"You look like the cat that's eaten the canary, what's so amusing?" Bill asked.

She shrugged slightly. "Nothing really, it's just this is the first *real* time that they're all listening to you. It seems you're disagreeing with the bald man and his friends did more to elevate your status as leader than anything else you've done since we found ourselves massed together."

He frowned at that. "You know, I never asked to be in charge of anything. I'm no better than anyone else around here," he stated flatly.

"That's right, Bill, and that's why you're perfect for the job." Then she held up her hands to quiet the others down. Bill stood silent, not quite understanding what she meant. He decided if they had a chance later, and if they weren't dead from trying to escape, he would ask her more about what she'd meant, but for now he had a meeting to finish.

When Marie had everyone quiet, all of them waiting with eager eyes to hear what Henry had to say next--with the exception of Mike, who stood with his arms folded across his chest and jaw locked tight-- he cleared his throat and stepped into the middle of the group.

"All right, look, I'm no leader, but if you'll let me, I'll give it a try. This means with the exception of something we put to a vote, you have to listen to what I tell you." He held up his hand when some of the others prepared to say something. "Now before you answer me, let me explain. If we need to do something quick out there or hide or what-ever, I need to know that you'll do it and not start arguing about it every time. There's a reason why on a battlefield there's only one man in charge and this is pretty damn similar. If you don't want me to lead, that's fine, but I tell you what. If we don't make someone the leader soon, then most of us will never make it out of here. We need to stick together and fight; it's the only way we're going to make it through whatever the hell's happened to the world both alive and in one piece."

Finishing his speech, he waited for their answer. If what Marie said was true, then they would agree with him. If not, well, that was fine with him. Let someone else deal with the responsibilities of taking care of the half-dozen ragtag survivors still left.

It was Melissa who stepped forward first. She walked away from the main group, pulled Bill with her, and stopped a few feet from the others. She turned to face the others, and with her head held high and a fire in her eyes to match her flaming hair, she nodded.

"He's right, we need a leader and I say Bill's the one for the job. Who's with me?" She asked them.

Marie came next, followed by Elizabeth and Janice. Janice held out her hand to the two boys and they walked over to join their growing group, now a few feet away from the original circle.

When the boys had stopped next to Janice, the entire group looked at Becky and Mike. For a brief moment everyone was quiet, only the howls of the Changed coming from the street below. Then Marie spoke up. "Well, Mike, what do you say?"

Mike stood there looking at each individual face until his gaze rested on Bill's. Though he was talking to Marie, his eyes never wavered from Bill. "Don't see as I've got any goddamn choice in the matter," he stated quietly, his voice barely carrying to the others.

Becky squeezed his arm slightly and placed her head on his shoulder. "Aww, come on, honey, don't be like that. Forgive and forget, please?" Becky pleaded.

Mike turned his head to look at Becky and sighed. "Fine, whatever, he's in charge," he said with a wave of his arms. Then he walked away, leaving Becky to stand alone in front of the rest of the group.

She smiled at Marie and Bill. "See, I told you he's not that bad of a person." Then she ran off across the roof to catch up to her boyfriend.

"All right then, meetings over for now. Everyone think of a way to make a distraction and get back to me or Marie. The sooner the better, people," Bill said with a clap of his hands, shooing them to different parts of the roof. Once everyone was dispersed in groups of twos and threes, talking animatedly amongst themselves, Bill looked to Marie.

"Well, there you have it, the first meeting of Survivors Anonymous. All in all, I think it went well."

She chuckled. "Suppose so. After what happened with Mike last night, anytime you two don't get into a fight, I'll call it a success."

"Very funny, you're a riot. You know, you should take that act on the road, you'd be rich. Hell, I bet the Tonight Show would even book you," Bill jibed back playfully.

The two of them started walking to the rear of the roof together, deciding to check the area one more time before deciding on a course of action. As they walked together, Marie slipped her arm in Bill's and looked at him slyly and winked.

"You joke, but when this is all over I may do just that, just to prove you right."

Bill shook his head and laughed a little. Though they were in dire peril and their chances for survival were slim, he still felt the need to laugh, no matter how trivial the reason.

Marie chatted with him and he listened politely, nodding when appropriate or giving her a soft grunt in agreement, but inside his own head he re-evaluated his laughter, realizing if he didn't laugh, he'd probably just start crying.

CHAPTER 6

Bɪʟʟ ᴄʜᴇᴄᴋᴇᴅ ʜɪs wristwatch for the fifth time in as many minutes. Gazing up at the blazing orb high overhead, he squinted and held his hand over his eyes to shield them from the worst of the sun's rays. It was going on noon and they still had not come up with a reasonable distraction to get them safely off the roof.

Despite this, though, the group of survivors had each donated a piece of clothing to make a rope. Most of the women now were without shirts, their white bras a weird contrast to their otherwise clothed bodies. Bill, too, was minus his shirt, his white t-shirt already wet with perspiration.

His mouth tasted like sandpaper and he really believed he would have given the next twenty years of his life for just one glass of water. Watching the faces of the others, he could easily see they were all feeling the same as him.

Marie walked up to him, and despite the fact that she was more than ten years his senior, he couldn't help but notice her breasts still appeared firm inside her white under-wire bra, and her waist was still slim, only the barest amount of extra fat exposed above her waistband.

Realizing he was staring, he quickly turned his gaze to look at something else. A tree, one of many, was across the street from the school, the branches full of leaves, waving in the wind. That seemed as good a place as any to concentrate his gaze.

Marie stopped when she was next to him and just stood there for a moment, looking out over the roof the same as him. Bill knew she was there, but feeling embarrassed and hoping she hadn't seen him staring at her chest, he decided to play stupid.

"So, you like my boobs, do you? I guess I owe you a thank you, especially with all the younger women bouncing around up here," Marie said, cutting the silence between them.

Bill was shocked, his jaw dropping so low he thought he might kick it with his foot accidentally. "Excuse me?" Was all he could muster.

"I'm just messing with you, Bill, don't worry," she chuckled. "You should see your face; you look like a teenager who's just seen his girlfriend naked for the first time…priceless."

"I'm sorry if I offended you, its just…" he debated how to say it, so he just said it. "It's just you look pretty good without your shirt on. I never would have guessed you had that kind of figure under your clothes."

She shrugged. "Well, now you know. I never got into wearing sexy outfits. Always wore things that weren't very flattering. Guess that's why I never landed a man."

Bill moved around a few pieces of gravel with his foot, feeling very uncomfortable with the conversation, especially with her standing there in nothing but her bra covering her upper torso.

Luckily, Marie was the one to change the subject for him.

"So, I've talked with the others and no one has come up with a way to distract those raging lunatics down there long enough for us to leave. How about you, anything come to mind?"

Shaking his head, he kicked the gravel he'd been toying with away from him. The small stone rolled until it reached the edge of the roof, slid over, and then dropped away to land on the crowd below. The stone struck an angry man on the forehead and he let out a savage scream that was lost with the roar of the rest of the mob.

"I got nothing, but I'll tell you this, whether we come up with something or not, we need to go soon. Are you as thirsty as I am?"

She nodded, wiping her brow with the back of her hand. The sun was hot on their heads and without shelter, plus the heat from the roof itself, reflecting the sun's rays; it had to be over ninety.

"Thirstier, I'd give my left boob for a drink right now."

Bill opened his mouth again, shocked. "Marie, where's all this coming from?" He asked her, surprised.

She sighed. "I'm sorry, Bill, I'm just tired and when I get tired I get a little loopy. Just ignore me; once we get out of here, I'll be okay."

Bill grunted, then looked beyond her to see the group now finishing the makeshift rope. Melissa and Janice were pulling on it, trying to see if the knots were solid and wouldn't unravel when the first body tried to climb down.

Melissa had finished with the line when she tugged on one of the last shirts. The knot wasn't up to the task and it unraveled, sending her falling to the hot rooftop in a spray of gravel. An instant later however, she was back on her feet, brushing the hot stones from her skin. From where Bill stood, he could see small red dots on her back where the hot stones had burned her slightly. Otherwise, she appeared to be fine.

She saw him looking her way and she waved to him, signaling she was fine, then with Janice's help, she went back to testing the rope again.

"She's a tough one," Marie stated next to him.

Bill looked at Marie and then realized she was talking about Melissa.

"Who, Melissa? Yeah, I guess so; she seems to be able to keep a level head, smart, too."

"That she is, if we need someone to help with keeping the others in line, she's the one to ask," Marie said.

"Well, I just hope it doesn't come to that. Besides, once we're out of here, I wonder how many of us will just go their own way?"

Marie crossed her arms and looked into Bill's eyes. "Why do you say that? You don't think we'll all stay together once we're down from here?"

"That's right, you just watch. Once we're away from here, everybody will have their own ideas of what we should do. We'll break apart quicker than a cardboard boat in the middle of the ocean."

"You might be right, but I guess it won't really matter until we're down, and if we can't find away to keep those bastards from the rear of the school, then it won't matter at all. They'll be on us the second our feet touch the ground."

Bill grunted; a low sound in his throat that Marie barely heard. "Then I guess we better come up with one."

Two more hours had passed and still no one had thought of a suitable distraction to keep the murderous crowd below busy while they escaped off the rear roof. Bill was really starting to give up hope when a rumbling sound, followed by the sound of gunfire, caught his attention.

Running to the front of the school, followed by the others, he looked through the waving trees at the end of the street.

At first nothing could be seen, though the rumbling and sounds of gunshots slowly grew louder. But soon the front bumper of a green and brown military truck pulled into view.

The murderous crowd below, seeing the truck approaching, quickly turned away from the unattainable prey on the school roof and moved off, towards the new target.

"Oh my God, it's the Army! They're coming to save us!" Elizabeth said, from his side."

"About damn time, they should have been here days ago back when all this shit started," Mike snarled to whoever would listen.

The staccato of gunfire filled the street, M-16s shooting at every target the soldiers could find. But as they moved closer and Bill was able to see inside the truck, he quickly realized their salvation might not be coming as soon as they had all hoped.

Squinting in the sun, he could see the truck had less than five men inside, at least two in the front cab, all wearing white biological suits. When they moved closer to the school, Bill saw one of the men remove a tarp from the rear bed and expose what looked like an M-60 machine gun. A soldier who looked no older than eighteen if he was a day, jumped behind the weapon and prepared it for battle. Another soldier, who looked only slightly older, had his back to the machine gunner, trying to keep the ever growing crowd of attackers off his back.

The soldier sent the first rounds over the raving crowd's heads, as if he was only trying to control them, warn them off, not destroy them. But when none of the raging killers seemed to care, he quickly lowered the barrel of the weapon and started to fire into the attacking mob.

Bodies danced a macabre jig as bullets ripped into flesh and exploded organs. The street ran red with blood and blasted body parts as the soldier continued firing. But then, just as suddenly as the weapon had started firing, it stopped. The area around the school seemed almost preternaturally quiet after the deafening sound of the machine gun. Bill watched as the soldier tried to un-jam the weapon, but it was hopeless. In the seconds the machine gun had stopped firing, bodies swarmed around the truck, and though the soldiers fought valiantly, they were soon outnumbered.

Bill could only watch helplessly while the men retreated to the middle of the rear bed of the truck to try and hold off the murderous horde. Bill watched for another instant and then snapped out of his trance. His heart, too, was filled with a false hope that was now quickly dashed away. But despite this, he saw one bright star in the darkness that was their reality.

He saw the distraction they so sorely needed.

Looking to Marie, he pointed down at the swamped military truck.

"Marie, we have to go now, while those soldiers are keeping the crowd busy."

"Now?" She asked, still thinking they were somehow about to be saved. "But we're not ready yet."

"Yes, right now, this second. Those soldiers are dead and in less than a minute they'll be overwhelmed, but until then they're the distraction we need."

Marie looked at the truck and back to him, then at the truck again, as if she couldn't comprehend what he was saying. But then her eyes went wide with the realization that he was right.

Marie looked at some of the others who were listening intently to the conversation, and then she nodded. "Bill's right, if we want to get off this roof alive; this is probably our best chance."

"All right then, what are we waiting for? Let's get going," Melissa said, slapping her hands together for emphasis.

Melissa, Bill and Marie herded the others away from the edge of the roof, while Mike hung back to watch the truck. Becky had left his side, and after a moment realized he wasn't with her. She stopped and ran back to him, grabbing his arm to get him to leave.

"Come on, Mike, we have to leave. We don't want to be last," she said pleadingly.

Mike held his hand up to make her stop. "Quit it, Becky, I want to see what happens to the jarheads. They are so screwed."

Mike was right and when Becky followed his gaze she saw the last soldier become overwhelmed by the crowd of screaming killers. The soldier managed to pull his sidearm and fired point-blank into the closest attackers, but there were always two more to take the fallen killer's place.

Then the man disappeared under a wave of bodies and was pulled from the truck and smashed to the street, his white suit soon turning red. There was nothing but a large mass of swirling bodies, each vying for a piece of the beleaguered man, his cries of pain and fear soon buried under the shrieks of the beastlike crowd.

The truck's driver had been pulled from behind the wheel and the vehicle drove onward, still in gear. One of the crowd jumped inside and tried to steer it, but it appeared to Mike that the man couldn't seem to comprehend the controls. The truck soon swerved and struck a tree, the motor still idling.

Becky pulled on his arm again and she pointed to the rear of the school where even now, Bill and Marie were going over the side.

"Come on, Mike, everyone's gone, we need to go," she wined, hoping for once her boyfriend would listen to her.

Mike finally looked away from the truck, the show over. Swiveling his head to see the rear of the roof, he saw she was correct, everyone had evacuated.

"Shit, they left us, come on, Becky, what the hell are you waiting for? We have to leave," he said, running away from the front of the roof to the makeshift rope.

She sighed, frustrated. "That's what I've been trying to tell you," she gasped and ran after him.

Reaching the edge of the roof, he looked down to just catch the back of Marie before she ran under a thicket of tree branches. As for the rest of the group, they were far from sight. Sliding over the edge, he let his feet dangle for a moment until he knew he had a firm grip on the rope, then he began to shimmy down it, one foot at a time. He was young and strong and was down in seconds, then he looked up to see Becky's head as she peeked down at him.

"Come on, damn it, what are you waiting for?" He yelled and whispered at the same time.

"I'm scared. I've always been scared of heights. You know that," she said, clearly intimidated by the climb down.

Mike looked around himself, expecting to see a crowd of raving lunatics come running around the corner at any second and overwhelm him, but so far all was quiet at the rear of the school.

"Look, if you don't get your ass down here now, I'm leaving you up there!" He spit, aggravated.

That seemed to be enough motivation for her and she carefully swung her right leg over the edge. She winced as the heat of the roof burned her hands and she slowly swung her body over the rest of the way. She reached out for the rope, tied to a pipe vent sticking out of the rooftop like a spear.

She started down slowly, much too slow for Mike's taste, and then it happened. She almost slipped, her hands losing her grip. She screamed in fear; managing to get a firmer grip, but her scream echoed across the area.

Mike cursed under his breathe, knowing what was coming, but praying he was wrong.

Becky had managed to make it almost halfway down, when the first attacker came around the school's left corner, his shoulder brushing against the manicured shrubs that lined the school's corners on all four sides.

The killer let out a piercing yell, signaling to the others he'd found more prey. Mike could only watch as more people, now bloody from their recent slaughter of the soldiers, ran and hopped into view.

Mike watched them for an instant, reminded of a National Geographic special about an indigenous species of man that lived deep in Africa and still practiced cannibalism. As the crowd prepared to run at him, flashes from that documentary came to mind.

"Keep coming, Becky, you're doing fine," he called to her. Then her pants caught on a jagged piece of metal sticking out from the bricks. If she'd had time to ponder what the metal might have been used for, she might have guessed it was an old hook or a broken eyering, but as she felt herself slam to a halt and then looked over her shoulder to see the crowd of screaming people running at her position, she was far to preoccupied to care.

All she knew was she was stuck and her arms were already too tired to pull her up enough to unhook herself.

"Mike, help me, I'm stuck," she pleaded.

"Damn it, Becky, there's no time, they're coming. We've got to go!" Mike yelled, his head constantly watching the oncoming people. He had only seconds before he would be overrun and Becky, too.

"I can't, I'm stuck. You've got to climb up here and help me, please!" She screamed, realizing she was in deep trouble.

Mike looked up at her and then at the crowd now halfway to his position, then back to Becky. Though he wanted to help her, he knew it would be suicide for them both, so he decided on the next best thing for himself.

He decided if he wanted to live, he needed to leave now, and hopefully, Becky would distract them long enough for him to make his escape.

"Sorry, baby, but you're on your own," he said quickly, backing away from the wall. "It's nothing personal, good luck!"

Then he took off at a run, away from the school. Whether he was moving in the same direction as Bill and the others was irrelevant. All he knew was he needed to go now before they were on top of him. Some of the crowd hesitated, deciding if they wanted to chase him, but when Becky let out a howl of loss as he sprinted away, all attention was focused back to her.

"Mike, where are you going? Don't leave me, Mike!" She screamed when the first killer reached the bottom of the rope and began to climb up the few feet to reach her dangling feet, wanting to pull her to the ground.

Without realizing it, she had helped Mike to escape unscathed, the infected happy to play with her while Mike disappeared into a nearby yard.

He sprinted across the street, only once glancing over his shoulder to check on Becky. He regretted leaving her; she'd been a nice piece of ass and had done whatever he had wanted. He'd totally controlled her. But that was all right, he thought, as he darted into a perfectly manicured backyard, there were plenty more women in the world.

He slowed for only a moment and turned to check on her one last time.

The ravenous crowd had reached the make-shift rope and was even now climbing up it. As for Becky, she was hanging on for her life, a growling, snarling blood-covered man hanging from her foot, the man's body only reaching halfway to the ground as he swung back and forth.

Just before Mike disappeared into the hedges of the yard, he saw her trying to kick her first attacker away from her, but she was hopelessly outnumbered and was soon pulled from the rope, her pants ripping free of the metal shard as she fell into the ravenous crowd.

With her death screams filling the air, Mike continued running, and was soon lost in the multiple yards of the neighborhood surrounding the school.

Becky's screams followed him for longer than he would have preferred.

CHAPTER 7

BILL CAUGHT UP to the last person in their rag-tag line. It was the other man that had been on the roof, the man with the picture of his wife. Jogging along side him, Bill tried to smile.

"Hey, I'm Bill, we were never introduced," Bill said in an upbeat, though gasping for air, voice.

The man continued jogging, but looked to his side at Bill. "Bruce, Bruce Greenwood," he stated, his voice only wavering slightly from the exertion of running.

"Nice to meet you, Bruce," Bill said, waving. "I'd shake your hand, but I think it's better if we keep moving."

Bruce didn't answer, but instead slipped through an opening in a thicket of shrubs. Once through, he slowed to a stop. The others were ahead of him and Bill moved past him and slowed once he was near Marie. Everyone was bending over, trying to catch their breath or just plain laying on the ground.

Bill smirked at this. Evidently his group wasn't in that great of shape, but then neither was he, and he bent over and placed his hands on his knees, sucking in another gulp of air. He closed his eyes, the white spots slowly diminishing as oxygen flooded his system.

"Looks like we lost them," Elizabeth said, one of the first to recover from their three block sprint from the school.

Once Bill had made it over the grass surrounding the school, he was pleased to see everyone running away at a good clip. Whoever had been in the lead had picked a winding trail between multiple backyards that filled the neighborhood, and in no time they were three blocks away.

The savage screams of the raving crowd had diminished and could barely be heard. For just a second Bill thought he heard Becky scream, but waved it away as his imagination. On a normal day in the small town, background noise would have easily drowned out the sounds from the school, but with the streets literally empty with the exception of the infected, sound traveled further.

"So what's next? Where do we go from here?" Janice asked; lying on her back in the soft grass of the yard they had gathered in.

"That's a good question, dear. Where is a safe place to go? Should we keep running or should we seek refuge in one of these houses?" Marie asked the group.

Bill had regained most of his composure and he stood taller, looking over the survivors. That was when he noticed Mike and Becky weren't with them.

"Hey, where's Mike and Becky?" He asked.

He was answered by a multitude of shrugs and shaking heads.

"Couldn't tell you, he was still on the roof when I climbed down," Elizabeth said, standing taller and wiping sweat from her brow. Perspiration glistened on her chest, making her skin glow.

Bill averted his eyes, not wanting to get caught looking at the female form twice in one day. He turned and jogged back to the opening in the shrubs. No one was following them and it would be too dangerous to go after Becky and Mike. Had he in fact heard Becky, after all?

He double checked to make sure he still had his .38 in the waistband of his pants and breathed a sigh of relief when he felt the comforting grip of the weapon. If it had fallen, it would have been too dangerous to go searching for it.

Walking back to the others, he frowned. "I could have sworn they were right behind me. Well, it's no use now; we can only hope they just chose to go their own way."

"All right then, that still leaves the question unanswered, just where do we go from here?" Melissa asked, stretching her legs as she cooled down from their brisk run from the school.

Bill was about to answer her when a loud rumbling filled the air around them.

"What the hell is that?" Janice asked, looking around the yard, the others doing the same.

The whine was growing louder, but was still a mystery.

"A train?" Melissa suggested.

Marie shook her head. "Can't be, the tracks are miles from here."

Bill looked up and to the left and saw a white shape slowly coming at them in a downward descent and his heart stopped beating.

Above the group, losing altitude fast was a large passenger airplane. He wasn't a connoisseur of aircraft, but if he had to guess, he would have figured it to be something as large as a 747 or something similar.

The airport was miles from where they stood in the backyard of an abandoned home, and if a plane was cruising that low, it could only mean one thing.

"Holy shit, that plane's coming down! We need to get the hell out of here, now!" Bill screamed over the roaring of the engines.

Those who were lying on the grass rolled to their feet again. The two boys, Roger and Phillip were huddling around Melissa and Janice, the girls hugging them close.

"What're you talking about?" Marie asked, looking at the descending airplane.

Bill grabbed her by the arm and pushed her out of the yard.

"There's no time to discuss it, if you want to live past the next ten minutes, then I suggest you all shut up and do what I tell you." All faces were looking at him, waiting, still not comprehending what he'd just said.

"Listen I was right when those people went down into the school and I'm right now, now do what I say!"

For a moment everyone hesitated, not grasping the situation.

"Did you hear me? I said run!" Then he took off out of the yard and into the street, pulling his weapon out of his pants in case he met resistance.

The others filed out of the yard and followed him into the street. Bill looked over his shoulder to see the plane was getting closer with every beat of his heart. As he ran, a small voice was telling him to forget it, there was no way he was going to be able to outrun a downed airplane.

He pushed that voice down as deep as it would go and pushed his legs to run faster. The others were behind him, all spreading out and running at their individual pace. Both Janice and Elizabeth actually passed him, but not so far that they still couldn't see him. In truth, neither woman knew where she was going and was deferring to Bill.

Bill glanced over his shoulder to see the small boy, Phillip, falling behind. Cursing his luck and thinking back to when Walter and Kathy were run down and slaughtered, he refused to let that happen again.

Stopping hard, he waved the others forward and quickly scooped the boy in his arms. Phillip wrapped his arms around his neck and Bill realized the boy barely weighed anything, no doubt because he hadn't eaten for a few days.

Pouring on the speed, he felt his teeth vibrating from the whining engines of the plane. Risking another glance over his shoulder, he saw there was no way in hell he or the others would outrun the falling aircraft, so he changed his tactic.

As they ran down the street, numerous cars sat either in the road or were half-on, half-off the sidewalk.

Spotting a Toyota van still idling on the sidewalk, its front bumper wedged against a telephone pole, he ran over to it and jumped into the passenger seat. He ignored the blood on the steering wheel and dashboard, letting Phillip slide off him and crawl into the back seat.

Backing away from the telephone pole, the van screeched when the bumper was ripped away, then he slammed the transmission in drive and shot forward, catching the others, still running down the road, in seconds. The side panels of the van were open, the wind whistling in his ears.

"Get in, now! It's the only way we'll outrun what's coming!" He screamed over the deafening noise.

While some of the group couldn't hear him, they easily figured out what he wanted them to do, and with the van still rolling, one at a time the others jumped inside. It was crowded in the van, far too many people for the small seats, but they all managed to squeeze in.

Just as Bill was ready to floor it, a dozen people came running around the street corner at the next intersection. They saw the van, but barely paid it any attention. Their hands were held to their ears and some of them pointed at the descending plane.

Bill never hesitated. Just by their clothes and the way the crowd moved, he knew they weren't normal like him and the others. With a surge of the engine, he shot into the frantic crowd, sending bodies rebounding off the front end of the van.

A moment later he was through the crowd and he floored the gas pedal. The van darted in and out of abandoned vehicles littering the road and Bill opted to drive on the sidewalk and manicured lawns of the neighborhood instead. With mailboxes and trashcans bouncing off the hood and windshield, he revved the engine and shot forward. His eyes took in two things at the same time. One was the gas gauge on the dashboard read almost empty, the needle hovering over the **E**. The second was he could actually see the falling plane in his rear view mirror. It was only seconds away from striking the earth and he shuddered to think what would happen to them all if they were still in its path.

Going for broke, he floored the pedal again, the van surging forward. He was moving at over sixty, but still driving on the sidewalk. The steering constantly fought him and he jumped in his seat when the front windshield cracked from an errant mailbox, sending a hundred spider web-like cracks across the safety glass.

He was still able to see, though his vision was impaired drastically, so he stuck his head out the window and almost lost it when the van drove too close to a telephone pole.

The van felt like it was shaking apart as the rumbling turbines of the plane seemed to rise in pitch. Bill swerved around a car that had jumped the curb and shot down another side street.

He kept expecting the road to be blocked, both sidewalk and street choked with cars, but his luck held and he continued moving.

Then it happened.

Though he was ready for it, there was no way he could have ever expected the magnitude of the explosion that ripped across the small neighborhood on the outskirts of Chicago. The plane landed on top of nearly half-a-dozen homes, plowing through each one as it slid across the earth, never slowing.

Fuel from the plane's fuel tanks sent up a fireball that consumed the entire block, but it was when one of the gas lines under the street were punctured that the true hell on earth began.

Sounding like he was being shelled by mortar rounds, the street behind the van started erupting, foot after foot, block after block.

Bill swerved around the bumper of a stalled truck and tried to concentrate on moving forward, but his brief glances in his side mirror told him what he was running from.

Behind him was a massive fireball two stories tall, the street exploding outward like the demons of Hell had finally broken through the dimensions and were at last coming to earth to dominate humanity.

"Oh my God, Bill, we are so screwed," Marie gasped from behind him. He was so flustered he didn't realize she'd spoken, vulgarity seeming out of character for the sophisticated woman. But her words most definitely fit their predicament.

A small picture of a gas pump appeared next to the gas gauge, telling the driver he was just about out of gas. Bill cursed. The van had idled for days on the sidewalk, perhaps starting life with a full tank, when its owner had abandoned the vehicle or been pulled from it and slaughtered; now only having fumes left.

All he could do was pray to God, Buddha or Allah, at the moment he would take help from any one of them, that they would seek to give it to him.

The column of fire was nipping at the rear of the van and Bill could feel himself sweating, either from nerves or the rise in air temperature. Inside the van, the others were screaming, some crying as they watched the inferno grow closer.

Swerving around a sharp corner with a screech of tires, he plowed into a woman who tried to jump on the van. Bill saw her eyes, wide with rage for the briefest instant, before she was thrown off the hood of the vehicle to roll in the street. He looked in his rearview mirror to see her getting to her feet, albeit with more cuts and bruises than when she'd started. She raised her hands in front of her face, as if that could protect her, and was quickly consumed by a wall of fire.

Bill looked forward, swerving and weaving. He had no way of knowing how far he'd traveled or how much more he'd need to go to escape the roaring conflagration behind him.

As he swerved around a few bodies lying prone on the sidewalk, he was still amazed he wasn't dead yet; both him and the others consumed by the rolling flames, incinerated in a blink of an eye.

While he drove, his mind filled with scenarios of death by fire. He probably wouldn't feel a thing, the flames consuming him in an instant, his eyes melting, his skin peeling back and flaking off his bones as it became nothing but charred ash.

Shaking his head clear of perspiration and blinking hard to clear his vision, he let out a yell of elation when the road opened up onto an on-ramp to a highway. No cars were in sight, the road clear. Not caring why, but just thanking whatever deity had sent him this way, he turned onto the highway and floored the pedal yet again. The Toyota surged forward and Bill had to squeeze the steering wheel hard to control the bouncing tires.

As the van shot down the road, the fireball started to recede in his back trail. Still, he continued going as fast as the van would let him.

After the first quarter mile, the engine started chugging, and then suddenly died, the power gone. Fighting the brakes, not cooperating very well with the engine off, he steered the van to the side of the road, finally stopping it.

Placing the transmission in park, he stepped out of the vehicle and opened the sliding side door. One at a time, the others stepped out into the smoke filled air.

The smell of jet fuel and burning homes filled the air, causing them to breathe through their mouths to try and prevent coughing.

Bill took a few steps from the van and looked out on what was left of the town behind him.

Where there was once a neighborhood, now there was nothing but a giant crater, miles long. The underground gas pipes had continued exploding, one after another, street after street, until there was nothing left but flames.

Marie walked up to him, her feet crunching in the loose gravel and sand on the shoulder of the highway. He was surprised he could hear her footsteps over the roaring flames and secondary explosions.

"You saved us, Bill. I don't know how you knew it, but you did. If you hadn't thought quick and got us moving, we'd all still be in there." She leaned over and stood on her tip toes and kissed him on the cheek. "Thank you, from all of us."

Bill touched his cheek. "Thanks, I guess, but I just got lucky. If I hadn't found this van we would've been toast, literally."

She smiled. "Maybe, but you did find it and you did save us." She turned when the others walked up behind him. Bruce slapped him on the back, his face cheerful. Bill could only assume that though the man had lost his wife and had been morose for days, when he'd seen his own life almost taken from him, he'd had a change of heart.

One at a time the others hugged him, their sweaty bodies sticking to his mostly bare chest, his t-shirt hanging ripped from somewhere on their flight. The heat from the massive fire blew toward him, causing him to wince.

"Come on, everyone, we need to go. The fire will keep on spreading until there's nothing left to burn and I don't want to be around here when that happens." With one last glance at the raging inferno behind him, he started up the highway.

One at a time the others set out after him, their faces exhausted, but cheerful. Each step they took and each lungful of air they breathed was a gift; a gift given to them by Bill.

If any of them had doubted his ability to lead them, all concern was wiped away, like the smoke from the fires as the wind caught the massive black pillars and carried them across the land.

CHAPTER 8

Dean looked up from the man he'd been torturing on the ground below him. Off in the distance, at least five or six miles, a huge explosion rocked the city. At first he thought it was an earthquake, though it would have been unlikely, but once his eyes saw the giant fireball rising into the sky, he realized it was just more wonderful chaos.

Evidently, something had happened in one of the suburbs surrounding Chicago, the growing fireball filling the sky to the east.

Dean climbed off the *normal* lying in the street, now dead, and tried to fix his clothes. They had become disarrayed while he'd killed the man. Not realizing it until now, he quickly tucked his shirt in and straightened his shirt sleeves.

Just because he was a homicidal maniac didn't mean he couldn't still look good.

He walked down the street, the fireball in the distance like a magnet, drawing him to it. He felt like a moth, slowly circling around the flame until at last it just flew into it, destroying itself in the process.

Shaking his head clear, he broke out of his stupor. Whatever had happened, it was over now. There would be nothing left to investigate even if he had chosen to do so.

Turning to look back at the supine body of the normal, the man's arms and legs bent at unnatural angles from the pain he had suffered, Dean got an idea.

With the fire burning, any normal that had survived would be evacuating, trying to find a safe haven to go to.

His mouth curved up into an evil grin.

Why try to chase down every normal in the city. Instead, he could just set the city ablaze at the west end and let the fire flush out every normal still in hiding.

Clasping his hands together and rubbing them quickly with excitement, he got control of himself again. Sometimes it was hard to stay focused. He always felt the rage inside him, threatening to come up from below, deep down in his mind and fully take over, like the other Changed surrounding him.

Only through sheer willpower had he managed to stay Dean Carlson, despite the tendency to want to kill and maim.

Calling the other Changed in the area to him, he headed off to the edge of the city, gathering recruits as he went. He wasn't quite sure how he'd get the deed done, but he'd always been a resourceful man.

He would need all hands for what he was intending. If everything went well, the city would be ablaze by sunset and every normal left alive would be running to him, like lemmings over the fabled cliff.

*   *   *

Mike, too, had seen the airplane falling out of the sky. When Bill and the others had escaped to the north, Mike had turned south.

With the roaring of turbines filling his head, he had managed to find a useable motorcycle lying in the street. The small 200cc Kawasaki engine more than enough to help him make his escape from the growing fireball that swept through the quiet neighborhood behind him.

With the heat roasting his back, coming so close his shirt became singed, he'd drove as fast as he could through the debris strewn streets until coming upon a roadblock. Military Hummers and large open bed trucks blocked the road and the sidewalks on both sides, preventing Mike from passing. As for the personnel, they were nowhere in sight, although many maroon bloodstains covered the asphalt and the sides of the trucks.

He'd abandoned the motorcycle and had run as fast as his legs would allow, slipping through the barricade and darting into a two-story house bordering the road.

Charging through the front door, heedless of what was inside, he ran to the kitchen, praying that was where the door for the basement would be. Luck was with him and he threw open the painted door and half-ran, half-fell down the set of rickety, wooden stairs.

A workbench was in the corner and he dove under it, covering his head with his hands as the world around him exploded. The shock-wave of the plane crash blew the military barricade away, causing the house above his head to nearly disintegrate.

It was like the mother of all hurricanes was blowing above him. He screamed while the world exploded above him, the first floor of the house falling into the basement, dust and debris flying everywhere and filling every crevice available.

Mike curled into a ball and prayed like he'd never prayed before; hoping God would answer his prayer this one time, though he was probably one of the worst Catholics ever to step into a church.

What seemed like hours passed, but was in fact only minutes, and the storm subsided and everything became preternaturally quiet.

Mike pushed away a large wooden beam that had fallen over the workbench, the sturdy bench having saved him from being crushed to death, and while coughing and spitting dust from his mouth, he started to dig himself out of the smoking wreckage.

More than an hour later, a hand filthy, ash-coated hand shot out of the top of the pile of rubble that had once been a house, the fingers moving back and forth as if they had eyes and were scoping the sur-rounding area before venturing further.

But then another hand punched its way through, and within sec-onds, a head appeared. Though covered with soot and dirt, Mike's head was unharmed and in short order he was able to drag his body onto the top of the debris.

He lay there breathing heavily, staring up at the ashen sky, the roaring fire behind him filling the sky with smoke. Numerous small fires burned here and there, looking like some cub scouts had gone crazy with campfires.

Rolling over onto his side, he vomited heavily. He hadn't eaten in days so was wracked by dry heaves. In time his stomach settled and he rose to a sitting position, dirt falling from his hair. Looking around himself, he was amazed at the devastation. If he hadn't seen the plane coming down for himself, he would have guessed that Illinois had been bombed, perhaps by a rival country.

Coughing from all the dust and smoke he'd inhaled, he stood up on unsteady legs. The wind was blowing the fire in all directions and he knew if he stayed where he was, he would be enveloped by the conflagration.

Climbing down off the pile of shattered wood beams and collapsed walls, he started walking, or better yet, shuffling.

At the moment he was still too dazed to even think of where he was going. He looked up to see the smoking Chicago skyline in the distance and it seemed to call to him.

Deciding the city was as good a place as any to go, he headed off in the direction of the towering buildings, not knowing what he'd find there, but hoping it might be better than what he was leaving behind.

CHAPTER 9

Bill AND THE others walked quietly down the highway, each lost in his or her private thoughts. Though wary of running into other people, so far they had been the only survivors of the explosion which had decimated the surrounding area.

The fires burned brightly behind them, turning the day into night as the ash from the flames floated higher into the sky. Hot embers floated on the breeze, also, landing on homes and structures that had escaped the brunt of the initial blast. Now these structures, too, caught fire, joining the massive conflagration as it slowly consumed everything east of Chicago.

Bill slowed his pace and turned around, starting to walk backwards, the others moving by him. His eyes, reflecting the orange and red flames, seemed to take on a life of their own. Marie walked next to him, not wanting to be the first to break the silence, but Bill did it for her.

"My house is in that hell back there somewhere," he said quietly.

"I'm sorry, Bill," was all she could think to say.

Bill looked at her as if for the first time and Marie realized he hadn't been talking to her, but had just spoken a thought out loud.

"Huh, what? Oh, thanks Marie. I know I shouldn't give a damn about my house, but it's one of the few things I have left that was both me and my wife's." He turned forward again, his head looking up at the sky. "Guess it all seems silly now."

Marie patted his arm. "That's not true, and you know it. Without our history we wouldn't know where we're going to in the future. One balances the other out."

Bill shrugged. "I suppose so. On the other hand, I guess there is a small bright side to all of this."

"Oh, and what could that possibly be?" She asked.

"Well, I did have a shitty mortgage. Interest was too damn high." His face lightened slightly. "Hey, I wonder if I'm covered under fire and falling airplanes."

Marie pursed her lips. "That's not funny, Bill, but I get your point."

"Yeah, I guess. Okay, but there is a real bright side to all of this."

"Okay, what is it?" She asked warily, wondering if he was just going to crack another joke.

"Well, it's a chance to start over, I suppose, start new and fresh. That is, if we can make it to somewhere safe."

Marie stepped over a dented hubcap that was in her path she nodded. "That's true, have you given it any thought? I mean, about where we'll go?"

He nodded. "A little." He pointed to one of the numerous highway markers. "Right now we're on Highway 23. If we keep walking, we'll come to the junction for Route 113. There's a big industrial complex there. Everything from toilet paper to textiles. I figure when everything started to happen and people started getting sick and going crazy, they would have abandoned their jobs and gone home. Hopefully, the place is deserted."

Marie grinned. "Sure, sounds good to me? Should we check with the others? Maybe one of them knows a better place, and if not it's good to know everyone's on board."

Bill agreed and the two of them sped up their pace, catching up to some of the others. The first two people Bill overtook were Bruce and Elizabeth. Bill had noticed them talking since everyone had abandoned the van. It looked like the two of them were hitting it off.

Bill approved.

If there was one thing the world needed right now, it was love. Since the viral outbreak, that emotion seemed to be one of the major ones in short supply.

Both Bill and Marie checked with the others one at a time until everyone agreed it was as good a place to go as any other. A few cars line the shoulder, some slanted at odd angles. The doors were closed, the engines silent. The small group moved passed them with barely a glance.

With a destination in mind, the pace was quickened just a little. So far the survivors hadn't come across another human being, either infected or normal like themselves.

But as the miles disappeared under their feet, all of them knew their luck would run out sooner or later.

Kenny Atkinson peeked out from the front seat of the abandoned car he was hiding in and watched the group of people walk by. Waiting until the last person was passed him and far enough away he wouldn't be noticed, he reached over the front seat and shook the shoulder of the young woman sleeping in the back seat.

Tessa Bateman opened her weary eyes and looked at Kenny.

"What do you want, it can't be my turn to stand watch," she mumbled groggily.

"No, it's not that. A bunch of people just walked by and they didn't look like they were crazy. I heard them talking and stuff and they sounded fine," Kenny said in a squeaky voice. He was just on the verge of puberty and his voice seemed to be changing every hour.

Tessa sat up slowly, making sure the area around them was clear. Scratching her hair and yawning, she looked over the dashboard at the once empty highway. Sure enough she could see the backs of the last people in the line as they continued moving down the lonely highway.

Sitting up, she stretched and looked Kenny straight in the eyes. "Damn it, Kenny, why didn't you wake me when you first saw them? If they're okay, like us, then we could have joined them."

Kenny leaned back in the front seat, his back touching the dashboard. "Well, shit, Tess', I didn't know what to do. What if they'd been crazies? What then? I figured I'd let them pass and then wake you; that way there was no way they'd see me."

Tessa climbed out of the dilapidated vehicle and looked behind the car. The fire was still burning brightly, the sun lost amidst the ash-grey clouds. Luckily, both she and Kenny had already been on the road when the first explosion had rocked the earth. It had been so bad she'd thought there was an earthquake or a bomb going off. She still had no idea what had started the massive fire and guessed it really didn't matter. She knew there was no going back, that's for sure. She also knew there'd be no fire department to even attempt to put out the blazing inferno.

Tessa stretched her lithe frame and looked to the other end of the highway, where the people Kenny had seen had just disappeared. She knew the road had a slight incline to it, causing the people to seem to evaporate from her vision, but she knew they weren't that far ahead of them.

She leaned forward in the seat, looking at her reflection in the rearview mirror of the car. Her light brown hair was a mess and her normally immaculate skin had streaks of dirt on it. But despite all these imperfections, any man would call her beautiful. She had met Kenny completely by accident. After her parents had gone completely nutso, she'd managed to barricade her bedroom door and sneak out her window. After that she had continued running, realizing the streets weren't much safer than her home had been.

That night she hid in an abandoned bakery and stuffed herself on stale bread and pastry. That was where she found Kenny. His parents owned the shop and when they, too, had succumbed to the infection, Kenny had run from their home only a few streets away to hide in the bakery.

At first Kenny had been frightened of her, thinking she was going to kill him, but after a lot of talking and reassurances that she was sane, he finally gave in.

Kenny had to be twelve to thirteen years old, only a few years younger than Tessa. The two had become friends quickly, both just glad to have someone else to talk to.

They stayed in the bakery for the next day and a half, only sneaking out the back door when a crowd of crazies came into the bakery looking for food.

Tessa had studied this. Although they were all raving killers, apparently they still needed to eat, to fuel the machine that was the human body. If they weren't intelligent enough to grow or raise food on their own, would it be just a matter of time before they died out?

Questions like these were what Tessa lived for. She'd always been a smart girl, always asking questions. She was a straight A student and had been planning on going to the college of her choice in another two years, though she figured that probably wouldn't be happening now.

Coming back to the present, she looked over at Kenny who was talking to her. She only managed to hear the last bit of his conversation, but it was enough.

"…are we going to follow them?" Kenny finished. "Do you think they're going to the Army camp?"

Tessa reached into the front seat of the car and retrieved a small backpack. It was all the food they had at the moment, and was more important to her than her Visa or cell phone. She thought it was funny how your priorities could change on a dime.

She ruffled his hair. "Calm down, squirt. Yeah, we'll follow them. Hopefully they are what you say they are and they won't end up tearing us to pieces when we catch up to them; but if they're going to the camp then forget it."

She was referring to a military camp that had set up outside of Chicago. A few other survivors had told her the policy was to shoot on sight and ask questions later. Not to mention how some of the survivors were nothing more than slaves, and others had been experimented on or put to work by the camp commander. From the looks on their faces, Tessa had no reason not to believe them. Tessa had decided she and Kenny should just stay as far away from there as humanly possible and keep on their own path.

Kenny folded his arms across his chest and scrunched his face up in anger. "I know what I saw Tess', and they looked okay."

Opening the rear door, she stepped onto the dusty shoulder of the highway, the odor of burnt rubber, wood and plastic suffusing the air like a living entity.

Backing away from the car, she moved towards the hot pavement, always ready to jump back into the tall grass lining the highway if she spotted something that could be harmful to the two of them.

"Well, I guess we'll find out either way, then, huh?" Then she gave Kenny her back and began walking away up the road like she was having a stroll in the park.

Kenny climbed out of the car and watched her walking away.

Kenny's face squeezed even more in anger, as if he'd eaten the biggest, sourest lemon in the world. Then he kicked a rock away from him and started to follow her.

"Girls," he said while jogging the few steps to catch up to Tessa.

*   *   *

Mike had been walking for more than an hour when he looked over his shoulder to see another highway meandering lazily to the south on his left a little more than half a mile away. He hadn't realized the highway he was on had looped around and was now parallel with another road.

He knew the area he was in pretty well and remembered the other road would end up curving away in another mile or so. He recalled there was a big industrial park out there somewhere. He didn't believe it was anything that could help him.

The highway he was on curved and sloped upward until he was a little higher than the other road, the open landscape allowing easy visibility in all four directions.

While he was looking around him, making sure he wasn't being followed, he paused and squinted harder, seeing movement.

Did he see other people walking on that other road?

Crouching lower, not knowing if they were dangerous, he ran to the guardrail and began walking while crouched over. The position hurt his back, the bruises from when the house fell on him, but he ignored the pain, not wanting to be spotted.

With the distance separating the people from him, plus the fact he was hiding, he was vaguely sure he was safe from discovery. He watched the other group closely, too far away to make out their faces.

He was about to give up and just go his own way when one of the walkers in the back of their little convoy stopped on the road and seemed to actually walk over to the guardrail and look gaze over the austere plain that separated both highways.

Mike stayed low, and when the sun peeked out from a bank of ash-covered clouds, the man's face was illuminated enough for Mike to get a good look.

Mike's jaw dropped. It was Bill. And a second later a woman walked up to him and Mike could tell by the gray hair that it was that bitch, Marie.

So they hadn't died in the fireball, like he'd thought.

Bill seemed to look around the plain, almost as if the man could sense that Mike was out there, but then Marie tugged his arm and the couple continued on. But before Bill left the guardrail, Mike saw the flash of metal, the dim light from the sun reflecting on the polished barrel of the .38.

Mike watched Bill move away down the road and pushed himself up, quickly moving to the far right side of the highway until he was walking on the shoulder.

From there, no one could see him from the other road.

Realizing whether he'd found them again or not was irrelevant, he continued down the highway.

Chicago was off to his right, the asphalt path soon curving away from his present position to join up with another highway further along. He spit into the gravel on the shoulder, cursing his luck for ever falling into Bill's group. They were a bunch of assholes, anyway. Rubbing his crotch, he wished Becky was with him. After all he'd been through, he could use a good blow job to let off some stress, and man could she do that like a pro.

Oh, well, he thought, there should still be plenty of pussy in Chicago. Hell, maybe he'd even see about doing one of the loonies. I mean, they might be crazy, but their bodies were still warm and soft like before.

With a smile on his face, he continued onward, feeling like he had a purpose, a destination.

Yes, sir, maybe finally splitting off from Bill and the others would turn out to be a good thing after all.

CHAPTER 10

"Shouldn't be too much farther now," Bill said when they passed a sign that read **Centennial Park, 2 miles**.

"Thank God, my feet are killing me," Melissa gasped askance of him.

A few other muffled groans of agreement filtered back to Bill as the rest of the group gave their two cents. They'd been walking for hours, what would have been a twenty minute car ride at sixty mph, now taking far, far, too long.

Most of them were walking in a daze, simply concentrating on placing one foot in front of the other. Luckily, the sky overhead had become overcast, threatening rain. Though the rain wasn't exactly welcome, it was nice not to have the sun beating down on their heads. With the arrival of the first rain cloud, the temperature had dropped more than five degrees with the possibility of it dropping further once the rain began.

Bill could only hope they made it to the office park before the first rain drops fell.

Turning around to check their back trail, Bill saw a brief glimpse of a small figure before it disappeared once again. He grinned as he turned back around.

He didn't know who was following them, but he knew it was only two of them.

Whoever they were, they certainly didn't act like they were infected.

Infected people would have simply charged at them, screaming and waving hands in front of them, prepared to attack, but the two people who followed them were sneaky, cautious. Two traits that were not synonymous with the crazies he'd previously had the displeasure to encounter.

Marie noticed him grinning and moved closer to him. "Did you see them?" She asked.

He nodded slightly. "Yeah, they're still there. Think we should just stop and introduce ourselves?"

Marie shook her head. "Nah, let them come when they're good and ready. They're just scared. Once they know we're friendly, I'm sure they'll come closer."

Bill was about to add something to that when a scream floated across the highway from behind him.

Turning quickly, he cursed under his breath and called out to the others to get their attention. As one unit, everyone turned and looked behind them, but it was obvious what had disturbed Bill.

Refugees from the fires had finally caught up to them. As they all watched from more than a half mile away, it was easy to see, even from this distance, the people running down the middle of the highway were definitely infected. They jumped up and down, waving their arms wildly, while crashing into each other. Some were badly burned, their clothes nothing but cinders, their single-mindedness to reach the survivors almost frightening in its intensity.

Their howls preceded them, while they charged at a full run toward the awe-struck survivors. Bill was the first to break from his stupor of watching the rampaging horde of humans.

"Shit, we need to run for it, now!" He yelled, turning and dashing down the highway. "Make for the office park, it's our only hope!"

Before he started running, he spotted the two people who'd been trailing them, now running full tilt, trying to escape the horde of murderers nipping on their heels.

The others followed him and in less than a heartbeat, they were all running for their lives.

Bruce scooped Phillip up in his arms, carrying the five-year-old so he wouldn't be left behind. They ran full out, their breaths rasping in their chests while they struggled to outrun the ravenous horde slowly growing closer with each tick of the clock.

The first mile passed under their feet in a blur of fear and terror. Bill quickly realized every second they ran, and every yard they tried to put between them, was for nothing; the horde was still gaining on them. Looking over his shoulder, he could clearly see the deranged faces as they galloped and jumped in anticipation of catching the survivors. It froze his blood in his veins, the sheer rage in those faces; the hate in those eyes.

Marie was one of the first to falter, her age and lack of real exercise slowing her down. Bill ran over to her, placing his arm around her, urging her on.

"No, go on without me, I'll only slow you down," she gasped, limping as fast as she could.

Not wanting to waste his breaths on arguing with her, he simply dragged her forward and gave her a quick: "No way am I leaving you, now shut up and run."

With less than a half mile to the office park, the two people who'd been trailing them caught up to the rest of the survivors.

Bill noticed in passing that they were nothing more than children, though on closer inspection, the girl seemed to be closer to adulthood. No one said welcome to them, but simply concentrated on running. Elizabeth picked up a cramp, and if it wasn't for Bruce by her side, the woman would have fallen to the road and been overrun, but the older man simply wrapped his arms around her and almost carried her to keep her moving, Phillip still wrapped in his other arm. Janice saw this and lent her help, too, both of them almost carrying Elizabeth between their running bodies while they ran for their life.

Tessa was now in front of the group and was the first to spot the first building that began the office park. She remembered something she'd heard from one of the refugees. The man had been a scientist and had commented on how he had worked at an office park nearby. Thinking it was possible they could find help there, Tessa waved to get Bill's attention, pointing to the buildings.

"Over there! We need to go there! There might be people inside that can help us!"

With no other options, Bill went with his gut and decided to follow the girl, hoping she knew something he didn't.

Bill pointed and waved everyone over the guardrail and had them cutting across the field separating the highway from the small road that led deep into the office complex.

With all of them on their last legs and the first of the horde of raving killers almost on top of them, they ran full tilt into the complex. Bill surveyed the buildings, knowing he only had one chance to find one that was unlocked. If he chose wrong, then they would all be trapped as the horde surrounded them.

He quickly read the names on the sides of the buildings. **FOREST TEXTILES**, **AND MCCULLANE PHARMACEUTICALS** were just the first two buildings he saw as the screaming murderous mob grew closer.

A piercing shriek came to his ears and he looked over his shoulder to see the first of the infected preparing to grab Elizabeth and Bruce. Pulling the .38 from his pants, and releasing Marie to let her run ahead, he slowed his gait, and with an almost casual aim, sent a round at a raving man.

The bullet only grazed the man's shoulder, but it was enough to cause him to stumble, off balance.

Bruce and Elizabeth poured on the last of their reserve strength and pulled away from the front of the mob. Satisfied, Bill turned and started running full tilt again.

His eyes caught the writing on a green awning on his left that overlooked a doorway. The words **STAR LABS** was stenciled in neat, white, lettering on the awning and he almost yelled in relief when he saw the door was partially open.

Tessa saw the sign, also, and remembered some more of the scientist's tale.

"We need to go in that one, there could be scientists and stuff that could help us in there," she said again.

"Okay, fine, it's worth a shot," Bill told her. He turned and called to the others who were almost to him. "Over there, go over there!" He called to the others, himself leaning to the left, and with Marie back in his arms, began running as fast as his waning strength would let him.

Pains shot up his left side and settled in his chest and he idly wondered if he was about to have a heart attack from the over exertion. Roger, Phillip's older brother, was the first to reach the doorway. He charged inside the building, the others following him one at a time. Bill pushed Marie into the building and then stopped. He needed to give the others the few precious seconds they needed to make it the last few feet, so with the .38 still in hand, he let off the last few rounds remaining in the revolver.

The mob of shrieking, screaming people was packed so close together he hit one with each round, causing the front of the line to falter for just an instant. His only good fortune was when one of them went down, falling to the grass in a tangle of arms and legs, the others following behind tripping over the prone body, causing a cascading effect.

But it only halted them for a moment, the others simply climbing over the bodies as they tried to be the first to reach Bill and the others.

The young boy and girl were the last into the building, and Bill was right behind them, closing the door and sliding the deadbolt, locking the door lock on its handle to prevent the infected from entering.

No sooner did he slam the door shut, then it rattled in its frame when dozens of bodies banged against it from the opposite side. The first of the mob were crushed as the people behind continued to push forward. Bill could see the door bending in its frame and knew it would only be a matter of time before it finally collapsed under the sheer pressure of the multitude of bodies pressing against it.

Blood began to seep under the bottom of the door as the first of the infected, crushed and killed by the mob pressing behind them, spilled their blood onto the cement.

Bill's eyes went down to the slowly spreading pool of plasma on the floor and he swallowed hard, a knot in his throat that wouldn't go down. That could have been him if he'd been slightly slower or had tripped in his mad dash to safety.

His eyes never leaving the shaking door, he began walking backward, only stopping when his heel struck the body of someone. He glanced down to see Marie lying below him on the floor, her shirtless chest heaving with exhaustion, her slim frame drenched in sweat. All of them had managed to run almost two miles non-stop, only their terror and adrenalin keeping them going.

Bill dropped to the floor, his head landing next to Marie. She flashed him a wan smile, her breath coming in gasps.

"Thank you," was all she said, her hand caressing his cheek.

Bill took her hand in his, squeezing gently. "My pleasure," he replied; then closed his eyes and simply concentrated on breathing. The pains in his chest were subsiding and he realized he was probably going to be okay.

"You know, I'm getting far too old for this shit," Bill joked between gasps of air.

That started Marie giggling, and she nodded her head in agreement. Soon the laughter became contagious and the others joined in. Phillip and Roger, the two brothers, didn't even know what was so funny, but joined in all the same, just glad to still be alive.

With the banging on the door continuing, sounding and feeling like demons of Hell were seeking entry, everyone chuckled, and laughed, just happy to be safe.

For the moment, the rest of the world was irrelevant, only sucking in the next lungful of air seemed to matter. At the edge of the small circle of prone bodies, both Kenny and Tessa looked at each other and moved closer together. They had no idea who these survivors were, but at the moment, with escape impossible, it appeared they were stuck with them.

CHAPTER 11

DEAN LEANED BACK in his self-made throne, enjoying the feeling of power. He'd cleared out the entire first floor of a clothing outlet, the room now one giant foyer which led to his throne situated at the back of the store.

To his right stood seven hostages, each one bound and gagged and tied to one of a dozen metal poles that held the roof up. All seven had tears in their eyes, though some were still too shocked to fully realize their present situation.

Scattered at their feet was the remains of hostage number eight. Body parts and entrails covered the white, tile floor, staining parts of it a bright red. The old man had been a screamer and Dean had enjoyed torturing him in front of the others. Thinking back, he realized he'd cherished the fear in the hostage's eyes as they watched the old man be slowly tortured to death, almost as much as the act of killing the old man itself. Relishing the feeling when each body part was pulled from the old man's ravaged body until his heart couldn't take it anymore and he expired.

The old man's eyelids were still open; the decapitated head staring up at the ceiling like the dead man was asking God why this had happened to him.

Dean leaned back in his oversized chair and smiled.

He remembered a saying from before, when he was a normal. "It's good to be the king," he'd heard people say it in jest. Well now that he was literally "the king" he had to admit it was good, in fact, it was downright awesome.

Leaning forward on his throne, he pointed to the hostage on the right, second from the end. She was a pretty little thing in her early thirties. Her blue eyes were wide with terror and he relished every second of it.

The Changed surrounding him saw where he pointed and immediately did his bidding, quickly untying her and throwing her to the floor at his feet.

"Please, why are you doing this to us?" The woman pleaded, through sobs of fear.

Dean stood up and walked down the three stairs leading to his throne. The woman was still prone on the ground, too frightened to move. Dean stopped when he was standing over her and placed his right foot over her neck, pressing her throat to the floor. With just a slight amount of pressure, he could snap her neck, like blowing out a candle. But what would be the fun in that? No, he wanted to make her suffer.

Releasing her neck, he knelt down. Leaning forward so his lips were almost touching her ear, he answered her.

"You want to know why I'm doing this? Well, I'll tell you. Before I was changed, I was nobody. People barely acknowledged my existence. But now, I'm a king. These people listen to me, obey me without question. So why do I do what I do?"

He leaned so close to her, she could feel his hot breath on the back of her ear. "Because I can, my dear, because I can." Then he had two of the Changed rip her clothes off, preparing her for him.

She cried and fought, but only half-heartedly. She knew she was doomed.

Dean stripped off his clothes and prepared to rape the woman, after which he would slaughter her like a pig being prepared for the Christmas dinner table.

Just before he mounted her, he called one of the Changed to him. The disheveled woman quickly ran to him, attentively waiting for instructions.

"Go out and find more normals. This can't be it, there has to be others. Take half of the men and women in here with you. Now go!"

The woman grunted and disappeared into the crowd, slapping men and women on the shoulder as she went, recruiting others to do Dean's bidding. The woman was one of the more intelligent in his present batch of underlings.

As the hall cleared out, half of them going out in search of more normals, Dean penetrated the woman, his hands wrapping around her neck and squeezing.

The woman's eyes bulged in their sockets as she tried to breath, the fear so strong in her Dean could smell it.

While he continued to defile her, holding her life in his hands, he realized perhaps he wasn't a king…perhaps he was a god.

With the other hostages either crying in empathy for the woman or perhaps weeping at their own fate that would soon be coming to each of them soon enough, he felt himself climaxing. Without realizing it, he squeezed the woman's neck too tight, crushing her trachea and cutting off her oxygen, the woman dying under him before he noticed.

Backing away from her, he kicked her with his foot, a frown creasing his face when she didn't stir.

"Damn it, I did it again. I simply have to stop killing them so quick every time I cum. Oh, well, there's always next time." He pointed to one of the Changed, a haggard looking man in his forties. "You, take her away, feel free to have some fun with her, she's still warm."

The man nodded and grinned stupidly. Picking up one of the dead woman's feet, he dragged her away by the ankle, a few others following him.

Dean started dressing again and walked back up to his throne. Sitting down, he looked down on the six other hostages, each one watching his every move.

"Now look, I know what you folks are thinking and it's really not that bad. After all, she's already dead." He grinned malevolently at the hostages. "Just think of it as recycling for the new world." He started laughing, his laughter carrying to the other Changed surrounding him. Pretty soon the store was filled with cackles and chuckles as the Changed laughed and hooted with their king.

Despite knowing they were doomed, the hostages squeezed their eyes shut and prayed to God that someone would save them from the hell they fallen into.

*   *   *

Mike slowed as he approached the city limits of Chicago. Across the road highway a military convoy, the trucks parked so that nothing could enter or exit the city without going by the barricade.

Raising the large lead pipe he'd found on the side of the road, he moved a little closer. Nothing moved; the prone bodies scattered around the barricade appeared to be dead.

All the soldiers wore white biological suits, though their gas masks were spread around them on the pavement like discarded beer cans at a frat party. All the bodies had been ripped apart, the wounds looking like a pack of hyenas or wild dogs had attacked them.

When he was no more than a few feet away from the first body, his eyes caught the reflection of the soldier's M-16 still lying under the corpse. With his heart fluttering in his throat, he moved the last few feet warily, and in a quick movement, reached down and pulled the weapon to him. The body rolled onto its side and Mike jumped two feet in the air, thinking the soldier wasn't dead and was about to attack him. But when the body remained still, he knew he was mistaken.

Though not an expert with firearms Mike had enough rudimentary knowledge to figure out how to eject the clip and find the safety.

Upon ejecting the clip, he saw the magazine was empty. Whatever had happened here, at least the soldier had given as good as he'd gotten. Mike searched the soldier's body, finding another full magazine. Slapping it into the empty weapon, he racked the arming bolt, sending the first round into the chamber. Feeling better now that he was armed, he climbed over the bumpers of two of the trucks where they'd been parked nose to nose to block traffic.

When he was on top of the trucks, he paused for a moment, taking in the visceral sight in front of him. If he had wondered where the soldier had expended his rounds, he now had his answer.

Bodies littered the street surrounding the barricade, all lying in odd directions where they had fallen. Infected and white suited soldiers alike covered the ground, so it would actually be a little difficult to traverse the street without tripping over a corpse. Flies and insects were everywhere, buzzing happily in the spilt blood. A murder of crows hopped from body to body, searching for tender eyes and soft tissue to feed on. One particular crow poked its head up when Mike stepped on the bumpers of the trucks. Its head swiveled to glare at Mike, the single eye in its beak hanging by a few optic ganglia.

Mike started counting corpses and stopped when he'd reached more than one hundred bodies. Evidently, the military had tried to contain the infected in the city and had failed miserably.

Looking at all the bodies spread out before him, and the empty city spread out in front of him, he realized maybe coming into Chicago was a bad idea.

Jumping back down onto the road, he was already deciding he'd go somewhere else when he spotted movement out of the corner of his eye. Before he realized what was happening, there were dozens of infected people coming from around the trucks and out of the nearby streets. Panicking, Mike raised the rifle, but forgot the safety was on. Squeezing the trigger again and again, he started shaking the rifle, not understanding why it wasn't working.

The first of the infected lunged at him, and he swung the rifle, butt first, at the man, and shattered his jaw. The man fell to the street, unconscious. That was when Mike's flailing fingers found the safety on the M-16 and he flicked it off with his thumb.

The rifle vibrated in his hand, spitting death, his shoulder absorbing some of the kick as the muzzle of the weapon started crawling upwards into the sky. Realizing he had to control the muzzle's climb, he overcompensated, the bullets now tearing into the asphalt in front of the infected horde.

A few of the attacking crowd were shot in the feet and legs, but it was only seconds later that the first one reached Mike, knocking him over, the rifle flying from his hands to clatter to the street.

Mike tried to fight them off, his screams filling the air. He expected to feel teeth and claw-like hands ripping into his flesh, but before the first attacker could do either, a sharp voice barked for them to stop.

"No, no kill. Bring to king!" The man's guttural voice said from the middle of the crowd.

"Holy shit, you guys can talk?" Mike said, surprised, despite his terror.

The man didn't respond to the question, but instead grunted and pointed back into the city. Mike was manhandled and pushed back over the trucks and onto the city side of the highway.

Rolling over the trucks, he came down hard on something squishy. At first he didn't want to look, but as he pulled himself to a sitting position, he found he'd landed inside the body cavity of a slain soldier. His right arm was wrist deep in viscera, the organs and tissue becoming entwined around his already shaking limb. With a yell of abhorrent terror, he rolled away from the corpse, shaking the blood and bile from his hand as he went.

Looking up, he found he was surrounded on all sides and if he'd even entertained the idea of escape, he would have easily been brought down and killed. Before he knew it he was pulled to his feet and pushed to begin walking.

With Mike in the middle, the mob of raving and screaming people pushed him deeper into Chicago. While he walked, Mike looked at the stores and buildings around him. A McDonalds was missing all its glass windows, the Burger King next to it in a similar state. A record store and a UPS store were still smoking from an old fire. The smell of smoke and burning debris was everywhere, and as Mike was pushed forward, he looked off to the other end of the city and could see flames reaching high into the sky.

It appeared the other side of Chicago was ablaze and Mike wondered how long it would take with the right amount of wind before the entire city joined it.

He continued walking until he was totally lost. He had never gone into the city very often, so its layout was a mystery to him. Bodies littered the streets and sidewalks, open eyes staring at nothing. Walking close to the corpse of a woman, Mike noticed the skin on her face was rippling. Slowing enough to examine this curiosity better, he almost vomited when a score of cockroaches spewed out of her mouth and nose.

With his stomach dry heaving, he continued onward, happy to put the vile scene behind him.

Rats were everywhere, enjoying all the free meat just lying out in the open. The corpse of a man lay on the hood of an askew car, the small rodents eating the cadaver's eyes. When the crowd was only a few feet away, the rats reared up on their hind legs and screeched at the intruders to their domain. Then each one picked up a succulent eyeball or other choice parts in their jaws and jumped off the corpse to disappear under a nearby postal truck, the doors opened wide, mail blowing everywhere. A letter blew across the road and landed at Mike's feet. He read the black script on the cover and almost wanted to laugh. It said he could be a millionaire if he just opened the letter. The top edge of the letter was a deep scarlet, and a small gobbet of flesh stuck to the corner. A few insane titters escaped his lips, but he managed to control himself, his stomach spasming inside his body from fear and dread.

Only sheer force of will kept him from vomiting all over his sneakers. Fifteen minutes later, the crowd halted in front of a clothing store. Mike noticed the windows were all intact, one of the few ground floor structures to remain so. He was pushed toward the main glass doorway and shoved through the swinging door. He tripped over his feet and fell heavily onto the polished marble floor.

Multiple hands grabbed him and dragged him deeper into the store. Though he wanted to fight, he knew it was hopeless. Whatever they were going to do with him, he could only hope it was quick.

With his feet dragging behind him, he was pulled through racks of clothing until he reached a wide open space. The racks had all been removed, leaving this section of the store now resembling a grand ball-room.

He was picked up and placed on his feet again and a hand pushed him toward what looked like a throne. The large chair appeared to be made out of boxes and crates, the high-backed, oversized chair held together with duct tape. When he was directly below the throne, his eyes trying not to look at the remains of six bodies lying to his right, the sole occupant of the chair stood up and walked down the stairs that lead to the throne.

"Well done, my people, you have done well bringing me another plaything. As you can see, I've finished with the others." He pointed to the closest metal post. "Tie him over there."

Mike was grabbed from all angles and pushed and dragged to the metal post. His arms were pulled behind him hard, causing him to yelp in pain.

The man walked over to him, chuckling. "Already in pain? My friend, you don't know what pain is, but I promise you, you will."

"Who the hell are you? You aren't like them, why don't you help me?" Mike begged; staring into the man's deranged eyes. If the man in front of him wasn't crazy, then he didn't know what crazy was.

"Oh, but I am like them, but for some reason I can still think, I'm still me, only better. I'm one of the new breed, the Changed. But not you. You're one of the normals, one of the last, I suspect. Even as we speak, I'm burning the city to the ground, causing any normals still alive to come to me like rats from a sinking ship as they try to evacuate the city. The military tried to quarantine us, keep us in, but I think you know what happened to them. When I'm done, every normal in the Chicago area will be dead, and then I'll spread out further until the whole damn country is mine. But don't you worry about it, you won't be around to see it," he said, raising his right hand to scratch Mike's face.

Fingernails that needed a good manicure cut deep into Mike's cheek, causing him to cry out in pain. The mob laughed and roared, enjoying his suffering. Blood dripped onto his chest, still bare from escaping the school. As his blood struck his chest, rolling into his pants, he started to shiver. He knew he was about to let go of his bladder, though he was doing his best not to.

The man raised his hand again, preparing to strike Mike again, when Mike yelled at the top of his lungs, desperate for a reprieve.

"Wait, don't kill me! I know where there's other people like me!"

The man's eyebrows went up in curiosity. "Oh really, I'm listening."

Mike looked over at the corpses piled carelessly in the corner and swallowed deeply. "First you have to promise me you won't kill me. I'll help you, I swear, and I'll do whatever you say. I know where there's almost a dozen people!" He said this while thinking of Bill and the others.

The man rubbed his jaw, thinking it over. "Hmm, a lap dog, a second hand man. I have to admit it would be nice to have someone to talk to, someone that actually knew what the hell I was saying." He waved to the infected around him. "Though the Changed do my bidding well, they've seemed to have lost about a hundred IQ points in the transformation. You know what, sure okay, why not." He leaned closer to Mike as if he was a confident. "Besides, if I get bored with you, I can always kill you later."

Mike nodded his head, eager to be liked by this man. "Sure, okay, that's fine, but I promise you, you won't be sorry."

The man stepped back and gestured to Mike. "Untie him, now," he ordered the nearest of the Changed. Mike was untied and he stepped away from the pole, rubbing his wrists. He reached up and touched his cheek, the deep scratch already clotting.

The man held out his hand to Mike. "My name's Dean, Dean Carlson, and I'm the new king of Chicago."

Mike hesitantly took the proffered hand. "Mike Fogarty."

Dean placed an arm around Mike's shoulders, and started walking to the front door. "So, Mike Fogarty, start talking, and if I don't like what I hear, then you'll be back on that post before you finish your last word."

CHAPTER 12

BILL ROLLED TO his feet, deciding he'd spent enough time recovering.

Besides, they were far from in the clear, the door still shaking like hellhounds were trying to gain entry.

"All right, everyone, that's enough rest for now, you can rest more when you're dead. Now we need someone to find something to put against that door. And the sooner the better."

Bruce rose to his feet, already moving out of the small hallway they had fallen into after entering the building. "I'm on it. Elizabeth, you want to help me?" He asked. She nodded and after climbing to her feet, the couple disappeared around a bend in the hallway.

The door continued rattling in its frame, and after watching it for another second, Bill was pretty sure it would hold; at least for long enough for them to decide on their next course of action.

"All right, people, on your feet. I know you're all tired, but we need to see what's in here and figure out how we're going to get out of here in one piece." Sounds of moans and groans filled the hallway while everyone rose on unsteady legs. Bill knew how they felt. Though he tried to stay relatively fit, going for walks after dinner and such, even his legs were sore after their two mile dash down the highway. Marie was using the wall to hold herself up, and when he looked her way, she shot him a weak smile.

"Don't worry about this old broad, she's still got some life in her yet," she joked.

A loud screeching sound filled the hallway behind him and Bill turned to see Bruce and Elizabeth pushing a heavy metal desk across the tiled floor. Long scratches were left in their wake, while the team of two struggled to keep the desk moving over the grout lines in the tiles.

Upon seeing the couple with the desk, Melissa and Janice joined in and in no time the desk was planted against the door.

Bill nodded. "That's good, but one more on top of the first one would be better.

"That's no problem, there's a room full of them back there."

"All right then, what are we waiting for?" Bill asked, moving down the hall, following the scratches on the floor to the correct room.

Stepping inside the large space, he saw it was used for office cubicles. Neck high cork walls separated each one, allowing the owner of his space a modicum of privacy. Bill grabbed the next desk in line and started pushing it out the door. Bruce was there a moment later, and the two men made quick work of sliding the desk to join the other one against the door.

Once the desk was on top of the other, Bill stepped away from their haphazard barricade.

"It should do, at least until we're ready to go," Bill told Bruce.

Askance of him, Bruce just grunted, then turned away to go join the others.

At the end of the long hall was a small break room which also served as the floor's cafeteria. Marie was already opening packages of noodles and others were munching on candy bars. The vending machine in the corner now had a shattered front glass, the survivors eagerly taking out its contents. The soda machine proved more difficult to open and Bill thought it the biggest irony that he had to actually put money in the machine to buy a Coke.

He handed the Coke to Phillip, the young boy taking it with a smile. Henry thought that was the sweetest thing. Have a Coke and a smile, and there it was, happening before him, just like the commercials said.

Though things were bad, he couldn't imagine what it must all look like to a child, watching the adults battle for their lives in a world turned upside down.

"We need to set a watch; someone needs to keep an eye on that door. If it starts to give, we need to know before they get in here." He looked around the room. "So who's first?"

All the survivors were silent, each concentrating on eating. Finally, when it seemed no one was going to volunteer, it was Melissa who raised her hand.

"Oh, fine, I'll go first. Christ, what is this, kindergarten?" Melissa asked the group.

"I'm in kindergarten, my teacher's name is Mrs. Milton," Phillip said from the corner of the room, where he was eating a candy bar with the Coke Bill had given him.

At first no one knew what to say, everyone so surprised to hear the boy talk. He'd said nothing since arriving at the school days ago, along with his brother. Marie walked over to him and gently rubbed his hair. "Of course it is, dear," she said nicely. "And I'm sure she's a great teacher."

"Will I ever get to see her again?" Phillip asked.

"Uhm, I don't know, honey, I sure hope so," Marie replied, stumped on how to answer the question properly.

Melissa stood up, her chair scraping across the floor. While wiping her hands on her pants, she moved to the door leading from the break room.

"Thanks, Melissa, I'll have someone relieve you in an hour or so," Bill said.

She answered with a quick wave and was gone, her footsteps echoing down the hall. Janice handed Bill a granola bar and he took it with a smile. Chewing, he sat down.

"Look guys, we're not safe in here. Once we rest up, we need to figure out how to ditch those bastards and go somewhere better. More secure," Bill said to the haggard faces in front of him.

"And where is that, exactly? Those damn nuts are everywhere, Bill. Where the hell are we supposed to go?" Janice asked, exasperated from across the table. "How can we fight a whole city?"

"I heard something about the military setting up a temporary camp outside of Chicago on the TV before I left my house. Maybe we could find out where they are and go there," Elizabeth suggested.

"I know where they are," a small voice said from the back of the room. It was the first time Bill had heard her voice and he realized no one had introduced themselves yet to their new arrivals.

"And who might you be? With all the commotion we never got properly introduced. I'm Bill and that's Marie for starters."

"I'm Tessa and this is Kenny," she said, looking at the others. Everyone said hi, and a round of introductions was made. Once finished, Bill walked over to Tessa and sat down next to her.

"Now, you were saying you know where the refugee camp is? And why exactly did you want to go into this building?"

"Uh-huh, sort of, but I don't want to go there. They scared us at that camp, me and Kenny. The soldiers wear these scary white jumpsuits and have gas masks on. But the worst thing is they shoot everyone on sight. If you went too close to their camp, they just shoot you, whether you were one of the crazy people or not. At least that's what we heard."

"Sounds like they're scared," Bruce said around a mouthful of Twinkie.

"And who isn't?" Janice said. "If this infection or plague or whatever keeps spreading, then the whole world could possibly collapse, but I don't see anywhere else we can go."

Bill nodded in agreement. "She's right. Despite the fact we might be turned away, or worse, shot, we need to try. It's either that or just stay here until either we run out of food or those bastards break in." Bill turned back to Tessa. "And what about why you said to come in here? You haven't answered me yet."

Tessa shrugged. "There was a guy there, a scientist. He said he worked at a place called Star Labs. I didn't even think of it until I saw that sign. I just figured maybe there's more scientists here and stuff, you know, to help with what's happening."

Bill frowned. "Well, if there's anyone here, they're keeping to themselves. We were making a lot of noise and all that banging those people are making…plus the door was unlocked. Still, we could check it out. Do the rest of you have any opinions?" Bill asked the others.

At the end of his question, everyone began arguing and talking at once, each person trying to give their opinion. Finally, Bill slammed his hands down on the table and stood up. "All right, okay, wait a minute. Now we don't have to decide right now. But we do need to make a decision quickly. So let's all sleep on it, okay? We all need rest, real rest, and now is the time with a roof over our heads."

Everyone agreed and after a few more minutes of talking amongst one another, Bill spoke up again. "All right then, now that we've gotten that out of the way, let's explore our new prison or haven, depending how you want to look at it. See what's in here. Tessa, in a little bit we can go see if what you heard was true."

She nodded, agreeing with him.

When everyone was finished eating, they paired up in groups of two. Bill grinned when he saw Bruce and Elizabeth pairing up. When they were all out the door and moving down the hall to explore, Bill called to them one last time.

"Try to find some weapons, anything that could be used as a defensive or offensive weapon!"

Turning back into the break room, Marie leaned against the wall while both Phillip and his brother Roger sat at the table below her. "I figured I'd keep these two guys with me," she said.

Bill shrugged. "Sure, whatever." He looked over at Tessa and Kenny. "What about you two, you want to hang with us?"

Kenny seemed to like the idea while Tessa was less enthusiastic.

"Sure whatever," she said, repeating Bill's answer to Marie. Her eyes drifted to Roger, about the same age as her and she looked away bashfully.

Bill chuckled and walked out of the room with the others in tow. Even in such dire circumstances as the one they were presently in, the human heart still looked for companionship; whether it was Bruce and Elizabeth or Tessa eyeing Roger.

"Well, come on gang; let's see what Star Labs has to show us."

CHAPTER 13

BILL AND MARIE, along with the three children walked down the deserted, debris strewn hallway; Roger had decided to stay in the break room and Bill had agreed it was all right. Doors lined each side of the hall, some open, others closed.

Bill slowed when he came upon a door marked: **Bio-genetics, Authorized Personnel Only**. Below that sign was another with smaller lettering that read. **Keep badges in view at all time**.

"This one looks interesting," Bill said, pushing the partially open door all the way open and stepping inside. The second his foot stepped over the threshold, the redolence of death struck him in the face. He held his arms out to his sides to stop the others from coming into the room.

"Marie, why don't you wait here with the kids until I make sure it's safe," he told her. "I'll be right back."

"Okay, but be careful," she said, pulling Phillip closer to her. The boy didn't resist.

Bill stepped into the room, his eyes already looking for a weapon other than his empty .38. There was a desk nearby, and on the desk in a holder for pens and pencils was a letter opener. Bill reached for the make-shift weapon, pulling it to his body like a drowning man would a life raft. With weapon in hand, he moved deeper into the office.

Once again, like the other room with the desks Bruce had found, the large open space was divided into cubicles. Bill moved down the main aisle, expecting something or someone to jump out at him any second.

With his pulse pounding in his ears, he moved deeper into the room.

Reaching the end of the space, he saw a leg lying on the floor, the rest of the body hidden from view. With the letter opener in front of him, he moved closer to what he assumed was a body, but was hesitant to take chances.

When he was even with the opening to the cubicle, he was able to look inside. He immediately turned away in disgust, having to close his eyes and try to think of better things, like a sunny day in the park or an ocean sunset.

Controlling his breathing, he covered his nose with his bare arm, realizing sooner or later they would all need to find new clothes, and leaned closer to what was once a body. The clothes were in tatters, bloody and ripped. The head of what Bill assumed was a man, thanks to the shoes, was nothing but a shattered mess of bone and brain matter, maggots squirming around in abject happiness. Both arms had been pulled from the body, like the man had been drawn and quartered, but had his left the legs intact.

On the man's blood-stained, white coat was an ID badge. Holding his breath, Bill leaned over and plucked the badge from the dead man's pocket, shaking the card free of the dozen or so maggots crawling on it. He quickly moved away from the corpse, almost running back to Marie and the others.

Now halfway across the room, with the odor of rotting meat behind him, the air smelled almost sweet. Once he'd reached Marie, he held out the badge for her to see.

"Found this," was all he said, stepping into the hallway. The sounds of pounding floated down the hall, the infected outside still doing their best to break inside the building.

"Yeah, and what are we supposed to do with this?" Marie asked while holding the card, but it was Tessa who took the badge from her hands and looked at it more closely.

"I've seen these before or something like it at my school. They just started using them. See this black line?" She said pointing to the magnetic strip on the bottom of the badge. "Well, I'll bet anything it's to get you into somewhere."

"You think that's an access card?" Bill asked, taking the badge from her and looking at it again. Now that he was in the hallway, away from the smell of death, he was able to think more clearly.

Tessa nodded. "Has to be. The question is, where's the door it opens?"

"Let's split up, look for a card reader outside one of the hall doors, odds are that'll be the one," Bill told them, enjoying the little mystery they'd discovered.

Elizabeth poked her head from the far side of the hallway and waved. "Hey, guys, guess what we found. A whole room full of clothes, probably from the employees that worked here before they took off. Guess they left in a hurry and didn't change."

"Hey, that's great, listen, keep your eye out for a locked door with a card reader next to it," Bill called to her.

"Sure, no problem, see ya," she said, her head disappearing like a ghost.

Bill looked at the others and grinned. "Well, what are we waiting for? Let's see if we can find that room."

Fifteen minutes later, Marie called from two hallways over with Phillip by her side. Bill, Tessa and now Roger jogged over to her and it was Phillip who pointed at the closed door with the card reader next to it. Bill smiled at that. Evidently, the boy was finally coming out of his shell after the trauma he'd suffered. Bill could only hope he could help to minimize anything else happening to the boy or any of them, for that matter.

"Excellent, Marie, great job," Bill said holding up the badge. "Now, to see if the slipper fits the right foot, said the Prince." With the badge in hand, he slid the card through the reader, the red light quickly changing to green. The door hissed for a second and popped open.

Before Bill could stop her, Tessa stepped inside the room. "Damn it, Tessa, wait, it could be dangerous!" Bill called to her back.

"It's fine. I'm fine. Come on in. Wow, you've got to see this stuff," she said, sounding amazed.

"Well, what do you think?" Marie asked askance of him.

"I think she's reckless and stupid, but I guess if there was going to be a problem it would have happened by now. So let's go see what she's found."

Bill stepped into the room, Marie and the kids' right behind him. The first thing Bill noticed was how bright it was in the room. More than two dozen halogen lamps hung from the ceiling, washing all the shadows away.

The second thing he noticed was that the cages were all filled with dead animals.

Moving into the spacious room, he was surprised there was almost no odor, then he saw the large vents on the walls and ceiling. With the air on full, the room was well ventilated. He didn't want to imagine what would happen if the power cut off.

The room was huge, about the size of four, three-car garages if they were put together like a square. While he walked through the center aisle, cages of dead animals on either side of him, he wondered what they could have been doing in here. What kind of experiments would have such a broad spectrum of animals? He saw the typical lab animals, such as mice and rabbits, but there were multiple cages filled with dogs, cats and one had a goat, all now dead.

"What the hell were they doing in here?" He asked the area around him.

"Usually they test cosmetics and vaccines on test animals, but this? I have no idea," Marie said, holding Phillip tight to her chest.

Tessa was still in front of them, and she stopped at the far wall, marveling at the table full of beakers and test tubes. She leaned down and stared at the multi-colored glass, her face distorting and magnifying her reflection.

"This place is so cool, it totally blows away the lab at my school," Tessa said.

"Aww, it ain't so great," Kenny mumbled, speaking up for the first time.

Bill glanced down at him. "Don't you like science, Kenny?" Bill asked him.

Kenny shrugged. "Guess so, but I'm not that good at it, so…you know."

Bill nodded in agreement, remembering his days in school. "Yeah, I know what you mean."

Bill's eyes tried to take in everything. Off against the far wall were half a dozen large hydrogen and oxygen tanks. The large cylinders always reminded him of torpedoes. Looking closer at the dead animals, he took an estimated guess and assumed some of them died from starvation and dehydration. When everyone evacuated, there was no one left to take care of the test animals. He shook his head, imagining the suffering the poor creatures had gone through as they slowly grew weaker until finally succumbing to death.

"Hey, I found something!" Tessa called from the corner of the vast room. At the moment, she was hidden from view, the cages blocking her waving body.

The others caught up to her and all stopped when she showed them what she'd discovered. In the corner of the room was another door, solid metal with one small square window set high in the middle. This door, too, had a card reader and Bill swiped the card, nervous when the door hissed and slid open like something out of Star Trek, the air escaping from the pressurized room.

"This looks important," he said. "Look at the rubber seals that line the frame. If I had to guess, this is one of those rooms where they mess with viruses and shit; like in the *China Syndrome*." He turned to Tessa. "Maybe this is what that scientist was talking about."

"That's impossible. Here? In Illinois? Marie asked, not believing it. "But it would be so dangerous to have a lab here in the middle of a populated area."

"Sure, why not here? The government loves to set up in unassuming places. That way no one suspects a thing," Tessa said.

"My, aren't we a conspiracy nut. And so young," Bill said to her, grinning.

She shrugged. "It was mostly my Dad, but I used to pay attention. Sometimes the stuff he found on the internet made sense."

"Do you think we should go in there? I mean, what if we end up letting out some kind of virus, like the Bubonic plague or Sars or Anthrax," Marie said, hovering near the door.

"Look, Marie, once the seals broken it's already too late. If there was something in there that was going to hurt us, we'd already be dead, so I say what the hell. If you want, we can send the kids back to the break room."

"I'd like that. They don't need to see this, especially Phillip," she said, brushing her hand over his hair.

"No way am I leaving, I want to see what's in there," Kenny said.

Bill sighed. "Jesus, I hate kids." He mumbled under his breath. He looked to Kenny, "Hey, Kenny, what do you say you bring Phillip back with you. It'll be a big favor to me. I'll make it up to you, I promise."

Kenny shrugged; disappointed. "Oh, okay, I could care less what's in that stupid room, anyway." He lied. "Come on, Phillip, lets go get some more candy from the break room," he said, addressing the small boy. He turned to look at Tessa. "You'll tell me what's in there later, though, right?"

Tessa shrugged like she was thinking about it.

"Forget it, then, I changed my mind. I want to stay here," Kenny said.

"No way, I want to see, too," Phillip said, excitedly.

Bill pointed to the way back out of the room. "No deal, Kenny, now get going. I promise if it's safe, then you can come back later, you too, Phillip," Bill said, coercing the boy.

Kenny hesitated, wanting to argue some more, but Bill gave him a look that would brook no more argument. With a slumping of shoulders, he gave in. "This sucks. Even when everything's all crazy I still get left out of stuff," Kenny said, walking away from the others. Bill followed behind him for a few feet to make sure he continued moving.

"Be careful, you two, don't do anything but go straight back to the break room, we'll be there soon," Bill called to them.

Kenny waved his hand, not looking back and Marie chuckled. "My, what a way you have with children," she joked. "Will you really let them come back if it's safe?"

Bill shrugged. "Doubt it, but at least Phillip seems to be getting better, at least he's talking now," Bill stated.

"Perhaps it's the arrival of Tessa and Kenny?" She suggested.

"Maybe, who knows what's going through his mind or Roger's, for that matter."

"Hello, are we going in or what?" Tessa asked impatiently.

"All right, hold your horses; we're coming, let the old folk talk for a moment, will ya?"

Tessa answered by stomping her feet in frustration, not wanting to wait.

"Shall we?" Bill asked Marie, holding out his arm as if they were going dancing, instead of venturing into an unknown lab.

"Why, thank you, sir, I guess we shall," Marie said, taking his arm and stepping through the pressurized door. Tessa rolled her eyes and wondered why adults had to act so weird, then she, too, followed them inside the chamber.

CHAPTER 14

STEPPING INSIDE THE airlock, Bill first saw another door in front of them.

"We need to close the outer door before the inner one will open. It's a safety feature," he told the others.

Marie turned to her side after stepping in and spotted a button on the wall. Pushing it, the outer door closed with a hissing of hydraulics, and once the chamber was re-pressurized, the inner door slid open.

The smell of disinfectant was the first thing to assail their olfactory senses; the second was the odor of stale death.

With Bill in the lead, the letter opener in front of him, they stepped into a smaller room, less than half the size of the one they'd just vacated; really just the size of one standard three-car garage.

It reminded him of something out of a mad scientist's handbook. The tables were covered with more beakers and test tubes, with the exception that this room had a large desk in the center and one computer terminal affixed to the middle of the desk. A chair was lying on its side near the door, but otherwise, the room appeared to be undisturbed.

Marie walked over to the desk and sat down. Bill moved with her and turned suddenly when Tessa shrieked in panic. Whirling quickly, the letter opener prepared to slash anything that moved, he realized she was looking at something on the floor of the room, hidden behind a large table.

Covering the few feet that separated him from her, he stopped when he saw there was no threat. But he did discover where the odor of stale death was emanating from.

On the floor, curled up in a ball was another dead animal. The dog had a tan coat and its ribs poked through its fur. Its eyelids were open, staring into the void of nothing. Bill leaned forward and turned its dog collar so he could read it better.

SUBJECT 11524B, it read in bold, black typing.

Bill turned to Tessa and placed his hand on her arm. "Looks like they might have made this one a pet," he said. "If I had to guess, I'd say the poor thing died from starvation. Come on, let's go back and join Marie, see what she's found."

Tessa nodded and let Bill lead her back to the center of the room. Marie looked up, curious about what had happened.

Bill waved it away. "It's nothing, just another dead animal, maybe the lab's pet dog."

"Oh, okay, well, you won't believe what I've found. The computer was still logged in, so it was easy to surf the menus. If it hadn't, I would never have been able to crack the password code."

"Don't look at me, I have enough trouble just trying to read my e-mails," Bill said looking over her shoulder at the flickering screen.

Tessa let out a huff. "Old people. Bill, get with the times."

Marie chuckled. "Yeah, Bill, either catch up or get out of the way. My daughter bought me a computer a few years ago and I self taught myself how to use it. It's actually quite simple once you get the hang of it. Windows inside of other windows, it's quite amazing actually, in fact..."

Bill cut her off. "Marie, please, a computer lesson later, okay? What did you find?"

"Oh sorry, I do go on. Well, I was able to access a video feed from a few days ago. Apparently it was a security camera that caught all the action, then it was supposed to be downloaded to the central processor, but that never happened.

It's not long, but it's quite shocking. Are you ready?"

"I'm ready, so go, will ya? Hit the button, start the show," he said impatiently.

Marie pressed a few keys. Starting the video again. The picture was grainy, but it was easy to see everything that was happening.

All three of them watched as a man in a biological containment suit, complete with oxygen tank on his back, moved across the floor of the lab. Without realizing it, the man accidentally knocked a beaker onto the floor, the glass shattering.

A moment later, lights began to flash and the other people began to run toward the door. The camera shifted position then, the view now of the chamber doors.

Just before the inner door tried to slam shut, a man pushed a chair in the frame, stopping the door from closing and sealing off the chamber. He quickly waved to the five others in the room to hurry, and one at a time they hopped over the chair, crowding into the airlock.

Then he kicked the chair away from the door and it slammed shut, the airlock cycled through and one at a time they ran out of the airlock and disappeared off camera. Before the last man was gone, Bill could clearly see the man's white suit had a large tear in its side, exposing the man to whatever was inside the broken test tube.

Marie hit a button and the picture went back to a screen saver. The picture of a gold star with the name *STAR LABS* inside the two sides of the star points floated around the screen, bouncing off the side walls of the monitor and continuing its loop again and again.

Bill looked away and dry-washed his face with his hands.

"Jesus Christ, if what we saw is true, then those idiots tried to escape when a biochemical lockdown started. In trying to save their own damn lives they let loose whatever was in that vile. This is where it all started, it's like we're living in a friggin' horror movie or a Stephen King book, now all I need are crazy dreams where old ladies talk to me and we're set."

Marie took his arm and squeezed. "It's all true Bill, there's a time stamp on the video. It coincides with only a few days before things started getting bad out there. Whatever they let loose spread in only a few days."

"But what was it? Some kind of plague?" Tessa asked, leaning on the desk.

"I don't think so, honey, in fact, I found a video diary of one of the scientists, but I haven't looked at them yet. Should I call them up?" She asked Bill.

He shrugged, still trying to wrap his head around what he'd seen. He was standing at ground zero; this is where the genie was let out of the bottle. Pandora's Box, he was actually standing inside Pandora's Box.

"Shit, do you think we're in danger of getting infected in here?" Bill asked.

Marie shook her head. "Doubt it. Whatever was in here is out there in the air now." She waved her hand to signify the world. "Whatever this bug is, it seems we're immune." She turned back to the computer screen. "So do you want to see the video diary or what?"

Looking down at Marie, he sighed.

"Sure, why the hell not, how bad could it be?"

Marie stroked the keys and another menu appeared along with a column of dates and names.

"Which one do you want to see? They're numbered by dates and names."

Bill read some of the names on the screens, one catching his eye. "What about that one? *Dead Rage*, it says, try that one. Doesn't matter really; try something about a week ago, before all the shit hit the fan," Bill said.

Marie highlighted the appropriate file and the screen went black. A second later a man's face filled the screen. He was short, maybe five-five by Bill's guess as he used the tables around the man for a reference. He had brown hair and brown eyes with a pair of wire rimmed glasses. The man removed the glasses for a moment, polishing them on his lab coat and Bill could see the indentation on his nose, proclaiming the glasses were almost always on his face.

The man flipped through a notebook and then spoke for the first time, his voice sounding hollow coming from the computer speakers.

"This is Dr. Theodore Donaldson, video log follow up for the *Dead-Rage virus*. I've given the feline the injection and have been waiting for almost five minutes for the first sign that it has worked. Now, I've placed the animal in the same cage as its mother. Before the initial injection, the cat was totally subservient to its mother, the mother being the dominant personality. But observe what occurred once the virus became active." The camera swung to a large glass cage where two orange and yellow cats sat inside, both docile.

"The mother is on the right, the infected feline on the left," the man's off camera voice said.

Bill, Marie and Tessa watched silently. At first the infected cat did nothing, merely licking its mother, showing the love it had for her, but after only a few minutes had passed, the cat slowly grew more aggressive until finally going crazy, claws and teeth attacking the mother. The mother tried to defend herself, tail doubling in size and claws out, but it couldn't take the constant onslaught and finally succumbed to death from too many bloody wounds. The infected cat never stopped attacking its mother, even after the animal was dead.

Finally, a hand reached over the cage and turned a knob. Smoke filled the glass cage and the violent animal slowed its attack and finally dropped to the cage floor. Bill could see its chest rising and falling slowly; the animal had been gassed to sleep.

The camera swung back to the man's face and his eyes were wide with excitement. "It works, the virus works! This could mean so much. Once we adapt it for humans, who won't take much fine tuning, we could in effect drop it on an enemy country and once the population turned, they would kill each other. Once most were killed, the rest would soon die of starvation, killing the virus at the same time. Just think, no longer would our soldiers have to go in on the ground and fight hand to hand, we could simply infect the water supply or the grain supply of a country and our problems would be solved!" The man's was ecstatic with excitement. "I'll win the Nobel Prize for this! I'll be famous! But first I need to deduce how long the virus will be viable in its host and how long it will take to take over said host. So much to do and so little time." The man started to giggle maniacally. Then the screen went black.

"Holy shit, that guy is a modern day Dr. Frankenstein," Bill said in awe. "That dumb bastard did this to all of us, he killed us all." Bill looked at the ID badge still in his hand and read the name on it again. Dr. Theodore Donaldson, the same face stared back at him from the small picture on the front of the badge.

Bill flicked the badge away from him, disgusted.

"Well, at least the bastard got a taste of his own medicine." He pushed himself off the desk and started for the door. "Come on, let's get back to the others and see what they've found."

Marie stood up and turned off the monitor out of habit, then followed Bill and Tessa.

"What do we tell the others? Do we tell them about the video?" Tessa asked him.

He shook his head, his face like stone.

"No way, no one says a word. They don't need to know what we found. Shit, if I could go back in time a few minutes, I would never have watched that damn video." He looked at the other two women, making sure they were onboard. "Do you agree with me? We keep what we know to ourselves."

Marie nodded assent, and after a moment, so did Tessa.

"Good, trust me, it's for the best. The others have enough to worry about without the burden of what we now know. We can shoulder the knowledge for them all."

Stepping into the airlock, they waited as it cycled through its program and then stepped back into the larger room.

The three walked through the room and into the main hallway, for the moment silent, keeping their thoughts to themselves. The pounding on the front door echoed off the walls, reminding them they were far from safe; the noise adding to their already melancholy moods.

*C*HAPTER *15*

WHEN BILL ARRIVED at the break room, with the others next to him, he was pleased to see everyone was back safely. Only Melissa was missing, still on watch near the front door. The others were now wearing fresh clot.

Bill, Marie and Tessa quickly put on some for themselves, and though still dirty and sweating from their escape down the highway, it still felt good to be wearing clothing again.

Bill chose a long-sleeve, button-down shirt that was about his size. Marie had on a New York Yankees polo shirt which caused Bill to smile. Tessa went out in the hallway, and now with a modicum of privacy, changed out of her worn clothing into a yellow t-shirt and a pair of faded jeans that seemed as if they were made for her.

Marie turned around in a circle, modeling her new wardrobe. "What, you don't like it?" She asked, noticing Bill's expression.

"No, Marie, you look fine," Bill said. Then he looked at the other faces around him and asked: "Can someone spell Melissa for a while, maybe for an hour or so? Then I'll come and do my shift."

It was Bruce who raised his hand casually.

"I'll go, Bill, I could use some time to think about everything's that happened." He looked to Elizabeth, taking her hand in his. "You okay?" He asked her.

She nodded. "Sure, I'm fine, go 'head. I'm sure Melissa wants to know what's happening, too."

Bruce squeezed her hand and then he was off, giving Bill a slight smile as he left.

Bill nodded in his direction, silently thanking the man for relieving Melissa and then sat down at the head of the table. Though the table was round, by the way everyone was sitting it just seemed that he was at the top. Bill didn't give it much thought, but instead slapped his hand on the table top, calling everyone to attention.

"All right then, so what did you guys find? Something useful, I hope," he stated blandly.

Elizabeth was first. With her face beaming pride, she pulled her hand from under the table and tossed Bill a box that rattled as it slid across the smooth Formica top.

"How's this, I think they're the right size," she said, looking into Bill's eyes.

Bill reached down and picked up the box, turning it in his hands.

"Well I'll be damned, bullets." He shook the box, the contents rattling back and forth. "And almost full, too." Opening the box and pulling the .38 from his pants, he quickly reloaded the weapon, shaking out the spent casings.

Once he was finished, he spun the cylinder and cocked the weapon. "Damn that feels good. I was out, you know; the damn gun was good for nothing but a club." He smiled at Elizabeth. "Thanks, you just might have saved us all."

She turned beet red, blushing. "Just glad to help," she answered back. "There were a few other boxes in a bottom drawer of one of the desks, but I was pretty sure they weren't the right size for your gun, so I only brought these with me."

"That's too bad, the more the better, but this is better than nothing. What we really need to do is find some more firearms; the more of us that are armed the better." Bill said.

"Did you guys find anything we could use?" Janice asked Bill and Marie.

"Not really, just a room full of dead animals," Bill said, giving Marie and Tessa a covert glance.

He looked up when Melissa walked into the room, glad for the distraction as the others all looked up when she entered, too.

"How's it going out there, honey?" Marie asked her.

Melissa grabbed a small bag of potato chips from the counter and started eating them while she dropped down in the seat vacated by Bruce.

"Not so good. They just keep banging on the door. The damn hinges are going to bend soon, we don't have much time." She looked at all the faces around her, and though she hated to say it, she did. "We need to get out of here before they break in; 'cause once they do, that's it, game over."

"Damn, what are we going to do?" Marie asked the room.

"That's not the worst of it," Elizabeth said. "When Bruce and I were checking out the other rooms we were able to see out the windows. There's more of them showing up every second. We're surrounded. If we try to sneak out the back or out a window, they'll just see us and run us down."

"Great, that makes things even worse than when we were on the school; at least there they couldn't get at us. But when we leave here where do we go? There has to be someplace secure from those bastards," Bill said, his right hand squeezed into a fist in frustration.

"So what do we do?" Tessa asked.

"What about the camp we talked about earlier? That's outside the city. Maybe we could go there?" Kenny spoke up; all faces looking to him, making him feel uncomfortable.

"Shut up, Kenny, you know that's not an option!" Tessa snapped at the boy.

"Tessa," Bill said, "I know what you said earlier about the camp, but it might just be our only option."

Tessa shook her head. "No way, forget it, we can't go there. It's a bad idea, trust me. Kenny doesn't know what he's talking about."

"Why, honey, why's it such a bad idea?" Marie asked. "Maybe they can be reasoned with. They're the Army for God's sake and we're American citizens," Marie finished, soothingly.

Tessa sighed and gave Kenny a look that said, "Wait till I get you alone later." Then she sat a little taller and told them what she knew.

"Me and Kenny met a few other people a day before we found you. They came from the camp. There was a woman with them, maybe my mom's age, and like I said before, she said the soldiers at the camp were shooting anything that gets near their perimeter, whether they're infected or not. They said there were people in the camp that were doing experiments on anyone who wasn't infected, like lab rats.

But the thing that scared me the most was that the guy in charge is running the place like a small country. If he decides he doesn't want you around anymore, he snaps his fingers and makes you disappear."

"What do you mean by 'disappear'?" Janice asked.

"She means they bring you to the back of the camp and shoot you, where they've dug a big grave. When there's too many bodies in it, they set it on fire. The lady that told us this, Carol was her name, wasn't it Kenny?" Tessa asked him.

Kenny nodded that it was.

"Yeah, well, Carol said you could smell the bodies burning day and night. She said the smell got into your clothes so you couldn't get rid of it."

"Tell him what else she said, Tessa, they might as well know," Kenny coaxed her.

Tessa nodded. "Well, she said the guy in charge is using people like slave labor, too. And if you don't agree with what he does, then he sends you to the back of the camp. Carol and her friends were lucky enough to sneak out, though some of them didn't make it."

"That does not sound like a place I'd like to visit," Marie said to everyone.

Nods and grunts of agreement filled the room.

Bill waved his hand, as if he could dismiss away what he'd heard. "It all doesn't really matter, anyway. The first thing is to get out of here before that door gives out. Any suggestions on how we're going to do that?"

Everyone sat quiet, trying to think of a way to get them out of the building in one piece. No one had any ideas.

"I think I have an idea, that is if you'll listen to a kid," Roger said from the corner of the room, finally speaking up. Since Bill had returned with Tessa and Marie, he'd merely sat quietly, watching and listening to the adults talk.

Bill began to chuckle a little, glad to see the boy joining in on the discussion. "Hell, Roger, I'd listen to anyone at this moment, I'm not proud. So, what do you got?"

Roger smiled, his eyes creasing a little. He wasn't used to people taking him seriously, especially adults. Pushing out his chest, he moved closer to the table, leaning against it with his hands. He slipped Tessa a quick look and she smiled, looking down at her sneakers bashfully. He smiled, too, then turned to face Bill and the others.

"Well, I think we need another distraction, like when we were on the roof of the school. Something so big those nut jobs out there will be too busy to worry about us."

"Okay, that's true enough, and…?" Bill asked.

Marie nodded, listening quietly. "Okay honey, what do you have in mind?"

Roger grinned the same way a teenager does when he knows he's doing something bad, but it's far too much fun to worry about the consequences.

"What do you guys know about making pipe bombs?"

CHAPTER 16

"Pipe bombs, are you serious?" Bill asked, shocked.

Roger nodded, took a deep breath and started in on what he knew. "It's not that hard, really. I used to go on the internet and search all kinds of stuff. All you have to do is Google pipe bombs and theirs whole instructions on how to make them and use them."

"And you did this?" Marie asked.

Roger nodded. "Yup, sure did. I mean, it's not like I would have or anything, but it's cool to know how."

"So, what do we do with them, use them like grenades?" Elizabeth asked.

Roger shook his head. "Yeah, sort of. We can put stuff in them like glass and nails. Thumbtacks would probably work pretty well, too. But they don't work like that. They're pretty unstable. If you don't know what you're doing, well…Boom," he said using his hands and mimicking a big explosion.

Bill leaned forward in his chair, his forehead wrinkling as he thought it over.

"Damn, Roger, that's not a half-bad idea. But what would we use for explosives?"

"That's the easy part. Elizabeth said there were more boxes of ammo in one of the desks in an office, right? We can open the bullets and use the gunpowder inside."

"But won't we need a lot of them? I mean, there's dozens of people outside, how will we be able to get everyone before they manage to rip us apart?" Melissa asked.

"That's true. The second we open that door or they bust it in, we'll be overwhelmed," Janice added.

Everyone started talking at once, each throwing out ideas and their concerns. The room became very loud with each voice trying to talk over another.

Phillip moved closer to Marie, not liking where the conversations were going. Marie held him close, telling him everything would be fine. She handed him a piece of a cookie she'd been munching on while they talked, the boy eating it up hungrily.

Bill held his hands up for quiet. "All right, enough, one at a time!" He said over the group.

"We can do this, Bill, I promise. Besides, you got any better ideas?" Roger asked. Tessa smiled, seeing the boy was in control of the argument, so she lent him her support.

"He's got a point, Bill, and we're short on time," Tessa added.

Bill sighed, slumping in his chair. "I know we're short on time. Fine, it's the best idea we have." He looked at Roger. "So, what do we need to get this done?"

Roger smiled. "All right, excellent, okay, this is what we need," and he started to list the items from memory.

When he was done, everyone stood up and headed off to see if they could find everything Roger needed.

Roger suggested they use a large room, so there would be distance from each person while they assembled the pipe bombs. Bill agreed and as they all set off on their individual errands, the survivors agreed to meet at the first large room they'd investigated, the cubicles the perfect way to isolate each person from the others.

Thirty minutes later, Bill walked to the front door of the building to check on Bruce. The man was leaning against the two desks, using his body as added weight to keep the door closed.

"Hey, Bruce, how's it going out here?" Bill asked.

"So far so good, but I don't think we have too much time left." He pointed to the hinges of the door as well as the top lip. "If you look closer, you can see where the paint is chipping as the metal bends. Please tell me you have a plan for getting us the hell out of here."

Bill shot the man a grin. "As a matter of fact, that's exactly what we're doing now. Elizabeth is coming to relieve you in a few minutes, what do you say you help out?"

"Sure, of course, whatever you need," Bruce said.

The two talked for a few minutes, making idle chatter. Bill found out Bruce was a lawyer and had worked in Chicago in one of the buildings in the Loop, the historical part of Chicago. He mostly took civil cases, though the man would sometimes dabble in criminal cases as long as they weren't too serious.

He was just about ready to begin talking about his wife when Elizabeth popped up. "Hey, guys, what's up? She looked to Bruce. "You ready for a break yet, Bruce?"

"Sure am," he looked to Bill and smiled shyly. "Ah, Bill, why don't you go ahead of me and I'll catch up to you."

Bill stood there for a moment, not quite understanding, but then it dawned on him. "Oh, sure, okay, no problem. First room on the right, at the end of the hall," he said embarrassed. Elizabeth waved slightly as he walked away, turning to talk to Bruce as soon as he was gone.

Walking away, Bill paused when he was halfway down the hallway. Turning around, he could just see the two silhouettes of Bruce and Elizabeth in the wan light coming in through a few small side windows. While he watched them, he saw the two bodies come together in an embrace. Bill grinned, happy for the both of them. When you had no idea if you would be alive the next day, it was good to see at least the two of them enjoying what happiness they could find.

A loud bang on the front door caused him to jump, the echo reverberating off the tile walls, reminding him of where he was and what he had to get done if he wanted to live to see the sun set that night.

Turning, he moved off, walking a little faster, now. He headed for the large space where the other survivors had gathered with the supplies to build the homemade bombs. When he was almost there, he decided to take a quick detour by the men's room to take care of some business.

The first thing Bill saw upon entering the room was that Roger was firmly in charge. The boy was moving from table to table, showing each of the survivors how to assemble their pipe bombs.

Bruce had already arrived and was at a corner desk, prying open bullets to use the gunpowder inside, while a few desks over was Janice, busy drilling holes in the middle of six-inch water pipes with a drill found in the janitor's closet.

Bill stopped when Roger moved up to him, the boy grinning from ear to ear. Bill pointed to Janice, curious about what she was doing and asked the teen.

Roger answered by picking up one of the nearby pipes and holding it near Bill's face, his finger pointing to the small hole drilled into the side. "She drills a small hole in the middle and then we use a shoelace for a fuse. Once the pipes full of gunpowder and you light the fuse…well, you know the rest."

Bill looked over to see Marie carrying a handful of nails. "What're the nails for?"

"Makes 'em deadlier. With nails and glass inside the bomb, when it goes off it'll cut anything around it to pieces," Roger said, proudly.

"Where'd everybody find this stuff?" Bill asked.

"There was a maintenance closet that had the tools and nails and Bruce took apart one of the pipes in one of the first floor bathrooms. Then we got lucky and found the pipe caps in another closet with supplies and light bulbs and stuff. That's why pipe bombs are so cool, if you have something explosive to put in them, then the rest is all household items," Roger beamed. "In fact, if we didn't have gunpowder, we probably could have made due with a bunch of matchbook heads. The heads of the matches does the same thing as the powder."

"So you learned all this on the internet?" Bill asked.

"Yup, you can find out how to build anything, but you have to be careful. Google the wrong site and the Feds will be on your ass. That happened to a friend of mine," Roger said sadly.

Bill only nodded, not really caring about some wild kid with too much time on his hands. "That's too bad. Uhm, listen what can I do to help?"

Roger pointed to two more boxes of bullets. "You can open those up, but be careful."

"Sure, okay," he said, moving to the desk with the ammunition.

The work went quick, like a small assembly line. In less than half an hour all the items were ready to be assembled. But before they began, Roger stopped everyone.

"Okay, now this is when it gets tricky. First, put the bottom cap on the pipe and then the gunpowder goes in. Put a piece of tape on the fuse hole so nothing falls out. Once the powder's in, make sure to pack it almost near the top, put the nails inside. But be very careful. One spark and the powder can ignite, and that's bad."

"Ya think?" Bruce said, clearly nervous.

"Bill, I think we should get the kids out of here," Marie suggested.

"You're right. Tessa, will you take Phillip and Kenny out into the hall? We'll tell you when it's safe to come back in."

"But I want to help," Tessa said, not wanting to leave.

"You will be helping if you look after Phillip. Please?" Bill asked, trying to sound sincere.

Tessa sighed, giving in. "Come on, little man, lets go back to the break room, I think there's some cookies left." She turned to find Kenny. "You, too, Kenny, let's go."

Phillip grinned and ran out the door, Tessa behind him. She shot Bill a look that said she wasn't happy. Bill only smiled back and said thank you softly as she passed him.

Kenny followed them out, his hands deep in the folds of his pant pockets, getting used to being sent away every time something dangerous was happening.

With Phillip and the other kids gone, the others started to get to work. Bill started assembling his bomb, sweat already getting into his eyes. If he made one crucial mistake, he would be nothing but a red stain on the ceiling. While he worked, he had to wonder if the homemade grenades would be enough. The more he thought about it, the more he realized though they would be helpful, they all needed a much larger bang.

Then he remembered the hydrogen and oxygen tanks in the lab with all the deceased animals. If they attached the pipe bombs to those tanks and set them off just as the mob outside charged into the building, they should be able to take them all out in one massive explosion, especially if he turned on the gas on the stove in the break room. The only question was would the survivors be able to make it out before they were overwhelmed? He still hadn't figured that part out yet and as he started to pour gunpowder into the pipe, he decided it could wait until he was done. He was using glass from a shattered soda bottle to pack the pipe with, and if what Roger said was true about sparks, then he wasn't looking forward to it.

Bruce was at the back of the room, moving along as he assembled his second bomb. He didn't understand what the fuss was about, the nails went in easily enough and then all he had to do was tighten the top cap, closing the pipe bomb.

He'd just started screwing the cap on, the adjustable wrench in his hand, when he turned the cap a little to fast, causing a small spark.

The gunpowder ignited, the pressure building up inside the small cylinder until with a thunderous roar the pipe bomb ignited.

Bill happened to be looking over at Bruce, checking on him and the others, trying to gauge how fast everyone was working compared to him, when he saw the man disappear in a blinding flash.

Janice was sitting nearby and she was thrown off her chair, where she fell to the floor in an unconscious heap of arms and legs.

Everyone started screaming, though the explosion had deafened almost everyone inside the room. After the initial explosion, Bill jumped to his feet, feeling a wet spot on his cheek. Wiping it away, he realized it was a piece of Bruce, though other than being red, it was unnamable.

He stumbled around his desk, feeling lightheaded. Reaching Marie, he helped her up. She had known enough to fall to the floor, the action probably saving her life.

"Are you okay?" He asked her, brushing her hair from her face.

She nodded and pushed him away. "I'm fine, go see to the others," she gasped. Melissa was unscathed and was already moving to help Marie.

Bill did as she told him, reaching Roger next. The boy was lying flat on his back, moaning. His face was peppered with small cuts, the shrapnel from the pipe bomb doing what it was made to do. Luckily, he'd been far enough away to only receive a few small pieces of flying debris for his trouble.

Bill helped the boy to a sitting position, the boy wincing in slight pain.

Roger held his hand to his head. "Oh, wow, what happened?"

"I don't really know. I was looking over at Bruce. One moment he was sitting there working, the next he was just…gone."

Roger shook his head. "Oh, shit, I told you the stuff is unstable, you've got to move slowly. The poor bastard blew himself up!" He was yelling, not realizing his ears were damaged from the explosion in the confined room.

Bill only heard the gist of it, then knowing the boy was okay, he left him and hobbled over to Janice.

She wasn't moving and he picked her up, holding her in his arms. She had a gash on her forehead and there was a small amount of blood seeping through her shirt, but her chest was rising and falling steadily; she was alive.

Bill situated her better in his arms, then left the smoke-filled room, going back to the break room. Tessa was already in the hallway, her face filled with fear after hearing the explosion. As Bill laid Janice down on the table, Tessa bombarded him with questions.

"What happened, are we under attack? Did the crazy people get in? Are we in trouble?"

"Slow down, Tessa, give me a second. No, we're fine for now; there was just a terrible accident." He hesitated for a second, gathering his thoughts when Elizabeth ran into the break room, her eyes wide in fear. She took one look at Janice and let out a small screech.

"Oh my God, what happened, it sounded like we're being attacked," she said, leaning over Janice.

"One of the bombs went off, Janice was caught in the blast," Bill said while wringing a rag out in the sink and washing Janice's face with it.

"Oh, God, no. Was anyone else hurt?" Elizabeth asked.

Bill decided now was not the time to tell Elizabeth that Bruce was dead. That he was nothing more than a red smear on the walls and ceiling of the office space.

"Help me with her, will you? I think her shoulder's bleeding," Bill said, focusing on Janice for now.

With Tessa and Elizabeth holding Janice steady, Bill removed her shirt, leaving the woman topless with the exception of her bra. Her right shoulder had a sharp piece of shrapnel in it, and Bill reached down, pulling the metal shard in one fluid motion. Dropping the bloody metal to the floor, he placed the wet rag on the wound, wiping away most of the plasma. He was relieved to see there was only a small gash, something that should heal on its own, given time. Tessa was wiping Janice's forehead, the woman's head wound was bloody, but not serious. All in all, she was a lucky woman to have been so close to the blast and come out with only minor injuries.

With both Tessa and Elizabeth helping him, Bill was able to bandage Janice up quickly. After leaving the woman under their care, he ran back to the office to see what else he could do to help.

The room smelled like blood and smoke, the blast leaving a black spot in the corner where the explosion had occurred. The desk Bruce had sat behind was shattered, splinters everywhere, only adding to the mess. The only good thing was the blast was localized to his corner, the other pipe bombs safe.

Marie and Melissa were standing, still shaken, but finding it hard to believe they had just lost one of their own in the time it takes to snap two fingers together.

Roger was already gathering what could be used from Janice's desk, knowing that despite the tragic event, they still had to keep going. Bill nodded as he watched the teen working. The boy was gathering his confidence back, realizing he was an asset to the group.

When Bill entered, all eyes turned to him. He had nothing to say to them, what could he say?

He turned to the sound of slapping feet and saw Elizabeth standing in the doorframe. Her eyes were wide as she looked from face to face; not finding what she was looking for.

"Where's Bruce? Why isn't he here? What the hell happened in here?"

Bill sighed, realizing he had to tell her. Elizabeth stepped into the room, her gaze going straight to the blackened desk and wall. She saw the red dripping from the ceiling and her eyes turned to look at Bill. She started to shake her head, slow at first, but then faster and faster as tears started flowing down her cheeks.

"No, no, it's not true, he's not dead, he's fine," she said quietly. She stared at each face, one at a time. "He's fine!" She screamed, her chest heaving as she tried to hold back the sobs of pain and loss.

Bill walked the few steps closer to her, taking her in his arms and holding her tight. She fought him at first, shaking her head in disbelief.

"No, he's fine, he's okay!" She yelled.

Bill hugged her tight, not letting her go. "I wish he was, God I do, but I'm so sorry, he's gone."

She struggled for a few more seconds as the words sank in despite her not wanting to believe them. Then she went limp in his arms as she sagged to the floor, crying. Bill let her go, gently easing her to the floor. Marie and Melissa were now over them and they, too, both knelt down and hugged their friend.

Elizabeth continued crying. Bill's heart felt like a lead weight.

He'd seen the way Bruce and Elizabeth had looked at each other. They had found each other in a world turned upside down. And now it was all gone.

While Elizabeth sobbed on the floor, her shoulders shaking as the loss of Bruce flooded through her, Bill let one tear roll down his cheek.

The tear was for many things.

For his wife; now gone and buried. For Bruce and Elizabeth, a love that would never flourish, and most of all for the rest of them that were still alive and fighting to see the future; especially when that future seemed so unsure at this point in time.

With Roger staring at the adults, wondering what the hell they were doing when they needed to be working, Bill knelt down and hugged Marie and Melissa, while the others held on to each other, hands squeezing together as tears flowed.

It wouldn't last.

Even in their grief, they knew they had no time for mourning, but for just a moment, a few minutes, everyone needed to be held, needing to know they weren't alone…at least, not yet.

Chapter 17

MIKE GAZED OUT over the devastation that was once the city of Chicago. Everywhere his eyes looked, he could see nothing but flaming buildings, some resembling giant torches, the tops burning in the falling dusk. The nickname "the windy city" was working against the metropolis as the winds spread the flames from building to building, the heat melting glass and steel.

Mike watched pieces of the Aon Center fall to the street below, the sounds of the destruction too far away for him to hear. The city that once contained over three million people was now crumbling, the flames consuming it piece by piece.

Mike looked over where the Loop, the historical part of Chicago, once stood and all he could see was smoke and soot, the old buildings like kindling for the flames, large black pillars of smoke soaring skyward where the high winds would decimate them. The Sears tower had fallen almost an hour ago, the blaze finally hot enough to melt some of the steel frame, until the weight of the building fell in on itself.

Now all that remained was a charred structure of molten steel and rubble. The parks were ablaze, as well, the lack of rain in the past few weeks contributing to the inferno. Rogers Park, Lincoln Park, Jefferson Park and countless others were now burning brightly, the conflagration spreading like water from a breached dam as the wind pushed the fire onward to its next victim.

Dean had been true to his word and had set the entire city of Chicago ablaze.

Using tanker trucks full of gasoline and setting gas stations and propane refueling stations on fire, he had managed to turn Chicago into Hell on earth.

With everything burning, all the survivors had tried to evacuate the city.

Survivors from the infection who'd been hiding inside apartments, basements of stores and back rooms of warehouses now had no choice but to run for their lives.

And when these terrified people had taken to the streets, the Changed had been waiting for them. One at a time, each person had been taken down and slaughtered. Teeth and hands mercilessly killed each and every one, until there was no one left.

Dean had managed to save a few for some fun and Mike's stomach still rolled when he thought about what Dean had done to them. He became further nauseous when he thought about how he could have joined them in death if he hadn't bargained for his life. Though with Dean's grasp on reality, tenuous at best, he had no real idea for how long that might be.

Now Mike had to lead Dean to Bill and the others, and the scary thing was he didn't exactly know where they'd gone to. He could only hope to stall Dean long enough to figure a way out of this horrible mess he'd gotten himself into, before he became another victim of the terrifying leader of the Changed.

Dean came up behind him and slapped him on the back. The man was smiling, his teeth red with blood from a young woman he'd just finished torturing, raping and killing. The woman hadn't gone easily, Mike knew, her screams still echoing in his ears.

"What's the matter, Mikey, my boy? Feeling blue?" Dean asked; his voice rough. When he was in a good mood, Dean had begun calling him Mickey. The only problem was, if Dean was in a good mood, then that probably meant someone was dying by his hands.

"No, I'm fine, just thinking about stuff."

"Stuff, what the hell's there to think about? The world is over, nothing to think about now, but how to enjoy what's left." He scratched his nose with his finger, leaving a bloody smear on his skin when he removed his hand. "Look, we're leaving in a few minutes, and you're on point. I want you to lead me straight to the others you told me about."

Mike turned around to look at Dean and tried to control himself at the sight of the skinny man. Dean was covered in blood, only his face relatively untouched, though his mouth had a few red rivulets dripping out of the sides, and of course his bloody teeth.

"What if I can't find them, what if they've moved on?" Mike asked hesitantly, his eyes looking anywhere but at the ghastly sight of Dean.

Dean smiled, his stained teeth flashing at Mike. "Well, then, Mickey, old chum of mine, I guess I won't need you anymore and I can give you to them," he said while pointing over his shoulder with a blood red finger at the monstrous crowd of infected.

Mike followed Dean's finger, his stomach jumping into his throat. Thousands of men, women, and children, filled the street, their bodies disappearing around the corner at the intersection a block away. Every infected person in the city was now standing behind Dean.

"Oh my God," Mike gasped, watching the shifting crowd of people, some of them barely old enough to walk.

"God has nothing to do with it, Mike, my boy. Mikey, who's gonna lead us to the rest of the normals. I'm God now and my wrath will be swift. With your help, I'll lead the Changed across this nation, sweeping everything in our path away like a dust bunny under a bed. When I'm through, this world will be mine and I'll be the sole heir." Dean looked into Mike's eyes, seeing the terror and concern there.

"What's wrong, Mike? Go ahead, you can tell me, I won't kill you, at least not yet.

Mike couldn't have stopped himself even if he'd wanted to, the words needed to come out, even if it was just so he could hear them with his own ears.

"You're fucking crazy, you're absolutely insane."

Dean chuckled and turned around to the giant crowd; his subjects.

"This man says I'm crazy! Am I?"

As one large entity, the crowd roared and pumped their hands, the nearby glass in the second-story buildings above seeming to shake from the ferocity of their screams.

Dean turned back to look at Mike, his eyes alight with excitement.

"Of course I'm crazy. But it's a good kind of crazy. I've never been as free as I am since I became one of the Changed. Insane? Perhaps. But I tell you what, I like it. I like this feeling and I'll give you a piece of advice. Do you remember the old saying, if you can't beat 'em, then join 'em?"

Mike nodded slightly.

"Good, Mike. You see, we are the new world, and if you don't become one of us, then there's no more use for you, so there's no need to keep you around anymore." He turned around to look at his people, raising his hands in the air, and they yelled and cheered. The crowd wanted something to kill, anything, and Mike had never felt so vulnerable since he'd first been captured by Dean.

Dean looked over his shoulder and flashed Mike a sly grin. "But don't worry, Mikey. I said I wouldn't kill you and I meant it. As long as you help me, I'll let you keep breathing." Mike thought he was done, but then Dean added one more tidbit. "However long that might be."

With a sly smile on his lips, Dean walked away to prepare his people for the evacuation of the city. They had all gathered near the city limits, the clothing store where Mike had first met him nothing more than charred cinders now. The inferno was spreading fast, and if Dean didn't leave soon, he and his followers would be threatened to be enveloped in his own fiery creation.

Dusk was falling fast, the darkness coming quicker thanks to the ash filled sky, but Dean didn't seem to mind. Besides, what did he have to fear from a dark world?

He was the predator, after all. The dominant species. The top of the food chain.

Mike turned away from the massive crowd of murderous people and concentrated on watching the flames as they slowly consumed the city.

Chicago was in ashes, a dead city, and Mike knew if he didn't figure out what to do soon, he too, would be joining that unfortunate metropolis in death.

Chapter 18

AFTER THE DEATH of Bruce, things went slow for a while as everyone tried to adjust to the loss of one of their own. The pipe bombs were started once again, this time everyone taking the utmost care to be more careful. While Bill finished tightening the cap on his last pipe bomb, he cringed, just waiting for the spark that would send him on the last train to Hell in little bitty bloody, pieces, right after Bruce. But luck was with him and the cap went on easily. When Bill finally laid the wrench down, he let out a sigh that the entire room heard; despite the fact each of them was sitting even farther apart than before.

After Bruce's explosion, all the desks were pushed well away from one another, in the hope that if there was another blast, the damage to the others would be minimized. Roger took up the slack lost by Bruce's death, the boy seeming to have a knack for building the small explosive devices.

"Are you sure you never did this before?" Bill asked Roger while he was helping him with the second bomb.

Roger had nodded, "Bill, I swear, I only read about them online, I never actually did anything. I mean, look at this face, I'm too pretty to go to jail."

Bill had chuckled at that and the two of them had quickly moved through the assembly of each device.

Bill set the last one down, and he looked over his shoulder at the others. Melissa was almost finished, her red hair plastered against her face as she perspired. Marie was working on her second, and Bill decided he'd go help her. Elizabeth was back on door duty, too fraught with loss to try to help make the bombs. She had been almost catatonic after the loss of Bruce, and though Bill had known they were becoming close, he'd had no idea just how close.

Janice was still in the break room. She'd come to a little while after the explosion and would be ready to leave in another hour or so when Bill decided they should try their escape. Tessa, Kenny and Phillip were with her, keeping her company.

With night falling, Bill figured that would be the best time to spring their trap. Once the infected mob poured into the building, the bombs could be set off, hopefully taking out the entire murderous horde. Even if a few didn't enter the building, it would be easy to slip away in the darkness and the confusion of the explosion.

Bill walked over to Marie and smiled, almost tip toeing across the floor while talking to her. "How's it going, need any help?" He asked softly.

Concentrating on packing the pipe bomb in her hands with nails and shards of glass, she didn't hear him at first. Bill knew enough not to disturb her and he waited patiently while she finished. Once the last of the glass was in the pipe, she let out a loud sigh, relieved she was still alive. Her arms were covered with a sheen of sweat, her nerves pushed to the breaking point as she dealt with the fragile device.

Holding the pipe in her left hand, she wiped her brow free of sweat, suddenly realizing Bill was beside her.

"Hey, didn't see you there, sorry, I was a little preoccupied."

"Not a problem, I figured I'd let you finish. Didn't want to startle you," he chuckled.

She laughed back, the laugh almost sounding forced. "Ya think?"

"You want any help?"

She shook her head. "No, I'm okay, why don't you do something else if you're done with yours. Are you?"

He pointed to the small stack of completed pipe bombs neatly lying on the desk he'd vacated. Each one had a piece of shoelace sticking out of the side, one of the many items found when Elizabeth had raided the locker room for clothing.

"Wow, you're fast," she said, "I've been moving as slow as molasses. I'm not planning on following Bruce into the big blue yonder."

Bill nodded, agreeing with her. "Okay then, I'll go get the tanks from the lab, that'll be the icing on the cake. See ya later… and be careful."

"I'll be nothing but, and you watch yourself, too," she replied.

He waved bye and started walking out of the room to retrieve the hydrogen and oxygen tanks. Roger saw him leave and nodded in his direction, then Bill slipped through the door and headed for the large research lab where he'd first seen the tanks.

Glancing over his shoulder, he could see the legs of Elizabeth as she sat on the floor near the front door at the opposite end of the long hallway. Though the banging had slowed a little, there was still plenty of noise to indicate the mob outside still wanted in. Bill debated going to check on her, making sure she was all right, but decided to leave her alone. Hopefully, she could come to grips with Bruce's death and be ready to leave when the time came.

Bill walked down the deserted hallway, the echo of his footsteps giving him the chills. It was eerie the way any building felt when it was deserted, like it was nothing but a giant tomb, waiting patiently for some archeologist to come and dig it out of the sands of time.

Upon reaching the entrance to the lab, he stepped inside, the animals in their cages still where he'd left them. Walking through the center aisle, he stared at some of the carcasses, sympathy welling up inside him for these poor souls. He had always had a soft spot for animals, and his late wife, Laura, had always teased him that he had a heart of gold.

Thinking of her made him pause. He missed her so much, but he knew now was not the time for dwelling on the past. He needed to stay focused in the here and now or all of their futures would be cut short very soon.

Spotting a dolly in the corner, he used it to easily transport the hydrogen and oxygen tanks back to the hallway. He'd even been fortunate enough to find a small propane tank used to fuel the Bunsen burners, and he took that, too. Though the gauge had read only half full, he was pretty sure it would only add to the blast.

Feeling good to have a task to accomplish that wouldn't blow him up at a seconds notice, he quickly moved each tank out of the lab, and without realizing it, found himself whistling, just happy to be doing a mundane task in a non- mundane world

Elizabeth sat on the floor and watched the front door shake in its frame. She knew what waited on the other side of the one-inch metal door.

Evil.

Though evil had taken the form of human beings, it was still evil.

Her heart ached terribly when she thought about Bruce. God how she missed him. Though they'd only been together for a short time, she had grown to love the man.

Sure, some people would say: "How can you love someone in such a short amount of time?" But she would answer if given the chance that when you find that one person, the only person, your soul-mate, it happens instantly and time is irrelevant.

That happened to her with Bruce and now, while she stared at the beleaguered door, she wondered what was the point in living at all.

Why keep on going, only to die a few hours or days from now?

She wanted to just stand up, walk over to the desks blocking the door, and push them out of the way, then unlock the door, letting in the ravenous mob. Though she knew it would hurt when they attacked her at first, she also knew it would only hurt for a short time before death took her into its warm embrace. Besides, how much more could it hurt than it did now, without Bruce?

But she wasn't ready to do it…not yet. She hadn't worked up the courage.

Tears started flowing down her cheeks again as the pain of loss filled her up inside.

She let it out and continued to stare at the door, knowing in time she would have the strength to end it once and for all. And when she did, she knew Bruce would be waiting for her in Heaven.

When Bill had finished moving the tanks and was satisfied with their positioning, he decided to go back to the large office space to see how the others were fairing. Stepping through the doorway, he was greeted by a smiling Roger. The boy grinned from ear to ear as he pointed to the table in the middle of the room.

"Good timing, Bill, we just finished," he said proudly.

Bill walked over to the pipe bombs, his eyes gazing over each one. There were nine in all, minus the three Bruce would have made. Bill couldn't tell his from the others, but he was sure if he had more time to inspect them, he'd be able to figure it out.

Marie quietly moved next to him, her breath coming in short gasps. "Frightening, isn't it, to think we actually made bombs."

Bill nodded. "New world, different rules. Not only did we build them, but we're about to use them and kill hundreds of people."

"Perhaps, but if we don't, those same people will be happy to tear us apart," she replied.

"True," he answered.

"So, what's next?" Melissa asked, while leaning against a nearby desk and rested her legs.

Bill had already discussed using the bombs in tandem with the gas tanks with Roger and now he turned and placed his hand on the boy's right shoulder.

"Now we make those tiny bombs into big ones, and hopefully, get the hell out of here," Bill said to them all while squeezing Roger's shoulder gently like a father to a son.

Marie moved toward the doorway, pulling Melissa with her as she went. "All right then, let's get started, time's a wasting, boys." Marie said this like an order and both Bill and Roger glanced up, each looking like their mother had just given them a command.

With a brief glance to each other, both Bill and Roger did as they were told, gathering up the make-shift bombs and a roll of duct tape to secure them to the tanks, then followed Marie out into the corridor while walking like they were carrying dynamite, which wasn't far from the truth.

The sun was almost down and when it finally set, they needed to be ready to move, but before they did, there was still a lot to accomplish and not a lot of time to do it in.

CHAPTER 19

BILL'S IDEA WAS simple and straight-forward. Strap the pipe bombs to the hydrogen and oxygen tanks and place them in the middle of the corridors against the support columns of the building. Then, while the rampaging crowd poured through the front door and into the long hallway, Bill would light the fuses to the bombs and high-tail it to the opposite door at the far end of the hallway. If things went as planned, then almost the entire crowd of raving lunatics would be inside the building when the explosions ripped through it, bringing the structure down, and hopefully killing most of them, if not all.

In the ensuing chaos of the explosion, they could slip into the darkness and with luck find a car or something to transport them away from the area. As to where to go after that, well, Bill hadn't figured that one out yet. Better to see if they lived through the first part of the plan before worrying about the second, after all, there were a whole lot of *hopefully's* to get through before the plan was a success.

Roger and Bill were taping the bombs to the tanks while the others patiently waited for them to finish. It was a two man job, the others fidgeting, wanting only to help.

Bill saw this and nodded to Marie. "Why don't you collect any food left in the break room, and when your done, bring Tessa and the others with you, we're almost ready to do this," Bill told her.

He then turned to Melissa who was fidgeting in the corner. "Melissa, why don't you go help, too."

Both women agreed and quickly left, feeling good to have something to do. When they were gone, Roger spoke up, while securing the last bomb to a tank.

"You really think this'll work?" He asked; looking at the tanks spread out across the main hall. Each tank was set near a support column. While Bill was no engineer, he had a pretty good knowledge of construction and demolition, thanks to reading a lot and asking questions when he was a spectator at a job sites where buildings were being demolished. Usually the demolition experts were happy to share their knowledge, enjoying a captive audience. Bill found almost everyone he had ever met would be happy to talk to you if they were either talking about their job or their own personal life.

Bill wiped the sweat from his brow and finished securing the final pipe bomb to an oxygen tank. He had positioned it between the other hydrogen tanks, hoping the different size explosions would complement each other, not that he would ever know for sure if it had worked, as he would be too busy running for his life.

The propane tank was in the middle of the hallway, where he hoped it would do the most damage.

"Honestly, Roger, I have no idea, but it's the best plan we've got," he said, walking over to stand with Roger in the middle of the hall. "Besides, it beats waiting to be slaughtered when they finally break in here, at least this way we're still fighting."

"I guess that's all we can do," Roger said quietly.

Bill rubbed the boy's shoulder. "If it'll help you feel better, I can lie and tell you everything's gonna be fine."

Roger shook his head no. "Nah, I hate being bullshitted. Just tell me like it is and I'll deal with it, that's all I ask."

Bill grinned. "Spoken like a true warrior. Come on, let's get the others and get this party started. It's dark outside, so there's no more reason to stay here."

Roger gave him a curt twitch of the head in agreement and the two men, because to Bill, Roger was as much a man as him, despite Roger's age, headed to the end of the hallway to meet up with the others.

Marie and Melissa were just coming around the corner, with Janice between them. Though the woman said she could walk herself, the other two women would hear nothing of it and insisted on at least half-carrying her to the departure point. Tessa, Kenny and Phillip were right behind them.

Bill looked at their haggard faces and realized how their group continued to shrink. He could only hope they had the same number of people when they finally put this place behind them.

Bill clapped his hands while they approached, smiling sincerely. "Fantastic, ladies and gentleman," he said looking down at Phillip, "you guys get to the rear entrance while I go get Elizabeth. Roger, seems you've got a lighter, I guess you're on fuse duty. Unless you want me to do it."

"No way, man. All this was my idea in the first place; it should be me who lights them. Besides, if the shoelaces don't take, I'll have to set them off manually with a hammer," he joked, though the others didn't find it amusing.

"You're not serious, are you?" Janice asked the boy, leaning on Marie for support, her voice weak, but growing stronger with each passing minute.

Roger nodded. "Damn straight. If the makeshift fuses don't burn, then this is all for nothing, someone will have to set the bombs off by hand."

Marie held up a hand to calm the others. "Relax, everyone, it won't come to that, I promise. You'll see in a few minutes, we'll all be away from here and on our way to someplace safe."

Though no one believed her, Marie's soothing voice put the others at ease.

Bill handed Roger one of the two-way radios that had been found in an office. If he had to guess, he would have assumed the radios were used for drills within a particular company or something similar. Now the radios were crucial to the plan. After Bill retrieved Elizabeth and unlocked the front door. He believed it would only be seconds before the infected mob figured out the door was unlocked and stormed inside. Roger would need time to light the fuses and then evacuate with the others, especially once the rear doors were clear.

With Elizabeth in tow, Bill hoped to race past the burning fuses and out the rear door just before the bombs went off, hopefully killing all that followed only seconds behind him. It was a long shot, but it was all they could come with on short notice.

"All right, Roger, be ready, I'll be calling you in a few minutes and then light 'em up." With a brief wave, he took off down the hallway, his adrenalin already pumping, preparing his body for the flight that would be only minutes away.

"Now all we have to do is wait for Elizabeth and Bill, then it's show time," Roger said, trying to psych himself up for the upcoming events.

Bill moved swiftly down the hallway, the banging on the front door becoming louder the closer he got to it. The first floor windows of the building they were now hiding in had all been covered in metal lattice for security, the only real reason why they weren't overrun by the murderous crowd after the first five minutes of entering the building. Now the same safety feature was a hindrance to their escape. The only way out of the building was the rear exit, and Bill could only hope once the crowd outside realized the front door was open to them, they would all quickly abandon the rear entrance and join their fellow brethren in the front.

As Bill approached the front door, he immediately noticed something was wrong and pulled his .38 revolver from his waistband. He had six rounds in the weapon and a pocket full of reloads, though he doubted he'd have time to reload once all hell broke loose.

One of the desks was not blocking the door, but instead lay on its side where it had been pushed. As he approached the door, he saw Elizabeth already pushing the bottom desk away from the shaking door.

Bill ran a few more feet, and yelled when he knew she would hear him. "Elizabeth, what the hell are you doing? We're not ready yet, stop!"

She turned to look at him after hearing his voice and Bill saw the bloodshot eyes and wet cheeks.

"Screw you, Bill, and screw everything. I'm sick of this shit. Bruce is gone and we'll be next. What the hell is the point? Sooner or later they'll get us. Well, fuck it, I'm ending it now, and sparing myself anymore pain!"

Bill slowed to a stop, not wanting to get any closer and spook the woman. He held up his hand, hoping she would stop. Luckily, she paused, as if despite her suicidal words, she didn't really want to commit suicide.

"Now, Liz, can I call you Liz? You're just distraught about Bruce and everything else that's happened, and who could blame you? Just come over here and I promise everything will be fine," he said soothingly. If he had to guess, he'd say she was having a nervous breakdown from all the stress, and losing Bruce had tipped her over the edge.

Elizabeth saw the gun in Bill's hand and gestured to it. "Fine, huh? If everything's so damn fine then why do you have a gun? No, Bill, nothing's fine and it'll never be fine again. You can keep fighting if you want, but I give up!" Then she turned and finished pushing the desk out of the way and unlocked the door in one quick, almost practiced motion. Bill had no way of knowing that Elizabeth had been going over the scenario again and again in her head as she sat on the floor alone, watching the door and hearing the pounding hour after hour.

"No, Elizabeth don't do it, we're not ready yet!" He screamed while taking two more steps toward her, but as the door opened and bloody hands shot through the crack, he stopped and started backpedaling.

It was too late for her, he realized this as he watched her body get pulled through the door, her screams filling the hallway.

"Roger, we've got a problem, light the damn fuses right now and get the hell out of there," Bill called into the radio.

"What, now? But I'm not ready," Roger's crackly voice said through the radio.

Bill was already turning around, starting to run for the other side of the building, the sounds of shrieks and screams already coming from behind him as the first of the infected poured through the door.

"Well, I'm coming whether you're ready or not, so get moving or we're all dead." Then there was no time for talking as he concentrated on running. Just before he turned the corner at an intersection of the east and west hallways, he glanced over his shoulder to see how close the killer mob was.

All he saw was a mass of bodies filling the hallway behind him and he thought he saw a head bobbing above the crowd. As he turned the corner, the crowd lost from sight, he was almost positive it was Elizabeth's head, seeming to float over the crowd like some kind of avenging angel.

Then the corner wall blocked his view and he concentrated on running, while behind him the crowd flooded into the building, with Elizabeth's severed head bouncing from hand to hand like a parody of a beach ball at a rock concert.

For the next one and a half minutes, Bill ran through the long hallway until he turned the corner where Roger should be lighting the fuses.

Sliding on the tile floor, he kept moving, his motion too fast to stop him. "We've got to go, Roger they're right behind me!" He screamed, scared shitless.

Roger lit another fuse and turned to look at Bill. "What the hells going on? What happened to the plan?"

Bill waved his question away. "No time, we've got to go. If you're not done then we'll just have to hope it's enough!" He yelled while pulling Roger with him as he ran for the rear door.

"But I'm not done yet, they won't blow up right!"

"Doesn't matter. We go now or we're all dead, just run!"

Roger did run, but only a few feet, then he ripped his arm away from Bill and stopped moving.

Realizing Roger wasn't next to him, Bill slowed. "What are you doing? We need to go!" Even as he said the words the first of the infected rounded the hallway intersection preparing to attack.

"No, if this is going to work and any of us are to live, then all the bombs need to go off at once and I didn't light them all. Just go and I'll make sure it happens!" Then he turned around and started running back toward the nearest two tanks that hadn't been lit.

"Damn it, Roger, no! Don't do it!" Bill screamed, though everything Roger had said made perfect sense.

"Just go, if these don't blow, then we're all dead anyway! This way some of you survive. Tell Phillip I love him! Tell him what I did to save him!" Then he ran, picking up a hammer from off the floor as he went.

Bill hesitated for only a moment, realizing there was nothing he could do for the teen. Already the infected were filling the hallway, and in only seconds would be on top of him. Cursing loud enough to fill the hall, he turned and ran as fast as he could, leaving a boy to do a man's job.

Roger reached the first tank as the first of the infected crowd reached him. Hands reached out and pulled him down, but he managed to kick the attacker away, only to have another behind the first one jump at him. He only had to keep them off him for a few seconds as Bill made his escape with the others. Though he was no fighter, he used the hammer as a weapon, cracking skulls and caving in foreheads as he fought for every last breath of his existence.

He imagined himself as a Viking warrior, battling a neighboring village, standing over his fallen foes, prepared to enter the gates of Valhalla upon his death.

No one ran past him, all seeking to kill him first, thereby keeping all the infected contained in the hallway.

Two of the mob got past his guard and a woman sank her teeth into his neck, another into his leg. He screamed from the pain, feeling his neck and shirt become wet with his blood. He hit her with the hammer, the point striking her left eye and caving in the soft orb, and then kicked the other away from his leg. Both the woman's eyeball and socket caved in under the weight of the metal hammer, Roger smiling as he was splashed with blood and ichor.

His vision grew blurry and he realized it was now or never.

Pushing the crowd from him, knowing he had less than a heartbeat to do what he'd set out to do, he swung the hammer at the pipe bomb, just as the fuses from the other previously lit pipe bombs burned down.

Other attackers pounced on him as he let down his guard, their hands and teeth sinking into his flesh. He screamed, but the pain lasted for less than a microsecond, because his body was consumed in the rolling fireball, the murderous mob with him.

His last thoughts were of his little brother. He hadn't always been the best older brother, always telling Phillip to get out of his room and lying to him about if he would play a game with him. He had realized too late that his little brother only wanted to be with him because he loved him and Roger had taken the small boy for granted. Now he hoped he gave Phillip the ultimate gift, a continuing life, hopefully safe from the crazy world he had been tossed into.

Then his lungs filled with fire and his face burned away from his skull as he was incinerated.

The bombs rocked the building, sending flames shooting through the hallways, and around corners. The shrieking mob was burned alive, the fire killing most, and the collapsing building and taking care of the rest.

Stone and concrete filled the blast zone, the building's foundation severely weakened as the last of the blast blew away any survivors.

Only a few seconds before the blast, Bill ran down the corridor, knowing time was quickly running out.

Marie was at the closed rear door with the others, waiting for Bill, Elizabeth and Roger to return. She was surprised and shocked when she started to hear Bill's voice yelling from down the hallway, too far away for any of them to hear him clearly.

"What's he yelling about?" Tessa asked curiously.

"No idea, honey, but we'll find out soon enough," Marie said nervously.

Bill rounded the bend and started to run towards them, waving his hands in front of himself like he was one of the infected.

"Go, go! Open the damn door and get out of here, the bombs are going off any second!"

"Where's Roger and Elizabeth?" Melissa yelled from the side, trying to see behind Bill.

"No time, just run goddammit, and hurry!" He yelled to Marie who did as she was told and opened the rear door. The night air poured into the hallway, caressing her hair, and she breathed in the fresh air.

Bill never slowed, but ran into the door frame, stopping sharply and breathing in quick gasps. "Come on, damn it, get your asses moving, or die where you stand!"

That got the others moving, though Phillip was hollering for his brother. Tessa and Kenny both dragged him through the door, the boy fighting them all the way.

"What's happening? Why are you alone?" Marie asked as Melissa slipped through the door and into the night. So far no screams of pain sounded, signaling the coast was clear.

"Tell you later, if we're still alive, now go, for the love of God, run!" Bill yelled, pushing her in front of him as he lunged out of the building. Marie flew through the doorway and Bill looked over his shoulder to glance back down the hallway. Deep down inside he was hoping to see Roger come running around the corner, waving his hands in triumph, but he knew that wouldn't be happening.

When he heard the blast, he knew his time was up and he turned, preparing to run through the door and the open area outside. The blast hit his back, sending him flying through the air as his arms and legs flailed around him.

His world was knocked askew and his ears were filled with an enormous rumbling as he hit the pavement and managed to crawl away a few more feet, hopefully out of any kind of blast zone.

Then his vision faded and he passed out for a few seconds. When he opened his eyes again, the world around him was eerily quiet, as if all sound had been sucked up in the explosion.

Moaning from the pain of his landing, he flexed his hands and moved his legs, amazed that nothing was broken, his eyes still closed. Reality flooded back to him and he knew he needed to get up and see to the others. He'd heard nothing of any of them and he started to worry.

He opened his eyes a little, wondering if any of their pursuers had managed to survive the explosion and were even now preparing to converge on him and kill him in very painful ways. The night was filled with dust, smoke and residual explosions as the collapsed building still settled.

Coughing hard, his lungs expelling any detritus he may have inhaled, he rolled onto his back, and looked up at what he expected to be the night sky above him.

Instead, he saw a man standing over him. The man wore a white biological containment suit and a military issue gas mask. The M-16 pointed at Bill's face was most definitely military issue.

Firelight from the destroyed building flooded the rear parking lot Bill was laid out on, illuminating it so that it appeared to be dusk. But then the night became day when the headlights from three military troop carriers were turned on, blinding him, making him close his eyes once more. When his eyes were adjusted to the bright illumination, or as good as he could possibly get them, he opened his eyelids again, very slowly. The man was still over him, the rifle never wavering.

"Don't move, you're under arrest by the United States Army. If you so much as twitch one pinky, you will be shot," a muffled voice from behind the gas mask said with authority. Bill had no reason to doubt the faceless soldier.

"I'm not one of those killers, none of us are. We're not infected."

The face nodded, the rifle never wavering. "Maybe you're immune or maybe you're just not showing signs yet. Either way, you're coming with us," he said, gesturing with the muzzle of the rifle. Bill noticed his .38 was now jammed into the soldiers web belt.

Bill rolled to his feet, moaning, a thousand nerves flaring in pain. He was pushed toward the last transport and forced to board it. He was pleased to see his fellow survivors were all there; their frightened faces looking out of the shadows of the troop carrier.

Every now and then a gunshot could be heard as the soldiers took down any murderous survivors from the explosion.

The soldier waved his hand to the other transports, giving the command to mount up. The dozen or so soldiers that were spread around the perimeter did as ordered and soon the truck was rumbling away, two soldiers with rifles readily aiming them at the group. More rifles shots sounded and screams joined the din as some of the surviving infected tried to attack the soldiers. Inside the truck, Bill couldn't see what was happening.

Bill sat next to Marie, holding onto a crossbeam so not to fall off her seat while the truck jumped and rolled.

"Do you think we're saved? That they'll help us?" Marie asked with a spark of hope in her voice.

Bill looked at the faces of Melissa, Tessa and the others; then he looked at Marie. He thought back to what Tessa had told them about the military camp and he frowned.

"I'd like to think that's the case, but you know the saying: Out of the frying pan and into the fire?"

She nodded, as did the others.

"Well, something tells me that saying is quite apt for our current situation."

"All of you, shut the fuck up or be shot," one of the faceless soldiers said, the rifle bouncing in his hands as the truck rumbled onto the main road. It was hard to tell which man had spoken, because with their masks on, they all looked alike.

Bill decided to do as he was told and remain silent for the time being. His fellow survivors glanced at one another, trying to comfort each other with their eyes, while the transport drove off into the night, their destination unknown.

CHAPTER 20

DEAN CALLED A halt when he saw the explosion coming from across the highway. The blanket of darkness made it easy to spot the eruption of flames and the noise of the collapsing building soon followed; the dust and smoke lost in the obsidian sky.

Dean felt himself cringe, sensing that a large group of his people had just perished. With every passing hour, he had found he was growing more attuned to his fellow infected. He still didn't know why he was granted a consciousness while the other Changed were nothing more than mindless killing machines, but he knew he would use the power well.

Perhaps that was why the Changed listened to him with such devotion. They, too, sensed his greatness.

Turning around to look behind him on the dark highway, he could see nothing but an eddying flow of heads and shoulders. Some would seem to rise off the ground as they swarmed over an abandoned car or truck. They had no choice but to go over the wrecks as there were far too many bodies crowding the highway to try and swarm around the objects.

Thousands of the Changed were behind him, following him on an exodus to where they knew not. With the city of Chicago in flames, Dean had left, taking all he could find with him. Chicago was nothing more than ash and rubble with the charred corpses of the dead to fill its streets. The suburbs of Chicago still burned, the great conflagration showing no signs of abating. As the winds grew, so did the flames, crossing roads and barriers to set neighborhood after neighborhood on fire until the landscape from the air would look like the gates of Hell themselves had broken open, allowing demonic fires to rage across the land.

So when Dean had left the city, there was really only one way to go.

South, toward the Midway International Airport or the *Midway Airport,* as the locals called it. The airport was situated near the edge of Lake Michigan and with the flames slowly consuming the entire state; Dean felt this would be a good a place as any to strike out for. Plus, it was a bonus that Mike believed the other normals had journeyed in the same direction.

Two birds with one stone, one of his foster father's had once told him that saying. At least between the beatings he had given poor Dean when the man was drunk.

Next to him stood Mike. The young man was petrified that Dean would lose interest in him and have him slaughtered, but so far Mike's directions had proved true, thus allowing him to live for another day.

The explosion less than a mile away proved it. Dean didn't know how he knew what he did, but he sensed that the normals had been within his grasp, but that they had eluded him.

The death of so many of his brethren only proved this assumption.

"Do you see that light and hear the rumble of destruction, Mikey?"

Mike nodded that he did.

"That was the normals you told me about, yes?"

Mike shrugged. "Could be, how would I know? All I know is they were walking this way when I saw them, before I turned off the highway to go into the city. The biggest mistake of my life." He muttered the last part.

Dean heard him anyway. "You think so? Actually, I think it was the best thing you could have done, finding me, that is. If not for me, the Changed would have ripped you to pieces long ago, so look at the bright side, even if I kill you, I can almost guarantee you'll be the last normal in the state of Illinois when I do."

Mike frowned. "Some consolation."

Dean chuckled at that. "Think so? Well, I guess it's all a matter of opinion. Shall we continue on? I'd like to see what survived that explosion if indeed there are survivors." Before moving on, he turned to

Mike and gazed into the blonde man's eyes. "I warn you, Mike, if I even sense your prevarication, I'll kill you."

"My what? I don't understand what you just said."

Dean sighed, frustrated. "I said, you better not be telling lies you ignorant normal."

Mike swallowed a large lump in his throat and nodded quickly. "Oh, ah, understood," he whispered.

"All right then, let's move out, there's a lot to investigate."

Dean waved his followers forward like the Jews following Moses out of Egypt. With all the refugees wandering the desert after escaping certain death, the exodus continued.

About twenty minutes later, Dean set his right foot down near the shattered building and the remains of Star Labs in the dark office park. The middle of the building had imploded in on itself, bricks and rubble strewn everywhere. Visibility was easy thanks to numerous small fires still burning. Dean was able to see arms and legs at odd angles in the rubble, and when he moved around the rear of the building, he spotted his first clue to what had happened here.

A dead soldier wearing a white suit lay prone on the black asphalt, his body covered by a pile of falling rubble and his head almost turned around to face the opposite way. It looked like the man was lying on his back, but his face was facing down.

"You and you; remove this debris from on top of this man so I can get a better look at him," Dean ordered three of the Changed nearby. The three men dove into the pile with gusto, tossing bricks and pieces of metal away from the fallen corpse. Some of the flying debris struck other infected and they screamed when they were hit, but otherwise remained where they stood. Dean rolled his eyes to the sky and asked, "why me?"

In no time the body was clear and Dean stepped over to the white-clothed corpse, kicking the body with his foot. The dead soldier rolled over onto its stomach, the bloody face now staring up at the sky.

"Soldiers, I might have known," Dean said, crisply.

Turning to Mike, he stuck his finger under the man's nose. "So help me, Mike, if you knew anything about this," he warned him.

Mike held his hands in front of him, trying to calm Dean down. "Whoa, there, Dean, I swear, I don't know anything about this shit."

Dean stared at Mike as if he was trying to discern if the man was lying or truthful, but after a full minute he looked away.

"Fine, I guess it's not your fault. That's okay, though, because when I catch up to them, they will all die horribly." Dean turned to stare at Mike one last time, the fires reflecting in his eyes giving him a demonic quality. "When everything first started to fall apart, the soldiers came into Chicago, you know. They'd just passed martial law and were trying to get the people under control. But there was one thing they didn't count on. The people were changing and didn't fear the men with their guns and trucks. The people swarmed over them, ripping the gas masks from their faces. Some of the soldiers joined us then, seeing the light, but others fought to the end and the people tore them to pieces. After that the military evacuated Chicago, at least what was left of them did, and never returned. If I had to guess, I'd say they gave up. But I know there still out there, watching and waiting for another chance to get us."

Mike only nodded, too afraid to say anything.

Dean grunted, satisfied, and then turned to the few hundred who had followed him to the building, the rest of his army was waiting impatiently on the highway. Dean pulled the closest Changed to him, a middle-aged woman with scraggly, light brown hair.

"You, gather a few other women and run ahead of us. You're my scouts. I want you to go at least three miles in front of us and then send one of you back to tell me what you find." He shoved the woman away from him. "Go, get going and don't stop until you've accomplished your task."

The woman grunted and ran off into the night; every now and then pulling a female to her, and with a few slurred words, said person would follow. Dean knew that if he sent male scouts out and they found any normals, they would quickly forget about their mission, wanting to hunt and kill instead, but he needed them focused. Usually the women were better at this, less bloodthirsty than the men, but only by a small degree.

Dean had already forgotten about them as he turned and started back to the highway.

"Come along, Mikey, There's a long road in front of us and a short time to get there."

Mike took one last look at the dead soldier and quickly ran after Dean. He'd already learned the hard way what the evil bastard would do to him if he didn't jump when ordered to do so. Dean's wanton lack of mercy had him breathing every second as if it was his last.

With the crowd of thousands starting to move again, leaving the office park and rubble of Star Labs behind, the office park grew quiet, with the exception of a few snaps and crackles from the still burning fires.

CHAPTER 21

"WHERE'S MY BROTHER?" Phillip asked from the front of the truck bed. One of the soldiers gave the boy a dirty look, but that's as far as the threat went, Bill was glad for it. At least the soldiers had some decency left underneath their gas masks and bio-suits.

Bill looked to Marie for support. How does one tell a five-year-old boy his only living family member had just given his life to save them all? Marie only shrugged, not having the answers he so desperately needed. Bill was surprised when it was Tessa who took the dilemma from him.

"Roger's not coming with us, Phillip. He's staying behind to help the soldiers. He'll be with us soon, though," she said this with a false smile.

One of the soldiers growled at her and Tessa answered by flipping him the finger. The soldier was about to stand up when the second soldier held his arm, stopping him.

"Leave it alone, Bob, the Sergeant-Major said he wanted them alive."

The soldier cursed under his mask and sat back down. "Alive, yeah, but he didn't say we couldn't bruise them a little."

The first soldier shook his head, exasperated, the gesture barely noticeable under his containment gear.

"Look, Bob, do what you want, but don't blame me when you're on corpse duty."

That seemed to make the man think for a second and he realized maybe he was getting carried away. Tessa on the other hand, acted like she'd scored some kind of moral victory and stuck her tongue out at the conflicted soldier in triumph.

While the insulted soldier grumbled under his mask, his hands gripping his rifle tighter, the second, more level-headed soldier only chuckled.

Bill leaned forward so only Tessa could hear him. "It might be better not to agitate them, Tessa. At least not until we know what we're going into," Bill suggested.

Tessa just grinned and looked away, hugging Kenny with her left arm. The boy had been quiet since they had boarded the truck, intimidated by the alien looking soldiers. Melissa and Janice were sitting near the opening of the bed, the wind blowing their hair wildly around their faces. Both women were subdued, not understanding what had happened and why Elizabeth hadn't made it out with them.

Bill didn't blame them. In only a few short hours they'd lost almost half their numbers. What would happen in another day, or a week, if the odds for survival were now this difficult?

"Where are you taking us, we have a right to know," Bill said to the soldiers, hoping for a response. He received one, but not the one he'd hoped for.

"You have a right to shut the fuck up, unless you want to be spitting teeth," the angrier of the soldiers said, sticking the rifle under Bill's chin.

"All right, take it easy. It's just that we've been on the run for a while now, trying to stay ahead of those people out there. Actually, it's great to see you guys," Bill said trying to smooth over any hostilities between the soldiers and his friends.

Soldier number two let out a loud sigh Bill could hear through the man's gas mask. "Lighten up, Bob, they're just people. Though for the life of me I don't know why you're not infected," he said, the last sentence aimed to Bill.

"Infected? Don't really know why we're okay. Just lucky I guess," Bill replied with a slight grin.

"Lucky my ass," the meaner soldier said, "if it wasn't for these masks I'd probably be one of those killers out there. I tell you it ain't right why some people are fine and some ain't."

"So there are others like us; that are okay?" Marie asked, hope filling her eyes.

Soldier number two nodded slightly. "Some are immune, like you, though most people, once exposed, become crazy and lose all sense of who they are. If it wasn't for the Sergeant-Major realizing what was happening and making us all don our masks, we'd probably be like the rest of them."

Bill nodded, glad to be getting some information from the soldier. The more they could find out the better off they'd be. Bill thought he'd try to find out their destination one more time.

"So, may I ask where we're going, please?" He said as politely as he could.

"All right, fine, might as well tell you. After all, once we get there you'll know anyway. We're going to Midway Airport."

"Midway Airport? Why? Why not a military installation or some kind of refugee camp? I heard there was one nearby," Marie said nicely.

The soldier nodded. "Yup, there was one, until more than five-hundred infected people overran it, causing us to evacuate. Luckily, we were already preparing to bug out and almost all of us got out of there. It was the Major's idea to set up at the airport. After all, they've already got fences and checkpoints and the terminals make a great staging point for the doctors, the research staff, and the rest of our unit. Not to mention where you're going."

"Where're we going?" Bill inquired.

"To the isolation ward that's been set up," the mean soldier said. Bill guessed the man was smiling under his gas mask. Bill wanted nothing more than to lean over and pull the mask from the man's face, but what would that actually accomplish? Either the man would shoot him or the soldier would turn into a raving killer and then attack him or his friends.

Thinking all this, he squeezed his hands into fists, holding his temper in check.

"Isolation ward, why? If we're not sick than we're not a threat to anyone," Bill said.

The second soldier shrugged. "Look, pal, I'm just a grunt. I leave the thinking to the docs and my superiors. Now, we're almost there, so how about piping down and letting me rest for a while, huh? I've been on duty for almost twenty-four hours straight."

Bill nodded; satisfied with the answers he'd received. Though some of the answers only opened up more questions, he was smart enough to know when to stop pushing. Looking out the rear of the truck bed, the city of Chicago faded away. Bill marveled how the skyline had changed, smoke and fire filling the night sky, the nearby, burning neighborhoods painting the horizon the color of blood.

At least they were moving away from the conflagration. That was something at least. And hopefully, they would be out of reach of the rest of the infected population that once lived and loved in the state of Illinois.

The truck slowed to a stop almost an hour later and Bill realized he'd dozed off. Not surprising, really. In the last few days he'd spent so much time running and fighting, sleep had been the last thing on his mind. His body felt like he was moving through molasses as he tried to shake the weariness from stiff limbs.

The soldiers were the first to disembark, jumping down to the tarmac where they were joined by three more men, all in white bio-containment suits and matching gas masks. It was all so surreal, Bill thought, looking around him. He was the last to hop down out of the truck.

It was still dark, sunrise a few more hours away, but it was easy to see where they were; an airport. Multiple planes sat silent on the tarmac, waiting for their chance to reach the skies once more.

Bill wondered if they would ever leave the ground again. If the infection was as bad as it appeared to be, then where would all the pilots be other than running around like rabid dogs?

"Move out, toward the terminal," one of the soldiers ordered. With their masks on, their voices were hard to distinguish, so Bill had no idea which soldier had given the order, not that it really mattered.

The survivors were herded like cattle across the open runway, with the soldiers flanking them on all sides.

"Kind of a little overkill for little old us, don't you think?" Marie commented dryly.

"I know what you mean, what do they think we're gonna do? Without weapons they'd slaughter us," Melissa added, askance of the others.

One of the soldiers heard the conversation and stepped a little closer. "I know it seems like we're being too cautious, but after what happened at the camp, the Sergeant-Major's taking no chances. You'll see once you meet him." The soldier moved away then, not wanting to be seen fraternizing with the prisoners. Still, it gave Bill hope perhaps not all them were dangerous, that in fact some sympathized with their situation.

In less than five minutes the terminal doors were in sight. Bill noticed there seemed to be some kind of tent on the other side of the doors and realized it was a pressurized air chamber, similar to the one they'd found at Star Labs, only this one was a temporary structure used by the CDC and other government authorities in times of crisis when airborne diseases were known to be prevalent.

One at a time, the group was ushered through the doors. Bill was the second, after Marie, and once inside the chamber, the sound of the chamber pressurizing filled his ears. Once finished, the other end of the tent was unzipped and Bill and Marie were told to exit. Once through, the seal was re-secured and they waited why the others were cycled through.

Upon exiting the chamber, Bill and the others then had to walk a ten foot tunnel. Bright lights, perhaps ultraviolet, lined both sides of the tunnel. Bill could feel the hair on his face actually burning slightly as he ran this gambit. When he stepped out the other side, he turned and waited for his friends. His skin felt slightly raw and he guessed the lights must have sterilized his clothing and exposed body, destroying any bacteria that may have clung to him from the outside world. Looking down, he saw his clothes were actually steaming slightly from the heat.

Another five minutes later had the survivors together once more, as were the soldiers. The soldier on Bill's right was the first to remove his mask, showing the blue eyes, and smooth, pale chin of a young man. If Bill was to guess, the soldier couldn't be more than eighteen or nineteen.

"Move along, this way to the Sergeant-Major," the soldier said. Despite the absence of the mask, Bill was sure this was the soldier who had talked to him on the walk over and the kindness in his eyes seemed to settle it for Bill. The other soldiers also removed their gas masks, showing a wide assortment of men. Spanish, Black and Irish were just some of the few nationalities represented by the men; and all seemed relieved to be breathing the canned air of the terminal.

With Bill and Marie in the lead, the group went where they were told, moving through the terminal. Normally, there would be thousands of people filling the terminal and the others connected by long walkways, now blocked off, all trying to catch their planes or waiting on a layover until their next flight would leave, but now the place was deserted. Bill moved through the terminal, noticing there were only a few soldiers moving about. All were armed with M-16 rifles and wore side- arms on their hips, a few having small knives on belts, too.

Bill slowed when they passed another temporary chamber. The doors were transparent, and as Bill watched, he could see men with lab coats moving about inside. Just before he was pushed away, he thought he saw a body on a table, but couldn't be sure. Then he was past the doors and had to leave it for later.

"Marie, did you see that?" Bill asked her softly.

"See what?" She asked curious.

"Never mind, I'll tell you later," he replied to her, his head moving left and right to make sure he wasn't seen talking by one of the guards.

After a few lefts and rights and up an escalator, Bill realized he was totally lost. They slowed as they approached a door. On the front of the door were the words: **SECURITY**, printed in bold letters.

One of the soldiers opened the door and Bill and the others were ushered inside.

The room was huge, full of monitor screens and computers. If Bill was right, this was the heart of the security portion of the airport, a pretty good headquarters he had to admit.

A man wearing a pair of BDU's and smoking a cigar walked over to the group, stopping when he was no more than three feet away. In front of Bill and the others there was a one foot high platform, and the soldier stopped just short of stepping down onto the main floor, and by doing this, Bill and the rest of the group had no choice but to look up at the man.

Psychologically speaking, it was a good ploy.

The young soldier with the kind eyes walked up to the front of their group, smiling as he gestured toward the man with the cigar.

"Ladies and gentlemen, I'd like to introduce you to our commander and savior, Sergeant-Major Thaddeus Deckard."

Bill gazed up at the man and wondered if he was supposed to clap, with such an introduction. Deciding that would be a foolish thing to do, he just stepped forward and held out his hand for the man to shake. "I'm Bill Thompson and I'm kind of the leader of our little group," Bill said.

The man let out a puff of smoke and just looked at Bill's hand as if he was deciding if he should shake it or not. Bill was starting to feel stupid and was about to let his hand drop when the man moved forward the other foot separating the two men, stepped down from his platform, and grasped Bill's hand. The handshake was nothing impressive and Bill was happy when the soldier let go. There had always been something unsettling to Bill when he shook another man's hand and the grip was weak. Said something about the character of the man shaking, Bill had always thought.

"Hello there, Mr. Thompson, I just wanted to meet you before you were brought to containment. It's good we found you. Your country needs you…all of you. For some reason, you people haven't been infected with the virus that's been released across America and we hope, no, pray, that there's something in your blood which will allow us to find a cure. So thank you in advance for cooperating and I hope to see you soon." He looked over at one of the soldiers, a large man with bright red hair and freckles. "Okay, Connelly, move them out."

"Yes, Sergeant-Major," the man barked and with rifle aimed at Bill and the others, the rest of the soldiers doing the same, the group was ushered out of the security room and back into the terminal.

"Wait, there's so much we need to know! What about the rest of the country, how bad is the contamination, wait, we need to know!" Bill yelled as he was pushed at gunpoint away from Deckard.

Deckard didn't hear him, the man was already moving deeper into the room, where a few soldiers sat at monitors, smoke billowing from his cigar as he walked away from a protesting Bill. The security door was slammed closed and the survivors were gathered in a circle in the middle of the terminal, the soldiers surrounding them. Bill's hand reached for his .38 out of instinct, but cursed instead, realizing it had been the first thing the soldiers had taken when they'd captured him before loading him and the others onto the transport trucks.

"Move along, don't make this any harder than it has to be. Cooperate and you'll be fine," one of the soldiers said. If Bill was right, the red-headed soldier was the leader for the unit; the other soldiers seemed to look to him for orders and assurances they were doing what they were supposed to be doing. Bill realized most of the men looked like they were just out of high school, only a few faces Bill had seen appeared to be older than twenty and only a few of them were women. It was like they were all cadets, still in boot camp and not fully prepared to enter the military and fight yet.

But the rifles they held were deadly and Bill knew when to do what he was told.

"Come on, people, let's do what they tell us, it's not like we have a choice," Bill said to the others.

"Smart man, maybe you'll actually live to see another day, especially after Dr. Frankenstein gets through with you," Red-Head said, the other soldiers chuckling.

"Dr. Frankenstein? Who the hell's that?" Melissa asked the soldiers, not caring who answered, but the fear clearly showing in her eyes.

"Don't worry, lady, you'll find out. If I was you, though, I wouldn't be in a hurry to find out."

More chuckles and soft laughter filled the terminal and Marie and Bill shared a look.

"All right, enough chatter. Everyone move out and no talking," Red-Head ordered, while waving his rifle aggressively.

Bill put his arm around Tessa, with Kenny and Phillip close by. Melissa was with Janice, the woman on her feet and feeling better.

"Fine, soldier; lead the way, won't you?" Bill said politely, as if he and the others were merely guests instead of captured prisoners.

Two soldiers went in front of the group and began walking deeper into the terminal, the survivors in the middle, then the other soldier's right behind them.

Marie moved as close as she could to Bill, and with her voice kept low, said: "What the hell are we going to do? What do they want with us?"

"I have no idea, but with the firepower they have, we're helpless to resist, so we might as well play along. At least we're safe here for the moment."

Marie nodded, not liking his answer, but understanding it was the best they could do in their current situation.

With a dozen footsteps echoing off the terminal walls, the survivors moved deeper into the airport, not knowing where they were being led, but praying it was better from whence they came.

CHAPTER 22

BILL AND THE others were ordered to stop when they reached the United Airlines terminal. The red-headed soldier jogged to the front of the line and continued moving forward into the terminal while the others waited, nervously.

No one knew what was happening or why they'd been brought to this place, but despite the rifles aimed at them, all were curious. The red-headed soldier returned a few minutes later and waved them onward through a set of double doors, his face set in stone.

Bill and Marie were the first through the egress and their eyes opened wide when they took in their surroundings. A massive hangar stood before them, totally enclosed. Large air filters could be seen surrounding the massive air conditioning units that kept the hangar relatively cool.

The survivors were instructed to move to the rear of the hangar where large steel cubicles had been erected. As they moved closer, Bill could see the metal had been welded together rather shabbily, but if he knew the military, then the welds would hold for whatever they were designed for, cosmetics notwithstanding.

He found out seconds later when he was told to stop in front of the first cubicle. Both he and Marie were told to step inside the small door built into the side of the small box, and once they had entered, the door was slammed shut without preamble. Bill immediately reached for the small handle and pushed, the door refusing to budge. He could hear the raised voices of his friends as they were placed in the other cubicles next to him.

Bill sighed, realizing he was now officially a prisoner and turned to look at Marie. She had taken a seat on the small cot in the corner of the room, the only other furniture being a small chemical toilet.

"Well, it looks like we're the official guests of the United States Army," he said sadly.

Marie leaned against the metal wall, the cool metal penetrating her shirt. "Well, at least we are safe for the moment, not like anything can get us in here. Did you see those fences when we came into the airport? I couldn't be sure, but I think they were electrified."

Bill shook his head. "I fell asleep, didn't see a thing. What else did you see?" He asked, moving to sit next to her on the cot. It creaked with both their combined weight, but seemed structurally sound.

Marie creased her forehead, trying to recall everything she'd observed when they'd entered the airport. "Well, for one thing, they had guards posted at the main entrance and there was large gate set up, and when we approached, they had to open it manually. Once we'd made it through, there were patrols that were walking around; I guess to make sure the area was secure. You figure we'll be okay here?"

He shrugged. "I'm not sure of anything. I mean, why are we prisoners? We've done nothing wrong and what was that crack about a doctor and using our blood to find a cure?" He stood up and walked the few feet to the far wall. He punched his right fist into the palm of his left hand, and spun around to look Marie straight in the eyes. "I don't like it, Marie, not one bit. I say if there's a chance, no matter how slim of getting out of here, we need to take it. Besides, if there's more of those killers out there, and there's no reason to assume there's not, then this airport is one giant target and I doubt even these soldiers could keep all of them at bay…electric fences or not."

Marie sighed, stretching out on the cot. "Well, whatever happens, I'm exhausted, what do you say we get some sleep and let the future come when it may?"

With the word sleep brought up, Bill felt a wave of exhaustion flood over him. He'd only drifted off for a short time in the troop transport and his weariness hit him hard now that he knew he could actually rest in relative safety.

Marie patted the cot. "Come here, handsome, there's room for two."

"Why, Marie, are you trying to get me into bed with you?" He asked slyly.

She chuckled. "Don't flatter yourself. I mean, have you smelled yourself recently? Not that I'm as fresh as a daisy mind you. No, I just want you to lie down next to me and let me pretend for just a little while that everything's fine and the world isn't falling apart."

He crossed the few feet and slid onto the cot, feeling her warm body next to him. She snuggled closer, closed her eyes and within seconds he could hear the steady breathing of her slumber. He lay there listening to her breathing, his own becoming in synch with hers, and like listening to the rhythmic sound of a metronome, he found himself drifting off to sleep.

He hovered on that fine line between actual sleep and wakefulness for a few more minutes, the thrum of the air conditioning units humming like the heart of a great engine. Then, he too, slipped into oblivion, lost in nightmares of running for his life while the beasts of Hell nipped at his heels.

But soon the nightmares dissolved into scenes from his past. He saw himself with his wife, Laura, on a sunny beach in Florida. They had gone to the sunshine state for their honeymoon and he smiled, recalling the joy he'd felt with her.

She had looked so beautiful that first night on the beach with the setting sun casting her in a halo of brilliance. He had taken her in his arms and kissed her long and hard, his passion for the woman almost to a boiling point.

After the kiss, they had raced each other back to their hotel room where they'd made passionate love for the rest of the night, only falling asleep when he was too exhausted to continue for the fourth or fifth time; frankly he'd lost count after the third.

Then the picture dissolved and shifted and a moment later he found himself standing in a wide open field outside of Chicago. He was alone and when he turned to look at the city behind him, a large blast filled the horizon. Bill was thrown to the grass by the shockwave and he threw his arms over his head as the world seemed to explode into a maelstrom of light and sound.

When he finally opened his eyes, he looked across the distance to see nothing but a vast crater where Chicago once stood. He didn't know how he knew, but he was aware that a nuclear bomb had just been set off within the city limits.

Nothing but devastation could be seen around him and he wondered why it was that he was still alive? Why hadn't he been vaporized from the initial blast with the thousands of other people in the city?

He reached up to rub his scalp and gasped when his hand came away with tufts of thinning hair in his fist. Reaching up again, he started pulling strand after strand away from his thinning scalp until there was nothing left but a bloody mess of flaking skin.

Before he could even wonder what was happening, he felt one of his teeth move in his mouth. His tongue poked at it until he finally reached in with two fingers and plucked it out.

The tooth came out easily, the bloody root staring back at him. His tongue inspected the hole where the tooth once was and soon his tongue pushed another one loose. His hand reached in, thumb and fingers wiggling one after the other loose. The entire top portion of his mouth seeming to fall out onto his tongue and he spit them out like an old codger with two much chewing tobacco in his cheek.

Blood spilled forth from gaping holes, wanting to drown him, the exposed nerves filling his head with intense pain. Spitting rivulets of red onto the dry, brown grass, he looked down at his chest and legs.

The skin was peeling away, his clothing having already disintegrated to tatters, and he let out a howl of anguish that floated over the countryside. His legs grew weak and he fell to the dirt, parts of his arms dissolving into the muddy soil his blood was making of the earth directly around him.

As his eyeballs turned to soup and flowed out of their sockets and down his face to land in the mud, he realized why he was still alive when an entire city had burned in radioactive fire. It was so he could suffer, not die in the blink of an eye while the superheated air burned him to nothing.

He screamed one last time, his tongue separating from his mouth and falling away to be lost below him. His shrieks soon turned to gargles as his consciousness faded, and he realized death was finally coming to take him.

Death stood over him, looking down with its gaping pale-white skull.

"You can't save them, they're all doomed!" Death screamed into his dissolving ear. *"I will have them all. Soon they will all join me in Hell!"*

Bill tried to yell back, to tell Death he was wrong. He would find a way to save them, he'd promised.

Tossing and turning in his cot, Marie tried to shake him awake.

"Bill, Bill, wake up, you're having a bad dream," she said into his ear, her own voice groggy from sleep.

Bill opened his eyes and Marie saw he seemed to be staring at nothing, a sheen of sweat covering his face and arms. Then he closed his eyes and went back to sleep, his chest rising and falling steadily.

Deciding whatever had been haunting him was finished, she closed her eyes and drifted back to sleep, comforted by the warm body next to her.

Bill slowly came back to consciousness, for a moment not knowing where he was. He wasn't sure what had shaken him from his slumber, but he was sure it had been loud enough to wake him. Wistful visions from his nightmares dissolved from his mind, like ghosts at the first cock-crow of the morning, becoming banished to the ether when the first rays of the newborn sun rose on the horizon.

He sat up, now snapping fully awake. He didn't remember what he'd been dreaming about, but for some reason his resolve to fight and see his friends through their ordeal was stronger than ever. Then he heard it again, a soft rapping sound coming from the left side of his steel prison.

Turning over, he saw Marie was still next to him. He carefully slid out from under her embrace, and after stretching, stood up. Wiping drool from his chin, he moved closer to the wall and placed his ear against it. He was regretful of the action as soon as he did it, when he was rewarded with yet another bang from the other side of the wall. He pulled his head back, his ear ringing as curses floated from his lips. Chastising his own foolishness, he noticed Marie waking up.

"What's up?" She asked; her voice groggy from sleep.

Bill pointed to the wall and moved closer to it, this time keeping his head and ears well clear of the cool metal. "Someone's banging from the other side. Maybe it's one of the others."

"Well, don't just stand there, answer them back," Marie told him, while she sat up and stretched aching limbs.

Bill did as she directed and tapped on the wall with his knuckles. "Hello? Who's in there?" He called to the unknown person.

"It's me, Tessa. I'm with Kenny and Phillip. Melissa and Janice are on the other side of me, but Melissa said they took Janice away a little while ago. The soldiers wouldn't say where they took her. Melissa is scared and so am I."

"How are the kids doing?" Bill asked.

"They're okay. They're sleeping right now. Phillip kept asking when he was going to see Roger. I didn't know what to say, so I lied again."

Bill nodded, but stopped when he realized she couldn't see him. "That's good, Tessa, we have enough to worry about right now; we don't need Phillip freaking out at the loss of his brother. If we get through this intact, there'll be time for that later."

"What do they want with us, Bill? I thought the Army was on our side? They're not doing bad stuff to us like I heard about at the camp, at least not yet," Tessa said, the worry in her voice easy to discern even through the metal wall.

"I don't really know, Tessa, but just stay strong for a little while longer and you'll be fine, all of you will."

Luckily, Tessa couldn't see the concern on his face, and that what he was saying to her, he didn't quite believe himself, but morale had to stay high or all was lost before they even started to try and fight.

"Okay, Bill, I'll be strong…for the kids."

"Good girl, okay now, go back and lie down and rest while you can," he told her.

She said she would and then the metal cubicle grew quiet again with the exception of the hum of the air units.

Marie stood up and walked over to Bill, placing her head on his shoulder. "That was the right thing to tell her. If we're in trouble here then let them find out when they have to. Worrying about what's coming won't change it for the better."

Bill stepped away from her and grabbed her shoulders. "Well, I'm not waiting; I'm going to find out just what the hell they want with us right now. If I don't come back, you'll know we're in trouble, so take your first chance and try to escape. Hopefully you can grab the kids and any of the others if possible."

Marie smiled wanly. "That's a tall request, Bill, who do I look like, Rambo? But I'll try. You just make sure to come back to me, to all of us." She leaned forward and kissed him lightly on the lips. Nothing sexual, just a show of affection. He took her hands and squeezed them hard, then he walked the few feet to the door and started to pound on it, the door rattling loudly. He continued pounding for five minutes straight until the door was finally opened.

"Dude, what the hell are you doing with all the noise? What do you want?" A blue eyed soldier--the same one as before they'd been placed into their cells, Bill noticed--said loudly. Behind him was another soldier with dark black hair. This man held his rifle at the ready in case Bill was trying to escape.

"I want to see Deckard, and if you don't take me to him, I'm gonna make so much damn racket I'll drive you guys crazy."

The soldier looked at Bill, seeing the conviction in his eyes and sighed. "All right, fine, just let me check to make sure it's cool, now give it a rest until I come back, okay?"

"Fine, but don't take too long," Bill said, the door closing once more.

"What do you really think you'll accomplish by talking to the Major?" Marie asked.

"I don't really know, but it's the best I could come up with on short notice," he said, pacing back and forth until he grew tired and he plopped down on the cot. Marie was leaning against the far corner, her arms crossed over her chest. Now it was a waiting game, hoping that Bill would be allowed to leave the cell.

"You know, you were having quite a dream earlier, do you remember any of it?" Marie asked, trying to break the awkward silence while they waited for a reply from the soldier.

Bill shook his head. "No, not really, though I do get the faintest feeling it wasn't pleasant. I think my wife was there…in my dream. She was young and healthy, before the cancer got hold of her."

Marie looked down at the floor. "I'm so sorry, Bill, I'm sure she was a good woman."

Bill smiled at her condolence. "Thanks, yeah, she was."

Twenty minutes ticked by and Bill was starting to worry that his request had been ignored when the door to the cell swung open once more. The same blue eyed soldier stood in the door frame and he waved Bill to come out. Marie tried to follow him, but she was told to stay.

"Just him, the Major's not much on the fairer sex, ma'am. He believes they're only on this earth for one thing, pardon my English."

Marie frowned. "Male chauvinist pig, I thought they were almost extinct," she turned and trudged back to the cot and sat down. "Don't worry, Marie, I'll be back, I promise," Bill said while exiting the cell.

"You'd better," she said as the door closed on her last words.

"If you're going to be guarding me, do you mind if I ask you your name," Bill asked the blue-eyed soldier.

The man shrugged. "Sure, no biggy. The names Private Chris Robinson and this here's Huff," Chris said pointing to the other soldier with the black hair.

"Just Huff?" Bill inquired.

Huff nodded. "That's right, never needed anything more, though first name's Shaun, but nobody uses it."

"Fair enough, Huff, and I'm Bill. So, shall we go?"

They headed off, and Bill noticed two more soldiers were replacing the men escorting him. The soldiers nodded to one another, Chris slapping his replacement on the shoulder in greeting.

The two soldiers escorted Bill back through the terminal to the security base once more. Upon entering it, Bill saw the Major was still in the same place and he wondered if the man had ever left.

The Sergeant-Major turned when Bill entered the security room and Deckard waved Bill forward.

Bill did so, leaving the soldiers to stand at ease by the door. Stepping onto the platform, Bill was able to see the monitor screens more closely. He could see the perimeter fence that surrounded the airport, as well as the main road in and the gate itself. Other cameras seemed to cover different parts of the terminal. Bill's eyes stopped when he saw what looked like a lab table with what appeared to be a corpse on top of it. The Major saw this and quickly flicked a switch, the monitor changing to one of the cameras aimed at the perimeter fence.

Sergeant-Major Thaddeus Deckard turned and gave Bill his full attention. "One of my men said you wanted an audience with me. He said you were being quite unruly. It was either let you see me or have you shot. Aren't you glad I chose the latter?"

Bill swallowed hard, not knowing his fate had been so carelessly decided. "Yes, I am, thank you."

"So now that you're here, would you mind telling me just what the hell you want?"

Bill cleared his throat. "Well for starters, how come only a Sergeant-Major is running this temporary camp? Why isn't there someone of higher authority, like a Colonel or a Captain?"

If Deckard was offended by the inquiry, he never let on; instead he lit the cold cigar in his mouth and leaned back against a bank of monitors.

"There was a General in charge, but he died at the last camp. Before this place was operational, we were set up just outside of Chicago. We'd been there for more than a week, since the outbreak first started. But then we were overrun by infected civilians. More than half of my men were either killed or had their gas masks removed and had then become infected themselves. We don't know much about this virus, but we do know its airborne, so to walk around outside exposed is a death warrant, that is with the exception of a small percentage of the population that appears to be immune to the virus. I took command when things at the last camp fell apart. I rallied the men and grabbed what we could and bugged out, taking as many eggheads as I could find. Now those same scientists are our only hope. Driving into the airport, I figured we could do a lot worse. After all, it already has fences and security cameras and it was already deserted once the FAA grounded all flights in or out of the United States. You see, once we were infiltrated by the infected, there was no way to leave Illinois. The entire state has been quarantined. So far, we've been able to limit the infection to Chicago and the surrounding suburbs, but its slowly spreading. By now it's probably everywhere across the damn planet. Barricades have been set up around the state and anyone trying to leave is shot on sight, infected or not, though I wonder how many of the roadblocks are still being manned by personnel. Communication had been spotty at best. So you see, if we don't find a cure, here and now, we're all dead."

"So what does that have to do with me and my friends being treated like prisoners?" Bill asked.

"Well, you seem to be part of the small minority that is immune to the virus. You need to be examined, blood work and the like. Hopefully, there's something in your blood or immune system that will help the doc's procure a cure."

"Okay, that's fine with me, I'm sure my friends will agree with me that we'll gladly help anyway we can. So then why are you keeping us locked up?"

Deckard shifted his feet, looking like a scolded child. "Ah, well you see, some of the procedures the doctors have to do are quite invasive.

It's possible some of you might die. At least that's what's happened to the few other immune people we've come across. But don't worry, your deaths will be for the greater good, in fact, you might be the one to save humanity." He grinned at the end of his speech, proud of what he was doing.

"What? Are you mad? Killing me or my friends won't find you a cure, no matter how much you dig into us. If it's not in a simple blood sample then it's not there to find!"

Deckard waved to the two soldiers at the door to come and hold Bill.

Bill struggled for a moment, but soon realized he was easily over-powered and decided to bide his time and pray for an opportunity to escape later.

Deckard leaned forward and blew smoke into Bill's face. "I'm sorry it has to be this way, I really am, but there's no other choice. I'm sure you've heard the saying, the good of the many is more important than the good of the one. This is one of those cases." Deckard turned to Private Chris Robinson while smoke rings surrounded his head like a sick parody of a halo.

"Private Robinson, take this man to the Doc now instead of later. Have him sedated and tell the Doc to make him his next test subject."

"Yes, Sergeant-Major," Chris said as he started to drag Bill out of the security base and back into the terminal.

"Oh, and Private, tell the Doc it would be nice if he left this one alive, but to do what he has to do. Results are the important thing."

"Yes, Sergeant-Major, I'll tell him," Chris said, exiting the room, with Huff on the other side of the slightly struggling Bill.

Bill wanted to push both soldiers away from him and run for it, but truth be told, there was nowhere to go. And if he did manage to elude his pursuers, he couldn't escape and leave his friends to a horrible fate at the hands of a mad doctor.

Shrugging the two men off him, he straightened his back and looked Chris in the eyes.

"Well, come on then, let's get to it, I don't have all day," Bill said, resigned to his fate, or so it would seem to the two soldiers.

With Bill almost dragging the two soldiers behind him, he moved off into the terminal, Chris telling him if he was going the right way.

While he walked between the two guards, Bill wracked his brain for a way out of his present predicament. To have survived so much only to be used as a lab experiment by his elected government was inexcusable. He had to find a way out. A distraction maybe, but what kind? What sort of a distraction could be so big that he would have free reign of the terminal and still be able to rescue his friends?

With all these questions floating around inside his head, he moved further away from the security office to a meeting with the revered Dr. Frankenstein of the camp.

He knew he wasn't going to like what was going to happen next, but he was powerless to stop it…at least for the moment.

CHAPTER 23

WHILE THE WALK to the lab was uneventful, Bill took full use of the time to try to get the lay of the land, so to speak. His eyes constantly scanned every door and access vent that led into the ceilings. He didn't know what he would do with the information, but he felt every bit of info might just come in handy if the right chance arrived.

As they walked down the center of the terminal, Bill noticed the lack of personnel. When he had first arrived he'd had the feeling there was a full complement of soldiers, but the more he watched, he realized he was actually seeing the same people more than once while they moved about the terminal on various errands.

"Where is everybody, why aren't there more soldiers around here?" Bill asked casually.

Private Chris Robinson only shrugged. "We lost almost everybody when we evacuated the camp. Most were killed, torn apart while they screamed for mercy. None of the infected gave them any. I witnessed our first commander dragged to the back of the camp by a large group of infected. His screams were so loud I could hear them over everyone else's." He seemed to hesitate for a moment and then he pushed on. "Then he stopped screaming and I didn't hear him after that."

Bill waited to hear more, but that was all the soldier was going to give him. Bill watched the young man's face while they walked; the soldier now lost in thought. Whatever he'd seen had shaken him up pretty bad.

"I'm sorry about your commander and everyone else that was killed, but I don't see why me and my friends have to die on the off chance some quack might find a cure."

Chris looked up, and slowed as he looked to Bill. "Oh, no, sir. Dr. Stevens is one of the leading epidemiologists in his field. If anyone can find a cure, it's him. It's just he's a little too aggressive with his research. I'm sorry about that, but the Sergeant-Major says it's for the better good. If a few people die and we save millions, billions even. Well, isn't that an okay price to pay?"

Bill stopped walking, the other soldier aggravated by the holdup. "Listen, son, I'm older than you and I hope you'll think about what I'm going to tell you. If I thought for just one second that if I gave my life there could be a cure, I would. But I won't just throw it away while some nut plays doctor on the off chance he might get lucky. Do you understand what I'm trying to say?"

Chris nodded and turned away from Bill's deep gaze.

"Yeah, I do, but it's out of my hands. My orders are to bring you to the Doc and that's what I'm gonna do, now if it's all the same to you, talk times over."

Bill was about to say something else, but the look in Chris' eyes said he meant what he said. The other soldier shoved Bill forward with the butt of his rifle and Bill started forward again.

No one talked the rest of the way to the lab.

When Bill reached the research lab, he saw it was the tent like structure he had originally passed when first entering the terminal with the others. Everything was a bright white and the smell of bleach filled the artificial room. Two soldiers stood at the opening, both seemed bored at standing guard duty.

After entering the tent, the two soldiers made him lay down on a metal table and strapped him down, then with an almost rueful look by Chris, both Chris and the other soldier left.

Bill lay there staring at the ceiling, his blood pounding in his chest, for the simple fact he was now strapped to a table like a frog waiting to be dissected in junior high science class. The actual ceiling was hidden by the tent's roof, the material sagging in places and billowing in others as the vents blew in fresh air.

Bill turned his head at the sound of footsteps coming from behind him. Though the person was coming closer, he still couldn't turn his head far enough to see who it was. He could only assume it was the fabled Dr. Stevens, or as the soldiers called him; Dr. Frankenstein.

Bill noticed another table was only a few feet to his left. The sheet was covering what had to be a body, and the material was stained red, the deep vermillion color a sharp contrast to the rest of the room.

Bill looked up as a shadow crossed his face and he came face to face with Dr. Stevens for the first time. From first appearances, the man was unassuming. He had a thinning hairline, with a heavy brow, thin cheeks and an almost nonexistent chin. His pale complexion stated to anyone he met he didn't get out much and that natural sunlight was alien to his skin.

Dr. Stevens looked down on Bill and grinned. The grin showed neither malice nor kindness. It simply was. Like the man had learned how to mimic the simple social graces from a book, but had yet to practice them on a real person.

"Good afternoon, sir. I'm Dr. Stevens," he said in a high-pitched, nasally voice. "Thank you for volunteering to help find a cure to this epidemic. If it wasn't for people like you, I fear there might never be a cure."

Bill's mouth fell open as he stared up at the man. "Volunteer? Are you crazy? I was forced to come here! I don't want to help you, now let me out of here or so help me…"

Dr. Stevens held up a hand as if he was silencing a young child short on manners. "Uh-uh, well, whether you volunteered or not really isn't the question. The question is why you seem to be immune to the disease while thousands, if not millions, have already succumbed to it." He reached around his back and pulled a table full of surgical implements closer to him. "Now, I'm afraid some of the tests I'll be doing are quite invasive, painful actually, but that can't be helped." His eyes scanned the tray for something he couldn't seem to find, then he sighed and stepped away from Bill. "Well, it seems I don't have all the scalpels I need to accomplish my task. Some of them are probably still being sterilized from the last specimen. I'll be right back, so you just try to stay calm and don't go anywhere." He chuckled at his poor joke and patted Bill's shoulder, almost tenderly. "Don't worry, the pain will be quick, I promise." He slipped away from Bill's sight, moving to the back of the room. He mumbled about the lack of manpower and how he had to do almost everything himself.

When he walked by the nearby surgical table, his waist rubbed the sheet covering the bloody lump. The sheet shifted enough that it slipped from the form, the doctor never noticing as he continued onward.

Bill turned his head to see what was under the mystery sheet and his face went white and a scream locked in his chest. Across from him, no more than three feet away, was the desecrated body of Janice. Her chest was peeled open in a macabre illusion of an autopsy, only her face was frozen in a mask of pain and terror. Whatever Dr. Stevens had done to her, she had suffered terribly before she finally expired. This must be the last specimen he had referred to.

Janice's eyelids were still open, her dead eyes staring up at the white tent ceiling. It was her eyes that seemed to unnerve Bill the most, and he became almost hypnotized by their deathly gaze.

He realized he would be next, and if it wasn't him, then Tessa or Marie would find themselves strapped to Dr. Stevens' table of horrors. If he had been the first one taken to see Stevens, then in all possibilities it would've been him lying dead on that cold, steel table instead of Janice.

Though he felt terrible for her death, deep down inside himself, where no one else would ever go, he breathed a sigh of relief that it was her and not him.

He struggled with the straps securing his arms and legs.

Similar to what you'd find in a mental hospital, the straps appeared solid. That is until Bill started to squirm as hard as he could. At first nothing happened, but then he realized the strap on his right arm, the one Chris had secured, was a little looser than the others. The Private had left the strap one notch looser, like buckling your belt on your pants with the number four hole when all you needed for a good fit is the number three hole. Bill pulled as hard as he could, knowing there was only seconds before the mad doctor returned.

His wrist started bleeding, the strap still not loose enough for an easy extraction, and the sharp leather began cutting into his flesh. He ignored the pain and pulled harder, hoping the blood would work as a lubricant and speed up the process. Pulling again, he bit back the yelp of pain wanting to erupt from his mouth and he grimaced when he started to see black spots in front of his eyes; but still he pulled.

With the blood covering the strap and his wrist, he couldn't see what was happening to his arm, but he knew if he failed, he would soon be joining Janice in death. They would be two matching bookends the doctor could place at opposite ends of the room, if he so chose.

With his teeth clamped from the excruciating pain, and sweat pouring down his face from exertion, he felt something give and his hand slipped free, his thumb cracking painfully the wrong way.

Breathing in great gasps, he looked down at his hand and was shocked to see the skin between his wrist and hand was almost completely peeled away, the skin hanging in ribbons. The blood covered the area, keeping the air from stinging the wound too badly, and though the limb felt like it was on fire, he quickly, but clumsily, undid the other strap and then quickly released his feet.

He heard rattling coming from behind him and he reached out, grabbed one of the half dozen scalpels on the nearby cart and lay back down on the table. He could feel his wrist still bleeding, but it couldn't be helped. He could only hope the doctor didn't notice until he was closer.

So far the two soldiers on guard duty were still oblivious, both of them talking amongst themselves, uninterested in the goings on in the lab.

Dr. Stevens came walking back to Bill's side, a tray of instruments in his hands.

"Ah, here we go, all nice and clean and ready for business. I'm sorry if I've kept you waiting, it's just that…"

But nothing but gargles now escaped his mouth, because Bill had sat up and swiped the scalpel across the man's throat, severing the carotid artery in one clean motion; blood shooting out and bathing Bill in the viscous fluid. The razor sharp knife almost felt like it was passing through air and Bill slowed his swing. He had been prepared for some resistance when the blade touched flesh, but there had been almost no resistance at all.

Dr. Stevens dropped to the floor, the instruments in his hands falling to the floor with a metallic clatter.

At the sound of the falling instruments, the two soldiers turned as one to see what was happening in the lab. What they expected to see was Dr. Stevens picking something up, what they ended up seeing was a man with a scalpel in each hand charging at them like a mad man, his face, chest and arms covered in blood.

Two things happened at almost the exact same moment. The first was the soldier's tried to bring their rifles up to point at Bill, but their reflexes were far too slow. The second was Bill charging at the two soldiers, his body plowing into the tent's fabric, the material giving way as the weight of his body caused it to stretch.

With his hands swiping the air in front of him, Bill stabbed both soldiers in the chest at almost the exact same time. The first soldier received a blow directly to his heart, the scalpel slicing the precious muscle almost in two, the soldier dead before his body struck the floor. The second soldier was luckier; the blade missed his heart and anything fatal, merely slipping through his ribcage and piercing muscle and veins.

Now if the soldier had been able to leave the scalpel where it was and had immediately tried to seek medical attention, his odds of living would have been excellent, but the man squirmed away from Bill, the blade coming free as he retreated. As an added bonus Bill managed to twist the blade when the soldier backed away, causing the wound to double in size.

With the blade out of the wound, blood shot outward and the man's chest was soaked in seconds. Though not fatal, the wound was still deadly if not attended to and Bill had just killed one of the only medical doctors in the terminal.

The soldier tried to crawl away from Bill, reaching for his sidearm. Bill used the scalpel to cut himself free of the tent, and with rage in his eyes like he was one of the infected, he fell onto the soldier and slashed and slashed until all he saw was red.

Only seconds had passed, but for Bill he was lost in limbo, time standing still as he vented his fury on the unfortunate soldier. Upon snapping back to reality, he looked down at the bloody mess that was once a human being and immediately felt sick. He had lost total control and had taken out all his anger and frustration on the poor soldier below him.

Standing up, he tried to wipe some of the blood from his face, but realized the effort was futile. Looking around the terminal, he saw it was empty. He knew it wouldn't last, though. Any second someone would come around the corner and see the mess and sound the alarm. Bill knew he needed to move, and fast.

The other soldier's clothes were relatively clean, the blood spray covering his lime t-shirt, but his green jacket and pants were mostly untouched; with the exception of the occasional heavy drops of blood here and there across the man's uniform.

Wasting no time, he stripped the soldier of his jacket and pants, grabbed his hat, and then with the soldier's rifle and sidearm, ran off down the corridor, not knowing where he was going, but just looking for a place to hide.

The hiding place appeared seconds later when he saw the signs for both the men's and ladies bathrooms. Deciding that with the lack of women in the terminal he would be less likely to be discovered in the ladies room, he slipped inside.

Leaning against the door, he tried to slow his breathing, his body shaking at what he'd just done. He'd killed three people in as many minutes and the shock of taking non-infected human lives was already hitting him, despite the fact that it was either him or them.

Stumbling to the sink, he washed his face and pulled his shirt off. His wrist was stinging something awful, now that his adrenalin was seeping away. His breathing echoed off the tile walls and he filled the sink with water, dipping his face into the cool liquid. He stared at his reflection in the mirror, staring deep into his own eyes. Is this what he had become now? A killer who would take a life without a moment of thought?

Pushing the troubling thoughts away, he focused on the immediate problems, his wound and his further escape.

When he felt he had control of himself, he quickly changed his pants and shirt and put on the soldier's clothes. The pants were too tight and the jacket was to short around the arms, but it would serve him if someone only gave him a cursory look. The hat worked well to cover his face, but it was far too big for his head and hung loosely over his eyes. Uncomfortable, but still useful.

Rinsing his bloody shirt in the sink, he ripped it to rags and wrapped some of them around his wrist wound. He held back the scream that wanted to escape his lips, not knowing who was outside the door to the bathroom, and closed his eyes to control his dimming vision.

He leaned against the long vanity counter and waited, concentrating on breathing and waiting for his vision to clear, relieved when his arm subsided to a dull throb.

When he was sure he wouldn't faint and he thought the shaking was under control, he slipped back into the terminal, and with soldiers already on the scene to investigate the attack on two of their own, he quietly disappeared around the next junction to the terminal.

One or two personnel saw him, but no one was looking for an intruder wearing the same uniform as them and Bill made it away free and clear.

Not knowing where he was going, but just wanting to hide and try to figure out a way to save his friends, he ran deeper into the airport.

Chapter 24

MARIE PACED BACK and forth in her small metal cell. She was worried about Bill. He'd been gone for more than an hour and she could only pray he was all right. Tessa kept her company, the two women talking through the thin metal. Tessa relayed words of encouragement to Melissa who was alone in her cell, also. Melissa kept asking about Janice, but none of them knew anything to tell her.

"How are the kids doing?" Marie asked Tessa.

"They're okay. They're playing in the corner. Kenny found a piece of paper under our cot and he made a paper plane out of it. Phillip loves it."

"That's good, the longer they stay busy the less we have to tell them," Marie said.

That was good; their lack of knowledge to what was happening to them a godsend. Marie could only hope it never came to the point the children would find out what their fates might be.

Sitting down on the cot, Marie stared up at the ceiling, high above her. Though the metal crossbeams would be easy to walk, on there was no feasible way to reach them. The walls of the cell were smooth and stopped long before reaching the first and lowest rafter. If there was some way out of her cell, it would have to be through the door.

"What do you think is happening to Bill? Do you think he's all right?" Tessa asked through the wall.

Marie let out a sigh. "Honestly, honey, I just don't know. These soldiers don't seem to care much for us or they wouldn't have locked us up like some kind of criminals."

"But we're safe here, right? I mean, none of those crazy people can get us in here. You saw the fences when we entered this morning."

"Yes, honey, we're safe here," Marie lied. "We shouldn't have to worry anymore. Once the government gets a handle on things, everything will be back to normal before you know it."

"That's good. I'm gonna lie down for a while, but just tap on the wall if you want to talk," Tessa told her.

"Okay, honey, have a good rest," Marie said and then added under her breath, softly. "You'll need it."

Stretching her legs out in front of her, Marie let out a sigh and tried to relax. Whatever would happen next was out of her hands, but she was pretty sure they needed to get away from the airport before something bad happened. She didn't know what would happen, but she had an overwhelming feeling of dread she just couldn't shake. She'd always had unsettling feelings when terrible things had happened in her life. When she was a little girl, she'd had nightmares for almost two weeks about her pet cat, Pickles. Her parents had told her it was just dreams and they didn't matter, but two weeks to the day, Pickles had been run over by a car. Though she had been an inside cat, she had somehow managed to get out, for the first time ever, and had been run down in the street. Her father had found the cat dead in the gutter, its intestines trailing behind it. She had run out to say goodbye to her father as he left for work and was greeted by her father with a shovel, her beloved pet lying dead on the edge of the wide, metal blade. She had cried for a week after that.

Years later, she'd had continuous nightmares of her mother dying only days before receiving a phone call that her mother had indeed died from a heart attack in the middle of the night. Over the years, she had learned to trust her instincts and had never told another soul about them.

Though she was in no way a psychic or some such nonsense, she nevertheless had always been sensitive to bad things happening. And now as she leaned her head back against the cool metal of her prison wall, she felt that same feeling again.

Whatever was coming, she knew it was gonna be big.

*   *   *

Dean slowed at the head of his massive army to rest for a while. One of his scouts had returned and reported there was activity at Midway airport.

"So they went to the airport, eh? Makes sense, it's secure with a large fence surrounding it. Since 9/11, airports are like small forts in themselves."

Standing next to Dean, relishing the time to rest, Mike raised a question. "So, you're really going to kill everyone you find? Why, how could any of the normal people like me threaten you?"

"How? By existing, that's how. Normals and Changed are different animals now. One is the hunter and the other is the prey. Guess which one you are?" Dean clucked happily.

Mike didn't answer, only turned to look back on the wave of human heads behind them. The hardest part of the forced march away from Chicago had been finding food and water to keep the people healthy. Luckily, a supermarket had been on their route and Dean had sent the Changed into the store to salvage what they could find. What they found were a family of normals that were hiding in the back. The family had been quickly slaughtered and thrown out the back, near a dumpster the store used for garbage.

The Changed had devoured everything in the supermarket, leaving only a few crumbs and a mountain of trash. The power was still on, some electric plant on automatic for the time being, feeding current to all the nearby buildings. The Changed had devoured every morsel of meat in the supermarket, ripping open packages and devouring the food whole.

Mike had watched them pour out of the doors with their prizes in their hands and wondered how many would get sick from eating the raw meat or worse, a serious case of the runs. Dean had handed him a box of pretzels and Mike had taken them, shoving them into his mouth in handfuls. With nothing to drink, his mouth had felt like a desert, but in time he'd been better, especially after they had come upon a small stream where almost all of the massive army had slaked their thirst, at least those that hadn't found something in the supermarket.

Deciding he'd rested for long enough, Dean started walking again, his army following behind their leader like love sick puppies. Their howls for blood and screams of rage drove Mike crazy at first, but now he barely heard them.

For the moment, Dean was quiet and Mike knew better than to break the man's ruminations. Sometimes Dean would talk for hours, sharing things that had happened to him and what the *change* had done to him. Mike listened to everything he said; not wanting to know what would happen if he appeared uninterested. Though Dean could think and reason, it was obviously clear he was insane. True, he wasn't a raving lunatic like the rest of the infected, but he had suffered all the same, he just didn't realize it. And Mike was not going to be the one to try and tell him different.

Mike wasn't an optimist. He still had hope he would somehow live through this ordeal he now found himself in. As he walked along the highway, he wondered if this was his punishment for leaving Becky to die. He doubted it, but the irony was still with him.

A stray dog ran across the highway and more than a hundred of the Changed broke ranks and dashed after it, howling and screaming for its blood. Dean threw his hands into the air in frustration.

This wasn't the first time this had happened. A few miles in their back trail a squirrel had darted from the shoulder of the road and more than two hundred had veered away from the pack and chased it into the scrub brush lining the highway. There had been a sharp incline and the bodies of the first of the runners had tumbled helplessly, the others following right behind.

When the dust had settled and the survivors had picked themselves off the ground, more than fifty of the Changed were dead, crushed by their fellow brethren; others were just wounded with shattered or broken limbs, with the white of bone poking through clothes to flash in the sun.

Dean had left them to rot in the heat and rays of the sun, too disgusted to deal with the situation. Though the Changed followed him loyally, they weren't very bright. The infection had given every man, woman and child a lobotomy with the exception of violent tendencies. This made them rather unpredictable sometimes.

Only with a firm hand had Dean managed to gather so many in one place, and he sometimes wondered if he would be able to maintain his control over them.

That's why it was important to reach the airport as soon as possible. Only when the Changed had prey to attack were they fully under his control.

Deciding the ones that had chased after the dog were irrelevant to his grand design, he let them go, waving the others onward. Though some hesitated, wanting to follow their brethren in the hunt for the dog, nearly all continued forward, their master leading the way like a medieval knight going to war at the head of his army.

CHAPTER 25

BILL WAS RUNNING and hiding as he made his way through the airport terminal. Whenever the sound of footsteps could be overheard, he would immediately dart into an alcove and wait while the approaching soldiers marched by him. So far, he had been barely noticed; his stolen uniform the perfect disguise.

He was slowly making his way back to the hangar where the others were being held prisoner. While he didn't know if they were still there for sure, he had nowhere else to go, so foot by agonizing foot, he kept moving, expecting to be discovered every time he turned a corner.

Less than ten minutes had passed since he'd left the bathroom and he almost fired the rifle when an alarm started to sound, filling the terminal with its loud shriek. Though he wasn't sure, he had a pretty good idea the soldiers had sounded some kind of an alarm once the two murdered soldiers had been found, placing the entire airport on red alert.

His supposition proved right as he rounded a corner at an intersection and walked straight into two soldiers who were running full tilt the opposite way. Bill hit both men head on and all three of them fell to the floor in a heap of flailing limbs and weapons.

Bill reached out for his rifle and pulled it too him just as the other two men sat up on their haunches and stared up at Bill with frustration in their eyes.

"You moron, why don't you watch where you're going," the first soldier said, a man in his late forties with thinning hair and a large wart on his chin. "The Sergeant-Major said the disturbance is happening behind you. Why are you going the wrong way?"

Bill's mouth hung open. He was caught flatfooted and couldn't think fast enough to cover his reason for moving away from the disturbance that he had, in fact, caused.

"Yeah, pal, you need to follow us, we know the way. Hey, what happened to your arm?" The other soldier asked. He was a short man in his late twenties with a pointed noise and thin lips. Bill noticed the bags under the man's eyes, showing the soldier hadn't been getting enough sleep lately.

"Uhm, sorry, I guess I got turned around," Bill said unconvincingly. As he answered them, the two soldiers climbed back to their feet, picking their rifles up and slinging them casually over their shoulders.

At that precise moment, Soldier Number One's radio squawked. "Attention, all personnel, the attacker is wearing one of our uniforms, be on the lookout for anyone who looks suspicious. Due to the amount of blood on the scene, he is probably wounded, over," the radio crackled.

Soldier Number Two's eyes looked down at Bill's wounded wrist and recognition sparked in his eyes, both orbs going wide with surprise. "Holy shit, this guy's…"

He never finished his sentence.

Bill swung his weapon toward the man and fired from the hip. The rifle barrel was pointed at an upward angle, the round striking the soldier in the neck and passing straight through to lodge in the acoustic ceiling tiles overhead.

The soldier instinctually reached up to the pain in his neck and was shocked to see his hand come away bathed in red. His mouth continued opening and closing like a landed trout and his knees gave out from under him. He fell to the polished floor of the terminal with a few more gargles of blood spilling from his mouth.

Bill only saw the bleeding soldier go down with his peripheral vision, his attention now focused on the other soldier in front of him. The man snarled a curse and tried to sling his rifle over his shoulder and aim it at Bill's chest, but Bill used his own barrel as a make-shift sword, blocking the man's rifle and stepping in and kneeing the man in the balls.

The air whooshed from the soldier's lungs and he let out a dry wheeze while he tried to suck in air. Bill never gave him the chance. With the man leaning over, his eyes squeezed shut in pain; Bill lifted the rifle stock over his head and brought it down with bone crushing force on the back of the man's neck.

The hard plastic stock vibrated with the impact and Bill winced as his arms absorbed the brunt of it. The soldier dropped to the floor like he'd been put down by a farmer slaughtering cattle. His fingers twitched while his brain tried to send signals which at the moment were being detoured thanks to a shattered spine.

Blood dripped out of the soldier's mouth to pool on the floor and Bill sighed at the sight. Counting these two men, he had now killed five people in almost the same amount of time give or take a few minutes. If things kept up like this, he would be adding many more to his list, barring they didn't get him first.

With his wrist throbbing, he looked up at the sound of more foot-steps from down the wide terminal. Quickly leaning down over the first soldier, he retrieved the combat blade from the man's hip, knowing it could prove useful as a stealth weapon.

Backing away from the bodies, he turned and ran to a side door lining the terminal's walls and started running down a small utility tunnel that moved parallel with the main terminal.

Not knowing if the soldiers used the tunnel for travel, he kept his rifle in front of him, prepared to fire at the first sign of movement.

With his footsteps echoing off the four-foot wide tunnel, he continued onward, hoping he was still moving the right way while he continued searching for Marie and the others.

The sound of his footsteps grew louder as he moved deeper into the utility tunnel. Some of the overhead lights were out in here, evidently the maintenance staff hadn't been on top of their game.

He slowed to a walk, periodically hearing shouts and boot steps coming from the other side of the wall on his left.

With the death of the last two soldiers, he was pretty sure the rest of the airport personnel would be out for blood. He wiped some of the blood spray from his face, residue blowback from the soldier he'd shot through the neck.

He sighed deeply, trying to get his breathing under control. How had it come to this? A week ago life had been normal. True, he hadn't been the happiest man alive. He had never been able to shake his wife's death, his love for her far too strong to stop just because she'd died.

Thinking of Laura made him smile wanly. The smell of her hair and the way little wrinkles would appear next to her eyes when she smiled came to him. And she had smiled a lot. Bill had always done his best to make her happy. There's had been a whirlwind relationship. He had met her on the "L" train one day and with the car incredibly crowded, they had been pushed so close together he could smell her perfume. Though they hadn't talked, their eyes had constantly met; an unspoken attraction of how when you found someone appealing, you couldn't help but want to look at them.

When the train had reached the next stop, she had poured out of the car along with twenty other passengers and Bill had watched her go sadly. He had chastised himself for not saying something to her, but what do you say to a woman on a train that you've just met that doesn't sound totally cliché?

Two more days had gone by and he'd searched for her everyday while he rode the train to and from work. He couldn't get her out of his mind. But she was nowhere to be found.

She was gone.

On the third day, he had given up hope when he'd looked up from his newspaper to see her standing at the rear of the car. Just as he spotted her, the train had lurched to a stop and she'd stepped out onto the platform. Throwing caution to the wind, he'd run out of the train, despite being three stops from his destination and followed her onto the street. They had both reached street level at the same moment, and with the John Hancock Center looming over them he had caught up to her, and though he knew he was crazy, had stopped her and introduced himself. At first she hadn't been interested, but Bill had continued charming her and making her laugh and smile and she finally agreed for coffee later in the day.

Bill had left then, off to work, late thanks to his detour. The rest of the day went agonizingly slow as the only thing on his mind was Laura. He hadn't gotten a phone number from her and if she changed her mind or had just outright lied, he'd never find her again.

Later that day, when the clock finally reached five, Bill had been the first one out the door. His heart had been beating so fast, as he rode the train back to the Hancock Center, he thought the other people in the car would stare at him, wondering what was wrong with him, but no one did and he reached his destination.

Taking the stairs three at a time, he had reached the street and wormed his way through the throng of pedestrians to reach the coffee shop. When the last person blocking his view had moved from in front of him, he had slowed and looked into the coffee shop and there, inside, on the other side of the large pane of glass that made up the front of the building, sat Laura.

She had come. He'd quickly moved inside and sat down, talking and making her laugh once more.

The rest was history, as they often say. Six months later they had been married and had lived happily together for the next twenty years.

He was pulled from his reverie by the sound of scraping coming from somewhere ahead of him. The tunnel curved to the right and he wasn't able to see what was beyond.

A hundred images flooded across his eyes as he slowed his stride. It could be soldiers, dozens of them preparing to come around the corner, guns blasting, seeking revenge for their fallen comrades. Or it could be some of the infected, hands out and teeth gnashing, ready to tear his flesh from his bones as they pounced on him like wild animals.

He swallowed hard and pushed the thoughts from his mind. Getting worked up now would do nothing but get him killed.

Taking small steps, the rifle ready to fire, he slowly crept forward, the scraping sound also slowly moving toward him. He stopped when he thought he heard the sound emanating from behind him, as well, but assumed it must be the service tunnel's acoustics playing tricks on him.

Reaching the slight curve, he poked his head around and his breath caught in his throat.

A large German shepherd was slowly creeping forward, its claws scraping on the cement floor of the service tunnel. The harness it had worn as a Customs dog was still hanging from its neck and shoulders. The animal's muzzle flared and its teeth shone white with a slight tint of red. This animal had tasted blood since the airport had been evacuated.

It growled menacingly at him.

Bill took two steps backward, bringing the rifle up, ready to put a round through the dog's head when the sound of shouting and footsteps could be heard on the other side of the wall.

Soldiers were patrolling the terminal, looking for him, and if he shot the dog, they would immediately know where he was and the game of cat and mouse would end, terribly if Bill was right.

Another growl came from his rear and he swiveled his head to see yet another Customs dog behind him. This one looked worse, its ribs showing through in places under the disheveled fur.

These dogs were hungry and Bill's ass was the blue plate special.

The first dog moved closer, hackles raised, its haunches high as it prepared to attack, while the other was moving low to the floor, evidently waiting for his brother to do the dirty work. These animals had probably been trapped in the service tunnels for almost a week and they were starving. Bill knew that any animal would turn to human meat if it was hungry enough, and Bill had stumbled right into them.

Turning the rifle to use as a club, he swallowed hard and waited, smiling to the dogs as he watched the feral animals move closer.

"Easy, boy, there's a good boy, now why don't we just be friends?" Bill said soothingly, hoping the dog would come to his senses and remember who had been the former master between the two species. But the dog would have none of it. Rear legs tensed and Bill knew what was coming next. He couldn't run, his retreat blocked by the second animal, and he thought it somehow amusing how after everything he'd been through, he was about to be taken down by a couple of domesticated, yet hungry, dogs.

And then it happened.

The dogs could smell the blood on Bill's cut wrist and what was soaked into his clothing and their stomachs rumbled in anticipation of fresh meat. The first one jumped at Bill, teeth flashing in the wan light of the service tunnel. But Bill held his ground, knowing if he was going to die here and now, then he would go down fighting,

Swinging the rifle as hard as he could, his hand receiving a slash from the gun sight at the end of the barrel, he swatted the dog away from him. Despite the blow, the animal's momentum was still enough to strike Bill on his right shoulder and he went with it, falling to the floor as the dog rolled over him, the rifle sliding across the smooth concrete to stop when it struck a pile of wires collecting against the far wall.

One of the dog's back claws had caught a fleeting purchase on his left thigh and he let out a short yell that he quickly quelled. Bad enough he had to defend himself against two animals in the small confines of the tunnel, but he had to do it without firing a shot and not uttering a sound.

Lying on the floor, the second dog pounced, the jaws going for his throat. Bill reached out with his free hand, his hand wrapping around a stray pipe lying in the tunnel. Pulling it to him, he thrust it into the dog's mouth, fending off the savage attack, while the other animal circled him, looking for an opening.

Not wanting to get to close, it would continually try to nip at his shoes, but the hard leather prevented any serious damage to his feet.

Bill struggled with the animal, its fetid breath enough to make him want to gag. The animal was lighter than normal, having lost most of its body mass from lack of nourishment, and Bill rolled to the side, throwing the dog away from him. The animal struck the wall with a yelp of pain and rolled back to its feet. Bill used the precious second to pull the combat knife from its sheath at his hip. The sheath had a simple clip on and Bill had wasted no time in securing it to his pants. Now, the small eight-inch knife might be the difference between life and death.

The first dog had jumped into the fray, only hesitating for an instant when it was sure its partner was still mobile.

Bill had a fleeting thought. If he was able to disable or even kill one of them, perhaps the other would leave him be and finish off the wounded animal. It was a chance he would have to take, as there was no way he could kill both dogs without being seriously hurt in the conflict.

Low growls from both dogs surrounded him and he waved the blade in front of him like a warrior from the distant past, fighting the wild animals of the forest for dominion.

With each slash of the knife, the dogs retreated. Evidently, they knew what it was and respected it. Bill tried to back away from the two dogs, but the skinnier one slipped behind him, blocking his retreat.

Cursing the dog's intelligence, he made a tough decision, realizing he was in a losing situation.

Crouching low and baring his own teeth, Bill flexed his legs, and before the first dog realized what was happening, Bill ran at it like a sprinter at the sound of the starting pistol. With blade leading the charge, he jumped onto the dog, barely avoiding the snapping muzzle, and plunged the blade into the animal's side up to the hilt. The dog screeched in pain and tried to escape, but he wouldn't let up.

Pulling the blade free, his other hand grasping the dog's control harness for leverage, he slammed the knife into the dog's body to the hilt again. The dog seemed to shake and then slow its snapping as blood shot out of the first wound, painting the wall a bright crimson. Blood started to froth around its muzzle and its breathing grew labored.

The second dog was hesitating, not quite understanding what was happening. This animal was mostly a follower, subservient to the wounded dog lying under Bill. Bill used the animal's cowardice and snarled at it, the wet blade throwing small droplets of vermilion across the tunnel to strike the dog's nose and eyes.

The dog's head went low to the ground, the smell of blood driving it wild, despite its cowardice.

Bill pushed away from the dog he'd jumped, crawling backwards on hands and knees, with the knife always in front of him. The wounded animal was unsteady on its feet, the loss of blood already slowing it down. The second animal moved closer, sniffing the air as it surveyed the new situation. It turned once to glare at Bill, its eyes flaring in the dim light, then it turned to watch its fallen brother.

The wounded dog had slumped to the floor, its eyes became thin slits while the breathing became labored, slowing in its chest with each passing second. Bloody bubbles pushed from one of the wounds, telling Bill he'd struck a lung.

Bill crawled away from the two animals, cursing his luck that the rifle was on the other side of them. Deciding it wasn't worth the risk, he continued backing away.

When he was almost fifteen feet away, he saw what he halfway expected. The second animal, now confident the wounded dog was no threat, attacked the first, teeth digging into the wounded dog's neck as it threw its head back and forth, shredding muscle and tendons. The wounded dog let out one muffled yelp and then was silent. Next came the sound of ripping and chewing, the starving animal slaking its hunger on its brother.

Bill didn't waste his chance to leave, but rolled to his knees and backed away as fast as was possible in his awkward position. A few times he struck the wall with his back, not having his bearings, but he refused to turn his back on the feral animals.

When he was far enough away that the sounds of feeding were only a distant echo, he turned and stood up; then headed off at a jog with legs and arms pumping.

When he was far enough away that he felt secure, he picked a door at random and exited the service tunnel, knowing to return to them again would risk another encounter with the wild animal or animals. He had no idea if there were more roaming in between the walls of the airport.

Sticking his head out to check the terminal, he was relieved to see it was empty.

A fine layer of dust coated the floor and he could tell no one had used this part of the airport for at least a few days.

Made sense, the soldiers needed to keep the part of the terminal they occupied airtight or risk the airborne virus infecting them.

Bill trotted out into the open, feeling vulnerable.

As he ran onward, he thought about the virus and the air containment. Maybe he could use that as a weapon to free his friends? But if he let the virus inside the protected airport terminal, he would still have to deal with the soldiers. Only then they would be infected and out for his blood even more than they were now. At least now they were under orders from their commander, there was still some semblance of humanity.

Private Chris Robinson was proof of that.

With all these ideas floating through his mind, and his wrist throbbing from his battle with the dogs, he ran deeper into the new terminal, deciding he needed to find a bathroom yet again to wash up and rest.

CHAPTER 26

"REPORT! WHAT THE hell is going on out there?" Sergeant-Major Thaddeus Deckard screamed at the two subordinates standing in front of him.

"Uhm, well, Sergeant-Major, we're still trying to piece together what happened, but it appears one of Dr. Stevens' patients got loose and killed him and then took out both of the guards." The man said this all with a sheepish look, not wanting to make eye contact with the furious sergeant-major.

"What, how? I want this place locked down now! Find out who did this and I want their heads brought to me," Deckard ordered the two soldiers, his voice rumbling with a threatening tone.

Both men saluted and turned to leave. When the last soldier had reached the door and was about to walk through it, Deckard called to the man.

"Private, one more thing," he said from his platform.

The soldier stopped and turned, waiting for further orders.

"When you bring me that head, I don't really give a damn if it's still attached to the body," he said grimly.

The man saluted and turned to leave. "Understood, Sergeant-Major."

Deckard turned to the two specialists monitoring the security system's monitors.

"We have all these damn cameras and no one saw anything? Why the hell not?" He demanded.

The man to his right, a soldier of no more than eighteen with acne still covering his cheeks, looked up at Deckard.

"It's not our fault, sir, I swear. There aren't any cameras where the temporary clinic was set up and Dr. Stevens said he didn't want any. He said they were an invasion of his privacy."

"Privacy? He's in the Army for Christ's sake! Well, look what he got for his damn privacy. If we had a security camera in there than maybe none of this would've happened."

He turned when another soldier entered the room, holding a piece of paper out for him. He meekly handed it to Deckard, and then quickly vacated the room, not wanting to bear the brunt of his commander's wrath. Deckard read the letter quickly, his face growing angry, his teeth showing as veins popped on his forehead.

"Jesus, damn, Christ, that son-of-a-bitch has killed two more of my men. So help me, when I get hold of him he'll pray he was killed when we captured him." Turning to the second man at the monitors, he leaned forward, the unlit cigar moving up and down while he talked.

"Sound the alarm. I want every available man and woman looking for that bastard. Shoot on sight, but try to bring him in alive."

"Yes, sir, I'll get right on it," the man said.

Deckard's face grew into a frown as he stared at the man, his eyes glancing at his partner. "Fine and the both of you listen up. Stop calling me sir, I'm not a damn officer, I work for a living!"

"Yes...yes Sergeant-Major," the second man said, the other man nodding in agreement.

"Good, carry on then," Deckard answered and walked away to the center of the room. A large office chair had been placed there soon after they'd arrived at the airport. They had suffered terrible losses at the overrun camp and it had been thanks to him that they had made it to the airport at all. Deckard had been in the United States Army for almost forty-two years. He had joined up right out of high school and had fought in almost every war since. When he wore his dress uniform, his chest looked like a rainbow salad with all the metals he'd won or received.

No, sir. No one would ever accuse Thaddeus Deckard of being a coward. He wished he could grab his silver plated Desert Eagle and join his men in hunting down the escaped prisoner, but he knew someone needed to coordinate the hunt. No, his days of fighting were mostly over. Now he would lead and let the young do the dirty work, though it burned him to allow them to do so.

Sitting back in the large chair, he stretched his legs and bit off a soggy piece of cigar. Though he had plenty, one of the finds from a few of the gift shops scattered across the terminal, he enjoyed making them last. It harked back to the days on the battlefield where he wouldn't know where his next cigar would be coming from, so he had to make the one he had last as long as possible.

Chewing contently on the end, he watched the monitors while his men and a few women moved about the terminal. They would find the fugitive, he had no doubt. After all, the airport was like an island surrounded by water. Where would the fugitive go? Chicago was ash, along with the surrounding suburbs, the conflagration still spreading. If rain didn't come soon, then the whole damn state could go up in a giant fireball.

Deckard leaned forward in his chair, the leather creaking with his movements.

"Mr. Batton, has there been any word from Washington or any of the other rescue camps that were set up around us?"

The man turned in his seat and shook his head. "Negative, sir…I mean, Sergeant-Major. The lines have been down for almost two days now."

"What about the two-way? Any chatter there?"

Mr. Batton shook his head again. "Negative there as well. All we've picked up is static. If there was someone monitoring our bandwidth, I believe they would have answered by now." The man sat up a little straighter and his face looked worried. "Can I speak freely, Sergeant-Major?"

Deckard nodded curtly. "Of course, I always value the opinion of my men; only a damn fool thinks he knows it all."

Mr. Batton seemed to wiggle in his seat as if he was sitting on something uncomfortable. "Well, me and the other guys have been talking and we all agree that we might be the only camp left in the entire Chicago area, and if so, what do you want to do about it. Should we stay here or try to make a run for higher ground? So to speak."

Deckard mulled over the man's words. He had been thinking the same thing, but hadn't wanted to alarm any of his men. Without hope, men fighting a war were lost before they began the battle.

"I think for the time being we should concentrate on finding the escaped prisoner and finding a cure for this damn virus before we all succumb and become stark raving lunatics. Now back to your station, if you please."

Mr. Batton nodded and turned back to his monitors, his partner relieved to only have to concentrate on his own now that his partner's eyes were facing forward once again.

Another soldier handed Deckard a report about what was being done to find the prisoner and he looked it over quickly, sending the soldier on his way. He barely noticed the departing soldier was a pretty thing in her early thirties. To him, she was a soldier, man or woman was irrelevant to him. Only competence mattered and Private Parsons was an excellent soldier. He tried not to think too much about how almost all the personnel below him now were Privates. There were a few Sergeants and one or two Majors but none of them had ever had field experience, so Deckard had taken the mantle of command. He had never risen high in the Army, satisfied to stay with his men. He always felt when you became a Colonel or General you lost sight of what really mattered. Those men dealt with statistics and collateral damages. But Deckard knew those same statistics were real men and women with real lives to lose.

So he had stayed a Sergeant-Major, despite the numerous chances to rise further in the ranks. And you know what? He never regretted it for a minute.

Leaning back in his oversized chair, he decided it was time to light his cigar. Puffing hard, he lit the tip, the wet end filling his mouth with the aroma of tobacco. He let out a sigh and closed his eyes for just a moment, trying to visualize himself on a beach in Hawaii, the surf moving in and out with the tide and the gentle breeze on his scarred face. And for the hell of it, a few island girls rubbing his shoulders and feet.

"Sergeant- Major, I think we've found him," Mr. Batton said, excitedly.

Deckard opened his eyes and jumped from the chair to loom over the man. "Where is he, report damn it!"

"He's back in the temporary cells, in the hangar," he said, pointing to the monitor that showed the man creeping out of an access door.

Deckard squeezed his hands into fists and patted Mr. Batton on the shoulder, heavily, the man wincing from the pain of the pat.

"I want all available men to the hangar at once. Take the bastard before he sets his friends free."

"Yes, sir," Mr. Batton said, Deckard overlooking the '*sir*' slip in his elation of finding the prisoner.

He leaned over the man, studying the monitor closely. The screen was only black and white, but the prisoner could be seen clear as day. In the light of the monitor, Deckard's eyes flickered with a life of their own, recognizing Bill Thompson.

"Soon, you bastard, soon," he said to Bill across the electronic air waves.

CHAPTER 27

Bɪʟʟ ᴏᴘᴇɴᴇᴅ ᴛʜᴇ service door to the hangar a fraction of an inch and surveyed the wide open area before him. Though he had been hesitant to use the service tunnels after his fight with the Customs dogs, he'd found he had little choice in the matter.

Soldiers were swarming through the terminal, leaving no hiding place untouched.

So back into the tunnels he went, praying he had seen the last of any stray animals. He had been fine, and had felt foolish later for straying back into the terminal. But hindsight was twenty-twenty, he'd always heard and now he knew it was correct.

So now he peeked through the opening in the door and tried to decide what to do to release his friends from their metal cells.

He watched two soldiers moving about the hangar, evidently guarding Marie and the others. Then one of them answered his radio, and with a quick wave to the other guard, ran out of the hangar to the actual terminal; Bill could only assume to help with the search for him.

Now the odds were better, one against one and Bill decided it was either now or never. He waited for the guard to stroll to the far end of the hangar, and then he slipped through the door and duck-walked across the wide area separating him from the cells. There was a large pile of shipping crates near the cells and Bill managed to reach them without being spotted. Looking up at the overhead rafters, he spotted a camera moving back and forth on its pole, watching and sending everything it saw to the security base and Deckard.

Ignoring the camera as irrelevant, he ran up to the end of the first cell just as the guard was returning. The guard spoke into the two-way radio, pinned to his shoulder, and then continued on.

Bill wasn't relishing what was going to happen next, but he had no choice. All it would take was for the guard to sound an alarm and all his efforts would have been for naught.

He needed to take the man down…and fast, before others arrived!

With the combat knife in his hand, he stepped out of hiding and plunged the knife into the man's chest, just below his ribcage, the knife slicing upwards.

The two men stood face to face and Bill held him as the soldier took in his last breath and his eyes glazed over. Bill slowly laid the man on the ground and Bill realized the man wasn't dead yet.

The soldier gazed up at Bill, though he didn't see him, his eyes not focused. His lower body was covered in bright blood as the man tried to take in another haggard breath. Bill leaned down over him and held the man's hand. He couldn't be a day over twenty and Bill's heart broke at what Deckard was making him do to these innocent soldiers who were only following orders.

"I'm dying, aren't I?" The soldier asked in a curious voice, as though he didn't quite believe what had happened to him.

"I'm afraid so, son," Bill said softly. "Hopefully, you shouldn't be feeling any pain."

The soldier eyes came into focus and he saw Bill for the first time.

"Pain? No, not really. Kind of numb, though, and it feels like I wet myself. Did I?"

Bill looked down and saw the wet spot where the man had emptied his bladder, but he shook his head, no. "No, son, you're fine. You're going to die with dignity."

"That's good. That's what my Dad would have wanted." His eyes became unfocused again and he looked over Bill's shoulder. "I hear music. Do you hear music?" Then his head slumped to the side and his chest stopped moving. Bill reached out and closed the man's eyes, realizing something had died inside him also as the soldier's soul left his lifeless body.

Standing up, he wiped the blade of the knife on the soldier's shirt, took the man's rifle, and got back to business. There would be time for reflection later if he and his friends somehow made it out of the airport alive. Stepping to the first cell, he unlocked the latch and swung the metal door wide. He was greeted by an empty cell, and he was about to go on to the next one, when Marie jumped out from the side of the door, desperately trying to scratch his eyes out.

"Whoa, wait, Marie! It's me, stop, damn it!" He yelled as he tried to fend off her claw like hands.

Marie swatted him a few more times and then recognition flooded her eyes.

"Bill? Oh my God, its you!" She shouted, jumping into his arms and hugging him. At first she hadn't recognized him, thanks to his soldier's uniform.

He embraced her for the briefest of moments and then disengaged himself.

"Look, let's save the hellos for later, right now they know I'm here and we need to go before there's a dozen soldiers in here, all out for my blood."

She nodded. "Okay, the others, we have to free the others." Her eyes went wide when she saw Bill's bandaged wrist.

"Your arm, Bill. Are you okay? It looks painful."

He chuckled at that. "Painful? Yeah, a little, but I'll live, now come on, let's open these cells, we don't have much time."

Marie went to Melissa's cell and Bill opened Tessa's and the kids.

Ten seconds later, everyone stood in front of the open cell doors as they prepared to leave.

"Where's Janice, we have to find her," Melissa said quickly.

"Janice is dead, there's nothing we can do for her now," Bill stated briskly. "I'll explain more later; but now we need to move, so all of you get across the hangar and go through that door at the far end." Bill pointed at the service door he'd entered from, and with a quick push to get Melissa going, they all ran across the hangar in single file with Bill in the lead.

Bill stopped at the tunnel entrance and poked his head inside, not wanting the surprise of another feral dog waiting for the group, then he pushed them in one after another.

When Marie was through, and they were all in the tunnel, he picked up a stray piece of pipe lying on the floor, and after closing the door, jammed it through the handle, hopefully slowing down pursuit.

"There was a camera on us the whole time, so they know where we are; we need to get as far away from here as fast as we can." He handed Melissa the rifle from the dead soldier he had just killed. "Here, take this and keep it ready. There are stray dogs running around the tunnels and God only knows what else, so shoot first and let God sort it out later," he told her. "You know how to use this?"

She nodded, popped out the clip to make sure it was full, slapped it back in and then charged the chamber. Then she ran to the front of the group, Bill taking up the rear. Bill watched her go, impressed by her knowledge of firearms.

"So where do we go from here?" Marie asked as they started down the tunnel. Bill shrugged. "Marie, I have absolutely no goddamn idea, so if you have any suggestions, now would be the time to share them. Actually, if anybody has an idea, sound off because I've got nothing. We're trapped in an airport with a bunch of heartless soldiers and outside there are blood thirsty killers who want nothing more than to tear us apart for the hell of it." He shook his head. "By the way, it looks like we are so screwed its ridiculous."

"Shhh, the children, we need to stay positive for the children," Marie scolded him.

"Don't worry about me, I know what's going on and I'm ready to fight," Kenny said his face set with grim determination. Bill patted the boy's shoulder, realizing the kid had had to grow up a lot quicker than he might have in a normal world.

He looked down at Phillip and tried to smile at the little boy. "Still, don't worry guys, we'll get through this, after all, we've gotten this far," he half-joked.

"You mean like my brother Roger got this far, Mr. Thompson?" Phillip asked softly.

Bill moved closer to the boy and rubbed his shoulder. "Son, we wouldn't be here now if it wasn't for your brother, and don't you ever forget that."

Phillip smiled, thinking of his brother and nodded.

"Good, all right then, let's pick up the pace, and Melissa, remember what I said."

She gave him a grunt of assent, then turned back to watch their front. Bill let the rest of them go a few feet in front of him and then, he too, moved forward with a quick glance over his shoulder to make sure the service tunnel was secure.

He could already hear the banging coming from the service door behind him, the soldiers trying to gain access.

Setting his jaw in determination, he took off at a jog to catch up to the others, praying a miracle would find them and help them break free.

CHAPTER 28

THE TWO WAY radio crackled and a man's voice floated from the small speaker. "There's no sign of the prisoners, Sergeant-Major, and we have another man down. Looks like he was stabbed."

"Dammit!" Deckard screamed into the radio. "Do you know where they went?"

"Ah, that's an affirmative. They ducked into the service tunnels that run parallel with the terminal. We should be able to pick up their trail just as soon as we get the door open. It seems blocked somehow."

"Enough, I don't want any more time wasted! Shoot the damn hinges off and find them, now!"

"Yes, Sergeant-Major." The radio went silent.

Deckard watched through the monitors as two soldiers shot the hinges off the door, the door falling outward to land on the hangar floor. Without sound on the monitors, the rifles and falling door were silent, but Deckard knew the destruction of the heavy metal door would have warned the prisoners that his men had broken into the tunnels.

While the service tunnels were internal, he was fairly confident that the air integrity of the terminal would stay sound, but he wasn't about to take any chances with the lives of his men. He had already lost far too many as it is.

Picking up the two-way radio, he set it so that all channels would receive his signal. "Attention, this is Deckard. As of now we are in a Code Red lockdown. All available personnel should don gas masks before risk of contamination, over and out."

"Does that include us?" Mr. Batton asked.

"No, we're fine in here. This room has its own ventilation filters and seals around the doors. As long as that door stays closed, we're safe from the virus." Batton and his partner looked over to the metal security door that led into the terminal, suddenly feeling the two-inch metal of the door didn't seem so strong.

Mr. Batton let out a shocked expression and he called Deckard to him immediately. Deckard had wandered away and was in close discussion with a female soldier and an older man who was closer in rank to him than most of the men in the terminal.

Deckard excused himself and walked back to the monitors. "What is it now, Batton? I'm trying to work out a strategy to find the prisoners."

"Uhm, sir, you should have a look at monitor four. You're not going to like it," Batton said, his voice trembling.

Deckard was about to scold the man for calling him 'sir' when his eyes lit up and he let out a gasp of shock, his cigar falling from his open mouth to tumble to the floor.

"Oh my God, it can't be," he gasped, unable to take his eyes from the monitor screen.

"I'm afraid it is, Sergeant-Major. There's an army out there and they're coming straight for us. Monitor four is about two miles out and was used for traffic control when the airport would become congested. At the rate they're moving, they should be here in about a half hour." The man's voice was trembling by the time he finished his report.

Deckard stared at the flickering black and white screen, the shock still hitting him. There were two men walking down the highway. One was young, with blond hair and a handsome physique. The other was an average looking man with brown hair and a skinny frame. In itself, not so imposing. But behind the two men was a sea of people. From the few marchers in the crowd Mr. Batton was able to zoom in on, it was apparent they were infected. Their eyes were wide with rage and their mouths were opening wide and snapping shut on empty air. They were yelling and screaming. With no sound coming from the screens, the procession of people had an almost ethereal quality.

Deckard backed away from the monitors and fell back into his over-sized chair. He dry washed his face with his hands and let them fall to his lap.

"After all we've fought through, to be taken down by a crowd of rabble. It's not fair, I tell you," he whispered.

"Seems like there's a lot more than a crowd out there, sir," Batton added.

Deckard shot the man a look that could have struck him dead. Batton swallowed hard, deciding to change the subject.

"What are you're orders, sir?" Mr. Batton asked, looking to his partner for any kind of moral support. Mr. Smith was a quiet man who preferred to let Batton do the talking. Smith was smart. After all, nobody usually shot the quiet guy when things fell apart. Such as the way things appeared to be heading now.

Deckard snapped out of it and sat up in his chair. Standing, he walked back to the monitors and studied them again.

"I want all available men to get to the entrance to the airport. Use the Hummers and transport trucks to shore up the gate. As soon as the attackers are in sight, tell them to fire. Aim for the head. Headshots will be better. Bring all heavy armaments; every damn grenade in the armory should be used, because if our perimeter is broken, then we are all dead." The last five words were spoken slowly, with emphasis on each one.

"But what about the prisoners?" Mr. Batton asked.

"Fuck the prisoners. Besides, if those infected animals manage to get in here, the damn prisoners will be just as dead as the rest of us." Deckard leaned forward and his eyes went wide when the man still didn't move.

"Well, don't just sit there, son, get started!"

Batton jumped in his seat and grabbed the two-way sitting next to him, calling personnel and diverting them to the main gate.

Midway Airport was surrounded by water on two sides, the other land boundary not an issue at the moment. High fences ran around the perimeter from the water to the highway and then continued further around the airport to be lost from sight. Only the main highway would gain you entrance into the massive austere landscape of asphalt and terminals.

The soldiers had made a temporary gate out of old fencing, now blocking the highway, but it was nowhere up to the challenge of stopping the thousands of infected now approaching the airport.

Their only hope would be to block the entrance with the large trucks and mow down any attacker stupid enough to attempt entry with the M-60's.

At least that was the plan. While soldiers ran about the terminal, gas masks now firmly secured on their faces, and trucks rolled across the tarmac to reach the gate, Deckard watched it all from the safety of his security base.

He felt like Patton on the brink of a great battle. Placing another cigar into his mouth, he waited for events to unfold.

While he waited, his eyes glanced at the small red button on the desk to the far right of Mr. Batton. It had been something his demolitionist had jury rigged just after they had arrived and secured the terminal. The small red button sitting under the glass covering was connected to dozens of packages of C-4, all scattered across the terminal in key places. When he had evacuated the last camp, he had known there wouldn't be many more places to fall back to, so when he and his men had arrived at the airport, he had decided to install a failsafe. If the terminal was overrun, and all hope was lost, he would make sure that with his last breath, he would press the red button and take all the infected to Hell with him.

Walking back to his chair, he sat down; making sure his gas mask was still hanging by the side of his chair. His hand went down to his Desert Eagle strapped snuggly to his hip, the oiled holster snapped shut.

Now all he could do was wait and let fate take its course.

CHAPTER 29

Bill called A halt when he saw a four-way junction at the far end of the tunnel. The tunnels went off and curved to the left or right, so Bill had no way of knowing what lay around each bend.

"Shit, I have no idea where we should go, any suggestions?" He asked the others.

"Maybe we should just go back into the terminal and talk to someone. Surely they'll listen to reason," Melissa said, hopefully.

Bill snorted. "Oh, yeah? And what should we say? Please, Sergeant-Major Deckard, don't cut me up and dissect me. I don't think I'd like it."

Melissa folded her arms across her chest and made a disappointed face. "Well, if you're going to say it like that, I agree it probably wouldn't work."

"No, it wouldn't and I'll tell you why. I was the one who saw Janice spread out on a metal table like a slab of beef with her chest peeled open like a chicken at Sunday dinner. These people are desperate and they think we're the Holy Grail. We need to escape from here and as soon as possible," Bill said; his eyes filled with emotion. He looked over at Marie for her support and realized she hadn't heard a word of it. Instead, she was holding her arms around herself like she was hugging her body. Her face wore a look of concern and she stared at the wall across from her.

Melissa forgotten, Bill moved next to her and placed a hand on her shoulder. "Hey, you all right? You look like you've just seen a ghost."

"Maybe I have. All our ghosts, in fact. Look, I don't expect you to believe me, but I get feelings sometimes, and I'll tell you what. I've got a feeling like some serious shit is coming down. Bill, we need to leave this place and fast."

Bill nodded. "What the hell do you think we've been trying to do for the past fifteen minutes? These damn tunnels are like a maze and we're the mice."

"What about that ladder, could we go up there?" Kenny asked from behind Melissa and Tessa.

"What ladder?" Bill asked.

"There," Kenny said, pointing to a metal ladder which was inset into the wall. If you were standing on the same side as the ladder, it would be invisible from view. Only when you were on top of it would it be seen. On closer inspection, Bill noticed the blue circle painted on the floor and ceiling. If he was right, then the circles were for identifying the ladders before you came upon them.

"Where does it go?" Tessa asked; looking up into the alcove, the ladder disappearing into the ceiling.

"Well, boys and girls, there's only one way to find out," Bill said and started climbing. After the first ten steps he was lost in darkness. He closed his eyes and waited a moment, and when he opened them again, he could just make out the outline of the rungs of the ladder. Climbing was difficult with his bad wrist, but he managed, gritting his teeth from the pain.

With what seemed like an eternity, but was in fact only minutes, Bill finally reached some form of hatch. Wincing as he tried to unlock it, he stopped and rested for a moment.

"How's it coming? Can we get out that way?" Marie's voice echoed from below him.

"I don't know yet. It's either locked or stuck, it's hard to tell in the dark. Just give me another minute and I'll know for sure!" He called back down.

Deciding he should try again, he pulled the combat knife from his hip and wedged it into the latch he'd found with his fingers. Prying at the latch, he wondered if the metal of the blade would give before the latch would. He had visions in the darkness as he battled with the locking mechanism of the blade snapping off and ricocheting into his eyes, blinding him. The blade would fly of the hilt, slicing through his closed eyelid and puncturing the orb beneath; a clear ooze dripping down his cheek to fall to the floor below.

He pushed the macabre thought away and focused on feeling the lock out. He shifted the blade a little to the right and was rewarded with something snapping. Involuntarily, he closed his eyes, like that would stop the rebounding blade from piercing his eyelid. But the blade was fine, the latch giving in first. The latch popped open, hanging downward. Bill pushed the hatch using his head and left shoulder and a moment later became blinded by the afternoon sun.

Blinking his eyes, temporarily blinded, he stepped out onto the large roof of the terminal. When the spots were finally gone, he saw he was on a wide, open roof, so large the edge wasn't easily discernable. Turning back down the hole, he called to the others to come up.

One at a time they made their way up the ladder, each one blinking while their eyes adjusted to the bright light of the afternoon sun.

Marie breathed in a deep breath and smiled. "Lord, does that feel good. After being in that cell, I honestly wondered if I'd ever be outside again."

"Aww, it wasn't that bad, Marie," Phillip said with a grin. Marie ruffled his hair and laughed. "Ah, youth, nothing bothers them."

Bill turned to the hatch and let it slam closed. "You know, when I cracked the hatch I destroyed whatever containment they had inside the terminal. The virus is probably already spreading in there right now."

"Who give's a shit," Melissa spat. "Those bastards killed Janice and would have killed us, too, if you hadn't saved us!"

"Yes, Bill, you saved us," Marie said kissing Bill on the cheek. "Again!"

He blushed for a second, unable to stop a smile from forming. But then he cleared his throat and tried his best to remain serious. "Now cut that out, Marie, we have to stay focused. Let's see if there's a way off this roof. Maybe we can hijack a truck and run the gate."

"You mean just like in the movies when the good guys have to escape from the bad guys headquarters?" Kenny asked, excitedly.

Bill patted Kenny's shoulder. "Exactly like that, and I'll need all hands to help me. Are you up for it? And you, too, Phillip?"

Both boys pumped their arms in the air, excited to help. Jumping up and down, both boys ran off to see if they could find a way down off the roof.

Bill glanced at Marie and saw the disapproval on her face.

"What?" He asked innocently.

"You know what. Those boys are five and thirteen and you want them running around the roof like commandos. What if Phillip falls off?"

Bill shrugged. "Then he'd die?"

Marie's frown grew longer and Bill waved his hand to calm her down.

"I'm only joking. Look, Marie, for the moment it's a new world. Even the young ones have to learn to fight. Phillip will be fine. He's a tough one. You know that."

She sighed, knowing he was telling the truth. "I know, it's just that I want to protect them. They've already seen and been through so much."

"Maybe so, but I bet before we get away from here they'll see a lot more."

"I sure as hell hope not," she said glumly.

Kenny was across the roof, his body a small shape in the sunlight, but it was apparent he had found something, because he was jumping up and down and waving his arms for attention. Phillip was at the other end, already sprinting across the roof to join his friend.

"See, I told you they could help, now come on; let's go see what the kid found."

Reluctantly, Marie followed Bill. Tessa and Melissa, who had been talking softly together, joined them, and the four survivors moved across the roof as Kenny continued to jump up and down excitedly, waving for them to hurry to his position.

CHAPTER 30

DEAN SLOWED WHEN the airport gate came into view at the end of the highway. He saw trucks and armed men lining the fence using old shipping crates for support.

He chuckled at their ridiculous attempt to stop him. Mike heard him laughing and turned to see what was so funny.

Dean pointed to the fence and sighed. "Look over there, Mikey, and see what your pitiful friends are trying to do. They somehow think they have the power to stop me because they have weapons." Turning to look at the thousands behind him, he raised his hands to the sky, yelling to the Changed all around him. "There aren't enough bullets in the entire state to stop us all! Am I right?"

Yells and shrieks of rage filled the highway, rolling across the grassy plain on all sides.

Less than a half mile distant, the soldiers on guard heard the chanting and screaming and each one shuddered with what was coming. Most of the men weren't combat trained, only pulled from bureaucratic posts to fill the personnel roster when the outbreak started. Now they would receive a trial by fire and no soldier knew for sure how they would perform.

"So you're just going to charge in there like cattle? You'll be mowed down. It'll be a slaughter," Mike said frankly.

"Oh, no, on the contrary. True, the first wave will go down, but the others behind them will use their corpses for stairs and tear down the fence and kill all of those foolish soldiers. Then we'll find every normal and wipe them from existence."

Dean turned to look at Mike, seeing the apprehension in his eyes "What's wrong, Mikey? You don't look like you agree with my plan."

"No, it's fine, I can't say that I care either way, it's just…"

"Yes, go on, spit it out," Dean cajoled him.

"Well, it's just that if you're going to kill all the uninfected, then where does that leave me?"

Dean nodded, as if he was thinking deeply, placing a finger under his chin. "Well, I wasn't rushing it, but you're right. If I want to kill all the normals, then I can't exactly let you live, now can I. I was going to wait until later, but I suppose now is as good a time as any."

Mike's eyes went wide. "What's a good time?"

Dean's mouth creased into a thin smile, his eyes gleaming maliciously. "Why, to say goodbye to you, Mike. I'm afraid your usefulness to me is over. Thanks for all the information, I really do appreciate it."

"What? No, you don't mean it. But you promised," Mike said hesitantly.

Dean shrugged slightly, almost casually. "I did, didn't I. Well, I'm the bad guy, I lied. Goodbye, Mike, enjoy your death, it should be painful," he said flatly and directed three men and a woman to take Mike by the arms. Before Mike could start to protest, he was pulled into the crowd of infected.

Hands shot out in all directions, reaching for any part of his body they could find. Mike was swallowed hole, like falling into a void. He sent a few shocked screams into the sky that soon turned to shrieks of agony. The infected ripped him apart, his arms going one way, legs another, head disappearing into the crowd to never be seen again. When there was nothing left but a bloody torn torso, some of the infected moved off to enjoy their prizes.

Dean watched it all with a solemn face. He had no empathy now; he was totally devoid of conscience. He saw a few of the Changed start to eat Mike's body parts and he made a face of disgust.

"Oh, gross, what are you people doing? Killing him is one thing, but eating him? That's kind of…" He mulled the next word over for a few seconds, feeling it out in his head. Then he finished the sentence with a smile across his lips. "That's kind of right. I like it. What better way to destroy your enemy than to eat him?"

One of the Changed heard him and brought over what was left of Mike's left arm.

Dean waved her away. "No thank you, dear, I had a big lunch, maybe later."

The woman grunted and jumped around, waving the arm over her head, red droplets of blood splattering the people around her, then she went back to eating.

Dean turned back to look at the large gate blocking the highway a little less than half a mile away.

It was time.

He held out both arms to his sides and screamed at the top of his lungs, his voice cutting through the din, silencing his people. Then with an almost preternatural silence surrounding them, thousands of infected moved toward the airport in complete silence.

Only their feet slapping against the warm concrete could be heard, sounding like an actual army was approaching. And an army was what Dean had gathered.

With the soldier's swallowing the spittle which had accumulated in their mouths, fingers caressing the triggers on their weapons, they waited patiently, knowing in minutes, the battle for their very lives would begin…and end.

CHAPTER 31

Upon reaching Kenny, Bill and the others looked down on what the boy had been so excited about. Below his feet, set into the wall was an emergency access ladder. The ladder was made of light aluminum and ran down the entire face of the building to reach the tarmac below.

"Fantastic, Kenny, you found our way down," Bill said, slapping the boy on the back.

Kenny beamed with pride and Tessa nudged him. "Don't go getting all full of yourself, any idiot could have found it," she joked, with a smirk on her face.

"Nonsense, he did great, now let's get down from here and see about finding a truck or something and leaving this place behind," Bill said. But before the first person could start down the ladder, shots rang out from the far corner of the building. The echoes of gun blasts were far away, the terminal deep inside the airport complex.

Everyone ran across the gravel roof to see if they could discern what was happening. Bill felt a strange sense of déjà vu while running across the roof, thinking back to the school he and the others had been trapped on only recently. Ruminating on the past made him think of the people they had lost since evacuating the school. Good men and women who had only wanted to survive and were now dead and gone.

Reaching the edge of the roof, he wore a taciturn countenance. Whatever would happen, he would make it through this Hell, and take as many of his friends with him as he could.

"Oh my God, it can't be!" Marie shouted, looking out over the runway to the gate in the distance.

Bill could only watch, too awestruck to say anything. Though the distance was too far to get an accurate idea to what was actually happening, he and the others could get the gist of it. Gunshots floated on the air like popcorn popping. Machine guns could be heard followed by the rolling blasts of hand grenades. There was a pitched battle less than a half mile away and all Bill and the others could do is watch helplessly. The sheer mass of people attacking the gate and surrounding fences was staggering. Already the perimeter fence was wobbling as the massive weight of human bodies prepared to push it to the ground.

"What do we do now? Look at how many people are out there; there's no way those soldiers can stop them all," Melissa said, the terror clear in her voice.

"There's so many of them," Tessa said softly. "We're doomed."

"Don't say that, none of you. We didn't come this far to give up now. Listen, we can use this as a distraction to escape. The soldiers will be too busy dealing with this new threat to worry about us. So now is the time to get off this roof and find some transportation out of here. Are you guys with me?" He asked.

Marie placed her hand on his shoulder and smiled. "Of course we're with you, Bill. You've managed to get us this far, haven't you?"

He frowned. "Perhaps, but I've lost a few on the way."

"That's not your fault, Bill," Melissa added. "Roger, Janice, Bruce, there was nothing you could do for them."

He looked her in the eyes and then looked to the faces of the others, stopping with Marie. She nodded and smiled, supportively. "It's true, Bill, don't beat yourself up. Frankly, I think it's a miracle any of us are still alive, at all."

"And we're gonna stay that way, come on, let's move out. Melissa, can I have that rifle?" Bill asked her.

She shrugged. "Sure, I'm not that great a shot anyway."

Taking the rifle, Bill placed it over his shoulder, cinching the shoulder strap tighter. "All right, I'll go down first and cover the rest of you, so just give me a minute or two."

He started down the ladder, the thin metal bending slightly. He slowed his progress and continued down. The ladder wasn't a permanent fixture to the roof, but used for maintenance. Though it bent slightly it was stronger than it looked, but Bill wasn't taking chances. As the largest of their group, if he could make it down okay, then the others would be fine.

Screams and gunshots floated over the building, reminding him he needed to keep moving. Once down, he waved to the others to start their descent.

"Come on, it's a piece of cake!" He joked, bringing the rifle around to watch the area around him. He was in the rear of the terminal. Luggage carts were spread about and a few stair cars were parked in the corner. He could just see the wing of a large passenger plane, though he had know way of knowing what kind it might be.

So far there was nothing that could be used as an escape vehicle.

Five minutes later everyone was down, Marie taking the longest. When she was finally on the ground with the rest of them, she looked to Bill bashfully. "Sorry. I took so long, I'm a little afraid of heights."

He nodded. "You did great." Looking to the faces of his fellow survivors, he grinned. "Okay, now let's get the hell out of here."

Smiles lit up the faces of Tessa, Melissa and the others and with Bill in the lead, they started out onto the runway. They hadn't gone more than a few hundred feet when a piercing voice shouted out. "Freeze or die where you stand!"

The survivors did as they were told and Bill turned slightly to see over his shoulder.

Three soldiers were double timing it over to him and the others, their faces set into hard grimaces of hate behind their gas masks.

"Drop your weapons, now. I won't ask again!" The first soldier in line barked.

Bill did as he was ordered, the others standing still with their hands out to their sides. "Now kick it over here," he ordered Bill. With the tip of his foot, Bill gave the rifle a shove and it slid a few feet before the drag of the cloth strap slowed it.

The soldiers stopped at ten paces, rifles held at waist level. Bill could only pray none of them had itchy trigger fingers.

"You people are the escaped prisoners everyone's been looking for." He turned to look at Bill. "You killed a friend of mine at the lab, you bastard. I was hoping I'd get to pay you back for it." He gestured for Bill to step away from the others. "Move over there, or so help me, I'll cut you and the others down together."

Marie held an arm out to Bill, but he pushed her away.

"No, it's okay, he's right. I took lives I had no right taking."

"That's bullshit and you know it!" Melissa screamed. "Those pricks were trying to kill you and probably us, too. Look at what they did to Janice! They should all burn in Hell!"

"Shut the fuck up, lady, or you can join him," the soldier snapped through his gas mask.

Melissa became quiet, though her face continued to show defiance. Phillip moved closer to Marie, hugging her legs. She patted his head and told him it would be all right, though she believed it would be far from it.

The staccato of gunshots and shrieks could be heard coming from over the main terminal and Bill gestured with his chin. "You hear that? There's a giant crowd of raving, murderous people coming through your little barricade and once they get through, this place is going to be overrun."

"I don't give a flying fuck what happens to this place. There's nowhere to go, anyway. And we can't wear these masks forever. We need to eat and drink. Once we take these off we'll become infected anyway," the soldier said angrily.

"Then what's the point?" Marie asked from Bill's side, more than ten feet away.

"The point is that I can take you bastards with me. That's the fucking point!"

"That's ridiculous. We're not infected. We can live through this!" Bill pleaded.

"And that sucks! Why do you get to live while so many of us die? Screw you, if I'm gonna die, then I'm taking you with me!"

Bill imagined a smile going across the man's face, though with the mask on there was no way to tell.

"Don't worry, buddy, you won't be alone in Hell for long, your friends will be joining you real soon, well, maybe not the women," the soldier said heavily.

The other two soldiers laughed at that, one of the men rubbing his crotch.

"But you can't do that! If you do, you'll have to take off your masks," Melissa said.

Shaking his head, the lead soldier stepped forward two steps. "Don't think so, I can do you just fine with the mask on. Sorry if you wanted me to kiss you."

The other soldiers laughed at his joke, Melissa hugging her body as she thought of what was to come.

"Enough of this shit, let's kill the bastard and have some fun," the second soldier yelled, his voice muffled under the mask.

"That's a damn good idea, Jake, a damn good idea." As one unit, the soldiers cocked their rifles and prepared to blow Bill off the face of the earth; the three man firing squad eager to finish and have some fun with the women.

Bill closed his eyes and waited for the crack of the rifles and the sharp pain as the bullets ripped apart organs and shredded muscle.

Sending him into pain induced oblivion.

CHAPTER 32

BILL HEARD THE rifles bark and braced himself for the impacts of the bullets that would be striking him in less than half a second. One bullet whizzed by his ear so close he felt the passage of it, the air becoming displaced.

A wide shot by a nervous soldier?

He'd always heard when you were about to die, your life would flood passed your mind's eye. Reliving past memories and perhaps regrets of the roads not taken. But all he could think of was the present, of how he wouldn't be around to see Phillip grow up or to help Marie lead the others. The face of his wife briefly hovered in his internal vision, and at least if he died, he would finally be with her again.

After taking three quick, panicked breaths, he cracked his eyes open. Though he wasn't complaining, he didn't understand why he wasn't dead yet. He'd heard the distinctive crack of the rifles.

His eyes went from slits to wide orbs and he looked down at the three soldiers in front of him. All three were lying face down on the tarmac, blood leaking out of small wounds in their backs, larger ones in the front of their torsos.

"What the hell?" Bill whispered.

From behind a stack of crates strode another soldier, the muzzle of his rifle still smoking. This man wasn't wearing a mask, but was acting quite normal. His stride was purposeful and he held the rifle in his hand casually. When the soldier was close enough for Bill to see him clearly, his eyes went even wider in surprise.

"Private Robinson?"

"Chris is better, but yeah, in the flesh, hope you don't mind me helping out, it seemed you were in a little bit of a pickle."

Bill shook his head. "Uhm, no, of course not. Thank you. But why?"

"Well, those things you said to me kept gnawing at me and when I saw these three ready to gun you down it really hit home. If this is how we're supposed to save the world, by killing and torturing innocent people, well then, maybe the world isn't worth saving."

"Amen to that, son," Marie said walking over to the man and kissing him on the cheek. "Thank you for helping us, you're a life saver."

"Yeah, literally, so has everybody forgotten or are we going to wait for the party crashers to arrive?" Melissa said with her hands waving animatedly in front of her while she talked.

"Shit, she's right. Look, Chris, we're getting out of here, will you join us?" Bill asked.

"Sure, I'd be honored, not like there's much of a future in the Army right now." He glanced down at the three dead soldiers. "I guess when I killed these guys I pretty much submitted my resignation."

"Bill, Marie, they're coming!" Kenny screamed and pointed to the far corner of the terminal.

"Shit, we need to go, now, or we're all dead!" Bill screamed, gathering the others into a group and starting to move across the runway. Marie, Melissa and Tessa picked up the rifles of the dead soldiers, Chris making sure to grab any spare clips; then they were off.

Behind them the first wave of infected had rounded the corner of the main terminal and were slowly spreading out like African army ants. They were running around mindlessly, but it would only be a matter of seconds before they saw Bill and the others and went for them.

"What's the plan?" Chris asked Bill, jogging next to him.

"No goddamn idea, I was hoping we could find a truck or van and use it to get out of here, but so far there's been nothing."

"And you won't find anything. All the transports were brought to the gate to reinforce it when the attacking army of infected was first spotted. The Sergeant-Major sent all available personnel to fortify it. There's nothing left that can be used."

"What about hot wiring something, like they do in the movies?" Kenny asked hopefully.

"It's not that easy, kid. In the movies, they pull a few wires and the engine starts, but in real life it's a little more complicated. Besides, I have no clue how to do it, does anyone else?" Chris asked.

Bill and the others all shook their heads. They were all everyday people with normal jobs and families. There had never been many opportunities to learn how to hotwire cars.

"Then we're screwed. Even if we run, they'll catch us eventually," Bill stated. He slowed down, the others following suit. "What's the point? We have no transportation and even if we did, the roads are jammed with wreckage and crazy people. It's hopeless." Bill sighed long and loud, giving up for the first time, the realization of their situation hitting home.

Chris was looking around the runway and his eyes lit up when he spotted something parked near a nearby terminal.

"Wait, I've got an idea. Instead of driving out, why don't we fly out?"

"Fly? Sorry Chris, but I left my pilot's license in my other jacket," Bill quipped in a sarcastic tone.

Chris shook his head. "No, you don't understand. I can fly. Or I used to."

"Really? Oh, my, that's wonderful," Marie exclaimed.

Chris held up his hands. "Now, slow down, it was a few years ago. I took a few lessons in high school. They had a program when I was in Aviation Science." He pointed across the tarmac to a small Cessna hiding amongst two other larger passenger planes. "I didn't know that was there, but if we can get it started, I should be able to fly it."

"Great," Tessa said, throwing her hands in the air. "Back to hotwiring something, but now it's an airplane, but I'm sure that's much easier to hotwire than a car," she snorted.

"No time to discuss it now," Bill said upon seeing the first of the infected had spotted them and were now running like sprinters in a marathon. "It's our best chance. Lead on Chris and we'll follow."

Chris nodded and the group started toward the Cessna. Bill sent a volley of bullets at the closest runners, watching when they went down hard. One woman fell straight to the ground, her hands at her sides. Her face impacted with the tarmac, shattering her nose and breaking teeth. She tried to stand again, her face a bloody mess, but fell back to the ground when others ran over her, their feet crushing her to a crimson pulp.

Bill nodded to himself, satisfied. The rest were still a little ways off and he could only hope he could give Chris the time he needed to ready the plane.

It was a double-wide twin engine job and Chris clapped his hands happily. "Hot damn, this is a lot like what I used to fly, though a little bigger."

"That's good, right? It means we can all fit," Melissa said from his side.

Chris nodded. "Hope so, but it'll be tight, we'll have to wait and see." He opened the door to the cockpit and motioned for Tessa to open the rear, side door, the others climbing inside one at a time.

Marie climbed into the co-pilot's seat, her mouth hanging open as she stared at all the knobs and controls. With Chris in the pilot's seat, he quickly started feeling all over the cockpit.

"What are you doing?" She asked, curiously.

"I'm looking for the keys. Most pilots leave the keys in the planes somewhere. That way if the plane needs to be moved, the keys are in it. Some pilot's leave them just so they won't lose them." His eyes lit up as he pulled down on the small visor and a set of keys fell into his lap. "Huh, guess I should have looked there first, but I didn't think it would be that easy."

From outside, Bill was firing round after round into the approaching mob. Now that they knew they were there, the crowd of people was growing. Already more than thirty were running towards the plane with hundreds far behind, just rounding the corner of the farthest building. Bill's rifle went dry and he screamed to the others behind him. "I'm out of bullets, I need another clip!"

Chris slid open the side window of his door and tossed Bill another one.

"Just give me a few more seconds and I should have us out of here."

Slamming in a fresh clip, Bill shook his head. "I don't think you have it, but I'll do my best." Then he couldn't talk as he sent a fusillade of rounds into charging bodies.

Chris slid the key into the ignition and started flicking knobs and controls. He turned to Marie and grinned. "I guess we'll wave the pre-flight inspection."

She only stared at him, not quite getting the joke. Melissa had jumped down from the back of the plane and was helping Bill keep the attackers at bay, her rifle firing continually. In less than two minutes there would be far too many targets to stop.

Bill sent the last of his clip into the screaming mob and then turned and pushed Melissa toward the plane. "That's it, I'm out again. Come on, it's now or never!"

She nodded and the two started to climb into the plane just as the twin motors surged to life. Just before Bill entered the aircraft, his eyes caught the wooden blocks behind the front wheels. Handing his rifle to Melissa, he dived under the plane, and removed them, thinking what a short trip it would have been if he hadn't spotted them.

As he backed out from under the plane, the first of the infected was on him. An arm wrapped around his throat causing him to gag as the smell of his attacker filled his nose. The man hadn't bathed in more than a week and with the mixture of blood and feces on his pants, he was ripe.

Breathing through his mouth, Bill bent at the waist, sending the man tumbling over his head. The man came to his feet quickly, but this time Bill was prepared. Pulling his combat knife, he jumped at the man, swiping with the blade. The man never slowed, either not intelligent enough to be wary of the blade or just not caring anymore thanks to the virus eating into his brain.

With teeth biting on empty air, and arms and hands out to grasp Bill, the man ran directly onto the knife. Bill didn't waste his good fortune, but pushed the blade in hard and twisted it sharply as he removed it. The man stopped for a moment, looking down at the sight of his entrails spilling out of his body and falling to the pavement. Then his eyes refocused on Bill and he started yet another charge.

A rifle cracked, sounding muffled over the engines of the plane, and the man's head snapped back as he crumpled to the tarmac. There were two other infected coming at Bill and one at a time each one fell to the tarmac, writhing from bullet wounds. Bill turned to see Melissa lowering the rifle from her shoulder.

He waved thanks and ran up to the rear door of the Cessna, Melissa helping him inside. She slammed the door closed and secured the latch.

Breathing heavily, Bill leaned forward so his mouth was only a few inches from Chris' ear. "Can we go now, please?"

Chris nodded and pushed the yoke forward, his feet working the pedals. The engine revved louder and the plane started moving. Another attacker ran at the plane, only to plow into the whirling blades of one of the engines. Blood and flesh sprayed everywhere across the tarmac, the headless body falling to the ground.

The others cheered at the sight, but Chris frowned.

"What's wrong?" Marie asked askance of him.

"The blades. It's not like in the movies. When a body gets caught up in the propellers, it could warp them or make them off balance. Shit, they can even snap off."

"But are we okay?" Marie said, looking out the front window at the massive amount of people running at them.

He nodded. "Think so, the blade only glanced that guy, we should be okay, plus, once we're up in the sky, I can easily fly with only one engine."

Everyone stayed silent as Chris started down the runway. He was moving at about thirty mph and he had to constantly drive around crowds of screaming people, most covered in blood like someone had dumped can after can of red paint on them. Bill had decided to open the rear door again, and while Chris maneuvered to the runway, Bill was taking pot shots at the closest of their attackers with his freshly loaded rifle.

He could feel the breeze drying the sheen of sweat on his brow as the plane moved about trying to escape the terminal.

Dropping one body after another, he quickly realized it was futile, but still, every attacker he took down was one less to block the plane.

With the plane zigzagging around the tarmac trying to fight its way through the throngs of murderous attackers, Bill continued firing, hoping it would be enough to get them to the runway and safety.

CHAPTER 33

"REPORT, GODDAMMIT! WHAT the hell is happening out there?" Deckard screamed into the two-way radio. More than five minutes had passed since the last check-in and despite his demands, no one was answering. Dropping the radio in frustration, he turned to look at the monitors. The small screens showed a massacre of unbelievable proportions. Bodies were piled dozens high in front of the gate and many of the soldiers lay dead or dying under a swarm of men and women.

When one of the transport trucks blew up in a fireball of orange and reds, Deckard actually backed away from the screen, almost as if he was worried he could be burned. The fireball turned into a black ball of smoke, the obsidian cloud floating into the sky where the wind cut it to ribbons and slowly dispersed it. When enough of the smoke cloud had cleared for him to see the gate again, he wasn't pleased.

The fence was knocked over on both sides of the highway, the twenty foot plus chain link; complete with barbed wire, trampled into the grass like it was nothing but a large piece of paper. Bodies were everywhere, some still twitching or crawling, most immobile.

Deckard zoomed in on the gate to find every last one of his men dead. Weapons were scattered across the gravel and pavement, the infected having no need for them. He watched as a man slowed his stride and looked up to the camera. This man seemed different, almost normal. He wasn't running around like a raving lunatic, but was calmly surveying the carnage around him. Deckard moved the camera so he could get a closer look at this strange anomaly in the middle of all the chaos. The man seemed to be looking through the glass of the camera directly into Deckard's mind.

Though he knew this to be impossible, Deckard still couldn't shake the feeling. Then the man did something almost shocking, and certainly unexpected. He raised his right hand to the camera and flipped the camera off.

Deckard's jaw dropped at the sight. This man was flipping him off!

"What a cheeky bastard," Mr. Smith said as he watched the screen.

"Shut up and do your job, dammit!" Deckard snapped. "What is the status of the infected mob, do we still have containment?"

Mr. Smith sat up straighter and sort of nodded. "Uhm, well, we sort of do."

"What the hell does that mean? Do we or don't we have containment!" Deckard snapped at the man.

"It'll be easier if I just show you, sir," Smith said, tapping the keyboard in front of him and changing some of the monitor screens. Deckard watched; his face set into a permanent scowl. The monitor flicked to an outside view of the terminal. The crowds were banging on the doors, some with steel pipes or rifles, using the latter as clubs. The thick glass doors were holding up against the onslaught, but if even steel would succumb to the wave of murderous humanity eventually, what chance did glass have? Even if it was reinforced?

"See, they're not in yet, but it's just a matter of time. We need to evacuate, sir, and as soon as possible."

Mr. Batton nodded in agreement, the sooner the better his face said.

Deckard ignored the man. "Evacuate? And just where the hell would we go? This is already our fall back camp. No one's answered us from Washington. The whole damn country is infected. No, we stay here and battle to the death. It's what any good soldier would do."

Mr. Batton looked up meekly from his chair. "But sir, I'm a civilian, I'm only contracted out to run the software. So is Smith."

Smith nodded as well, not wanting to rock the boat, but deciding if there was ever a time to speak up, this had to be it.

"I don't give a goddamn whether you're Army or not. As of now, you're all enlisted, and if you don't like it, tough shit. Besides, I don't think those people out there really care whether you're enlisted or not, do you?"

Both men looked at the faces on the monitor screens, the anger and rage and lunacy reflected within their eyes, and both men shook their heads no.

"All right then, we should be safe here for a while, maybe we can hold out until help arrives…if it ever comes. But we have no choice gentlemen; we're in it for the long haul."

Turning away from the two men, Deckard waved to his aid and another soldier, a woman with short brown hair and glasses. Both came to him immediately and he spoke to them in low whispers that neither Smith nor Batton could hear. When Deckard was done, both soldiers moved away to the back of the room, where a desk had been set up for their use. Looking back at the two men, he smiled.

"Don't worry, gentlemen, we're the United States Army. The most powerful military fighting machine on the planet. We'll prevail, we always prevail." Then he walked away to sit in his chair, relighting his cigar as he went.

Batton turned to Smith and leaned over so only the one man would hear him. "The mighty Army, never fails he said. Then what about Vietnam and Iraq, to name a few."

"Shut up, man. Don't let him hear you bad mouthing the Army. Just look at him, the man's losing it. If I thought I could get out of this room without him shooting me, I'd already be gone," Smith said quietly.

Baton made a face of disbelief. "Come on, you're not serious, are you?"

"Just look at his face and you tell me," Smith suggested.

Batton turned in his chair, slightly, so as not to attract Deckard's attention. He watched as the man caressed his Desert Eagle, mumbling nonsense to himself. Batton swallowed hard and looked back to Smith. Smith's eyes went wide in a: "See, what did I tell you?" look.

Batton's face fell as reality hit him. He was now trapped with a man who was slowly losing his mind, while outside, thousands of people howled for his blood.

All together, he couldn't think of a worst day in his life, and he wished he could just go back to bed and start over.

*   *   *

Dean stopped at the edge of the entrance into the airport and surveyed the death and destruction before him. The smell of blood was in the air, making him want to run into the fray and rip and rend with his brethren, but he knew he was better than that. Stopping near a metal pole, he looked up at the mounted camera that moved back and forth above him. Someone was watching him and his people, someone who would be dead very soon.

Stepping closer to the camera, he felt a little playful, so he flipped off the camera, showing his best smile.

Then he moved off, away from the gate, stepping over the pieces of bodies. A man in an Army uniform groaned off to his right. Dean walked over to him and leaned down on his haunches. The man reached out to Dean, his mouth opening and closing as he pleaded for help, blood dripping from the corner of his mouth to pool on the ground below him.

Dean did help the man, sort of. He leaned down over the soldier and squatted over his body, and with a hand on either side of his head, he twisted, snapping the man's neck and sending him to oblivion.

Wiping the blood on the man's uniform, he stood up and wandered away. His followers were well ahead of him, but Dean preferred to take his time and relish his victory. Once all the normals in the airport were slaughtered, he could move on to the next state and the next after that.

He grinned malevolently, thinking of the next state to invade. He had heard Indiana was nice this time of year, not a bad place to go next, with a few detours along the way of course to keep his people happy.

If they weren't killing, they weren't happy, and he liked to keep his followers happy.

What good leader wouldn't?

Whistling a tune on his lips, he strode down the highway into the airport, enjoying the day and the carnage that was to follow.

Off in the distance, the raging conflagration that was once the city of Chicago continued to burn, lighting the broken horizon with orange and reds; filling the sky with black, choking smoke that snuffed out the sun like the hand of God.

CHAPTER 34

"HOLD ON!" CHRIS yelled and turned the yoke hard to avoid a particularly large group of the infected mob. The plane leaned hard to the right and the engines whined as Chris increased speed.

So far they had been unable to reach the runway and taxi away from the terminal. The tarmac was now almost completely full of mad, screaming people, all wanting to do nothing more than overwhelm the plane and kill the survivors within.

Bill shot his last round in the rifle and leaned back in, closing the door. He still had more ammo, but it was now useless. He ran the risk of being pulled from the plane by grasping hands and decided it would be best to just give up.

The plane bounced and wobbled as Chris mowed down another person, the body falling under the wheels of the Cessna,

Leaning forward so Chris could hear him, Bill raised his voice to be heard over the engines.

"This isn't working; we'll never get out this way. We need a way to distract them long enough to make it to the runway!"

Chris glanced over his shoulder at Bill, then quickly turned back to the windshield of the plane, studying the ebb and flow of the mass of humanity on the tarmac. "What the hell do you think I've been trying to do? There everywhere, and if too many hit the propellers, they'll warp or break for sure!" He slammed the yoke to the left, sending Bill tumbling away from him as he avoided a knot of people. A few had taken to climbing on the wings, at the moment all they could do was hold on to the bouncing aircraft, but as soon as Chris leveled the plane, they would attempt to creep slowly to the cockpit and the people within.

Marie looked to her right, seeing the terminal. Doors were shattered and people were flooding inside. Hundreds at a time were doing their best to invade the building, the few soldiers remaining valiantly trying to hold them off.

"They're in the terminal," Marie said, barely loud enough to be heard over the engines.

Chris' ears caught the end of her statement and he, too, looked across the tarmac. "That's it then, once they get in, there's no turning back. We either get this baby off the ground or we're dead."

Footsteps on the roof of the plane caused everyone to look up at the metal ceiling. "Shit, they're on the roof!" Melissa screamed, raising the rifle to shoot through the ceiling at the attacker.

"No, don't, you idiot!" Chris shouted. "This isn't a car, if you put holes in the plane it won't pressurize properly and it'll cause problems."

"Pressurize? It's a damn Cessna, even I know we don't go that high!" She screamed back, her finger on the trigger of the rifle.

"Perhaps, but every hole will just add to the drag and we could even get a rupture, so please don't shoot any holes in my plane!"

She made a face of annoyance, but she lowered the rifle. Chris nodded and pressed the breaks, the plane jolting to a slight stop for a fraction of a second. The man on the roof flew over the plane, his raving, raging face appearing in the front windshield for a fraction of a second. His body flew like it had been shot from a catapult, slamming into a large group of infected and knocking them to the pavement. Chris slammed the plane to the right, avoiding the mass of arms and legs, clipping one man with the left propeller. The man's severed limb flew off, sliced cleanly, the bloody stump spraying the surrounding area like a fire hose. Then Chris was past, the mortally wounded man lost from sight.

"What's going to happen to all the soldiers inside the airport?" Tessa asked, both Phillip and Kenny next to her. Phillip had his head tucked into her chest, terrified by the noise and the screaming. Kenny was more controlled as he watched the tarmac through a small window, amazed at the ferocity of the people trying to get them. Only thirteen, he couldn't fully comprehend that he could die, feeling young and immortal. Tessa could only hope that his delusions would stay with him.

Chris continued driving in circles, desperately trying to reach the runway, but it was impossible, the mass of bodies were everywhere. He heard Tessa's question and shrugged, slightly. "Probably be killed or infected themselves. Once the containment seals were broken anyone without a mask on will probably become infected."

"Hey, that's right, how come you're not crazy? You don't have a mask on," Kenny stated.

Everyone's face in the plane lit up at that question and Chris looked back at them. "Jesus, I hadn't given it much thought. You're right, I'm not crazy."

"You must be immune, like us. Lucky Deckard didn't find out or it might have been you on one of those surgical tables," Bill stated blandly. "By the way, I never thanked you for helping me escape. If you hadn't left one of my straps a little loose…" He trailed off, knowing Chris knew where he was going.

Chris only nodded. "No problem. You made a lot of sense and I just couldn't do it in the end, strap you down, I mean. But if I had tried to help, I would have been shot, so I did the next best thing. Glad it all worked out."

"You and me both," Bill said with a smile.

"It didn't work out for Janice," Melissa said angrily.

"And I'm truly sorry for that, but I did what I could," Chris said over his shoulder.

Bill stared at Melissa. "Lay off him, Melissa, he's all right. Let him concentrate on flying. Later, if there is a later, we can talk about this some more."

She nodded. Not happy about it, but deferring to Bill.

The plane slammed to the right and Chris put the terminal behind him again.

The engines whined and Chris powered them forward.

"Hold on, I've got a small opening and I'm gonna try for it!" Chris screamed.

The plane shot forward, a small line of tarmac open. It was just dumb luck, the crowd dispersing everywhere, some running without purpose. Chris gunned the engines, praying the hole would stay open.

"Are we going to make it?" Marie asked from his side.

"Don't know," Chris shouted at her, "If this channel closes up, it's over. I might be able to knock a few out of the way, but if they get too compacted, the bodies will just choke the props. This is a light weight plane, built for speed, not power."

And then it happened. Two hundred feet in front of the plane, a large knot of people had formed, closing the gap the plane was shooting for.

"Get us in the air, or we're all dead!" Bill shouted, seeing the mass of people.

"I'm trying!" Chris said, redlining the engines. "I don't know if there's enough space to get up enough speed!"

"Shit," screamed Bill, watching as they grew ever closer to the crowd. The plane was still moving closer, faster with each second, but so was the wall of bodies.

It would be close, but as Bill watched, he could already see it would be too little, too late.

CHAPTER 35

"THEY'RE AT THE door!" Screamed Batton, turning in his chair to stare at the security door that led out to the terminal.

"No shit, dumbass, I can see that!" Deckard snapped at the man.

Holding his sidearm in his hand, the cool metal feeling comforting, Deckard waited for the seals of the door to give out.

The far right monitor showed the security door from the outside, the mass of people banging on it, some becoming crushed as their brethren pushed ever forward. The other monitors in the terminal showed the same thing. Infected were everywhere, overrunning his soldiers, trashing the research lab.

The door buckled inward and Deckard put on his gas mask. Turning to the others in the room, he told them to do the same. "And have your weapons ready. The second that door opens, start firing. Maybe we can hold them off."

"Not bloody likely," Smith said as he tried to count the number of bodies outside the door and gave up after reaching a hundred. "We are so fucked."

Batton finished securing his mask and looked at Smith. "Come on, man, put on your mask. They'll be in here any second!"

"What's the point? Hell, maybe it won't be so bad to be one of them, I mean, look at them. They don't seem too unhappy."

Batton did a double take and then pulled his sidearm. All personnel were armed, civilian or not. "Whatever man, do what you want, but I'm gonna make it out of here in one piece."

Smith chuckled at that. "Really? Well you just keep thinking that."

The door jumped in its frame and a small bit of light from outside seeped in.

"Shit, that's it, men, containment breach. I want a firing line over here, now!" He screamed, his aides and the few other personnel all doing as ordered. When he was finished positioning his troops, he had seven soldiers aiming weapons at the shaking door. Three were on their knees, the others standing behind them, able to fire over their heads easily.

Smith just sat in his chair, smiling.

Deckard turned to look at the man, his eyes wide behind the plastic shield of his gas mask.

"Smith, what the hell are you doing, man! Get into the firing line, they're almost in!"

"If it's all the same to you, sir, I think I'll sit this one out. Seems I'm about to die, I'd like to hand in my resignation."

"What, are you mad, son!"

Smith chuckled, the virus already affecting him. "Maybe, but I figure if I'm going to die anyway, I'd like to live my last few minutes free, and not working for an asshole like you."

Deckard's eyes went wide behind his mask, and he was about to yell at the man, when the door finally succumbed to the onslaught of bodies and fell in with a crash. Bodies of screaming, yelling men and women poured through the doorway like water through a broken dam.

"Fire at will!" Deckard screamed, himself picking targets.

Faces exploded and holes were blown out of bodies, arms were shot off and blood sprayed everywhere, bathing the walls in a bright scarlet. Bullet after bullet took down the infected killers, the bodies piling up like cordwood.

Deckard emptied his weapon and quickly reloaded. A crazed woman was only two feet away when he raised the reloaded weapon and blew her head off. She dropped to the floor and twitched while Deckard continued firing.

One after another, they poured into the control room, the soldiers taking them out one and two at a time. Despite their superior numbers, they could only attack in twos or threes, restricted by the small opening, and Deckard used this to his advantage, for the moment controlling the situation.

Then it happened, as he knew it would. "I'm out, Sergeant-Major!" Screamed a soldier kneeling below him.

"Me, too," one of his aides yelled over the deafening noise of weapons discharging and the yells of the infected.

Smith sat quietly in his chair, watching the scene in front of him like it was an action movie. He only wished he had some popcorn.

Deckard fired his last round and reached in his belt for more ammo, cursing when he realized he was empty. Throwing the Desert Eagle at the closest attacker, he backed away from the firing line.

"Damn it, this isn't fair!" He screamed as he watched his men, one at a time, expel their last remaining rounds of ammunition. Then it happened as it inevitably would and the first of his men became overwhelmed by the crazed attackers.

Batton went down under a pile of bodies, his screams muffled under his gas mask. So far Deckard was ignored, off in the corner of the security desk. One after another his men were taken down, their screams of pain mixing with that of their attackers. Then he saw a blur to his right and a figure plowed into him. He gazed down to see Smith, a feral grin on his face, trying to pull him to the floor.

"Smith, get a hold of yourself, what the hell are you doing?"

But Smith was oblivious, the virus infecting his brain and making him into yet another killing machine. Smith reached up and pulled the gas mask from Deckard's face, the soldier screaming as he breathed the contaminated air.

"No, you'll kill us all, Smith, stop it!"

Smith ignored his pleas and sank his teeth into Deckard's arm, hands like claws, reaching and scratching Deckard's face. With a heave, Deckard pushed the man away, a piece of his arm going with the man. Deckard never noticed it as a wave of attackers, now fully aware of his presence, charged him.

He saw his soldiers were all dead or dying, one stray arm shooting out through the mass of bodies. The hand made a fist and then went slack, the arm dropping away. Then Deckard was being pulled down, arms and hands covering him.

Clothing was ripped from his body as he tried to fight, but there were just so damn many. Pulling his combat knife from his belt, he swiped blindly around him, slicing flesh. He had no way of knowing what damage he was doing, but continued slashing blindly, until his knife became stuck, and it was pulled from his grip.

Blinding pain filled his head as someone pulled his arm the wrong way, snapping it from its socket. Teeth found his leg and his vision grew dim from the pain. It was like acid had been injected under his skin and his heart was even now pumping it through his body.

He was thrown across the security desk, and in his dimming vision, he saw the red button. His eyes went wide with recognition and he let out a bark of laughter that quickly turned to shrieks of pain.

He managed to free his left hand, and with one smooth motion, slammed his hand on the glass casing over the button. Glass shattered, shards of glass becoming lodged in his hand, but he didn't notice, more serious injuries overriding the small needle-like splinters.

Below the button a digital display flashed zero and two minutes flashed on the screen, the red number already starting to tick downward.

"Ha, you bastards, I win. Kill me if you want to, but I win!" He screamed loudly, his laughter mixing with his shrieks of agony. An older woman, at least seventy, darted in under his guard and bit his nose off. He slammed his forehead into her nose, causing her to back away, but only after she'd taken his nose with her. Blood poured into his nasal cavity and he began to choke, spitting blood at his attackers.

While he fought, losing with every tick of the clock, his eyes caught the red numbers flashing. Ten seconds remained, nine, eight,

He yelled at the top of his lungs. "See you in Hell, you bastards! I'll be waiting for you!"

The digital display continued ticking down, three, two, one…then a blinding flash filled the room and the surrounding terminal. The entire Midway Airport had been mined, the surplus of C-4 having been put to good use by the explosive's expert.

One after another, the blasts ripped through the building, taking out support columns as they went. Then the roaring inferno enveloped two refueling trucks, both tanks full to the brim with jet fuel. The intense heat of the inferno ruptured the tanks, the unleaded gas in the engines tanks also becoming bombs in their own right. The resulting explosion ignited the jet fuel, adding to the blaze. Gas lines below the tarmac ruptured, and the entire complex went up like a small sun had exploded right in the middle of the airport.

Everything in a half mile radius was incinerated immediately, the blast rolling across the open tarmac, engulfing the small humans running around frantically.

As the wave of living Hell flowed across the runway, a small Cessna valiantly tried to outrun the fireball, the flames slowly gaining on the tail of the aircraft.

CHAPTER 36

"OH, MY GOOD Lord!" Marie screamed as she turned and glanced over her shoulder at the resounding blast, watching the terminal go up in a blazing fireball.

Bill and the others turned, also, trying to see out the small glass windows of the aircraft.

"Uh, Chris, I really think now would be a good time to go faster," Bill said, trying to keep the panic out of his voice.

Chris only had eyes for the large group of infected blocking his access to the runway in front of him, and when he quickly glanced over his shoulder, his jaw dropped and his face went blank. "Oh shit, the crazy bastard did it!"

"Did what?" Bill screamed.

"I heard rumors that Deckard mined the entire airport with explosives, but I never actually believed he really did it. You know, guys like to make shit up!"

"Well, he did do it and he did set them off, so for the love of God, hurry up!" Bill screamed.

The flames were spreading across the tarmac, the first tendrils of fire licking at the rudder of the Cessna.

Chris tried to coax a little more power out of the engines, but they were already at their maximum output. Watching the dwindling gap that had been open, shrinking, he realized they wouldn't make escape velocity in time.

His mind was already playing through what was coming. The plane, propellers first, would plow into the mass of bodies, spraying blood and bone everywhere, then the Cessna would slam to a halt, moored down by all the bodies. Then the fireball would engulf them and they would all be burned alive.

Then multiple things happened at the same time. The heat of the rolling explosion, the air heated to the point that skin would boil on the bodies of its owners, shot over the aircraft and enveloped the mass of infected blocking the runway.

All at once, people began running away from the blast, trying to outrun the explosion. The solid knot of bodies dispersed as they ran for their lives. It seemed, even under the influence of the virus, some sense of survival instinct kicked in, making them run away from the encroaching blast.

But some ignored the heat, and with burning bubbles of flesh, melting faces and burning hair, they charged the Cessna, wanting to kill the people inside.

Protected from the heat, the Cessna rode the thermals of the blast, just staying out of reach of the fireball.

Then it happened.

Chris felt the wheels of the plane touch off, the plane leaving the tarmac, rocketing past where the knot of infected had been before they had dispersed, the wheels not more than a few inches off the ground.

Chris pulled back on the yoke and the plane slowly ascended into the sky. The tendrils of the massive explosion wrapped around the rudder, seeming to caress the fiberglass, scorching the paint. Then the plane was free, soaring into the air and out of the radius of the inferno.

Chris banked the plane high, and when he was satisfied with his altitude, he turned back around to survey the damage to the airport. Secondary explosions continued to rumble through the massive complex, each terminal collapsing under the residual blasts from gas mains.

From high above the area, only a few bodies could be seen, all supine on the pavement. Chris banked the Cessna and they passed over the edge of the conflagration. Bill and the others stared in shock at where they had been only moments ago.

"Jesus, that was close," Bill muttered near Chris' ear.

Chris nodded. "You know, if we hadn't got that extra boost from the explosion, and the crowd hadn't opened up when it did, we never would have made it. Deckard saved our lives by setting off those explosives."

"No shit? Son-of-a-bitch tries to kill me and then ends up saving my ass." Bill saluted the flames below him. "To you, Sergeant-Major Deckard." Then he turned the salute into a middle finger. "Thanks for nothing, you asshole."

"Bill, stop that," Marie scolded him.

Bill looked ashamed, like he'd been caught sneaking a cookie before dinner. "Sorry, Marie, but the guy deserves it."

"Maybe, but he's dust now, so let it be, okay?"

"Sure, Marie, okay." He turned to Kenny and Phillip, rubbing the smaller boy's hair. "Well, guys, what do you think?"

Kenny shrugged, the resilience of youth taking over. "No biggy, I knew we were gonna make it all the time."

Bill started to chuckle at that and soon the others were all laughing with him, enjoying the relief of being alive. When the laughter had died down, Bill turned back to Chris.

"So what now? Any suggestions, after all, you're the pilot," Bill asked while gazing out at the massive smoke cloud roiling into the sky over the airport behind the plane. The smoke cloud was so large the sun was snuffed out until the plane cleared the perimeter of it, then it was nothing but clear sky.

Chris' forehead creased as he thought about the question. "Well, we've almost got a full tank, so fuel is good. The rudder's a little sluggish, but still works. Probably damaged in the explosion. So where do you want to go?"

"How about Indiana? Maybe it's not so bad there, and if it is, we could just keep going," Melissa suggested.

No one objected, one place being as good as another.

"Indiana it is. Well, Chris, would you do the honors?" Bill asked him.

Chris nodded and banked the plane east, toward Indiana. There were maps in the plane, and once Chris was situated, he would have Marie do some research as to how far their fuel would get them.

The sun was just beginning to set, the scarlet hues painting the sky a molten red, and soon the small aircraft was swallowed by the horizon, leaving the charred remains of Chicago behind them for a brighter future.

Epilogue

DEAN CRAWLED OUT of the rubble that had all but buried him. A few slabs of concrete had landed in such an angle that Dean had been protected from being squashed like a bug under a child's heel. The raging fireball had washed over him, singing his flesh, but not killing him.

With smoking clothes and a few minor burns, he pulled himself free of his rubble prison and looked out at what was once a major airport in the United States.

Now all that stood before him was a smoking crater. Most of the secondary explosions had stopped, a steady fire still burning, fueled by the underground gas mains.

Walking on wobbly legs, he stumbled around the blast site, his eyes not focusing on any one thing just yet.

A low moan to his left had him moving off in the same direction. Five minutes later, after clearing the rubble away from the man; he helped one of the Changed to his feet. The man had an ugly head wound, but otherwise was unhurt. Dean brushed the ash from his clothes and patted the man on the back.

"There you go, fella, let's see if we can find anyone else, Hmm?"

Moving about the debris of shattered concrete and steel, Dean managed to find four more of his people. One, a young woman in her late twenties had lost all of her hair in the scorching heat, even her eyebrows had been singed away. Her skin was a bright red, and Dean had the urge to reach out and slap her, like you did when someone had a bad sunburn, but he resisted.

The other three refugees from the explosion were in an equal state of disrepair. One had a dislocated shoulder, and with one of the other Changed helping, Dean managed to pop it back into its socket, to the man's cries of pain.

No one else was alive, or if they were, they were in such bad shape they wouldn't be alive for long.

Dean looked up as a small airplane flew by overhead. He didn't know where the plane had come from and frankly didn't care. Watching the plane disappear on the horizon, he gathered his four followers to him.

"Well, folks, it looks like you're it. At least for now." Starting to walk away from the decimated airport, he turned to look at the four infected people, standing immobile, still wobbly from their bout with the blast.

"Well, what are you waiting for, come on. There's places to go and people to kill."

One at a time, the four moved into a single line, following Dean over the debris strewn runway, their feet shuffling along like drunks leaving a bar after last call.

An hour later found them moving through the airport blockade and back onto the highway. Dean stopped and looked back at the remains of the airport and his once great army.

Then he sighed, looking at the four survivors.

"Just four. Four people out of thousands, all gone in a flash. Oh, well, guess you have to start somewhere, right?" None of the four answered, each lost in a world of madness.

He began walking again, making sure they were still following him. His plans hadn't altered. There would be other Changed in other cities and he would gather them to him and start over again.

A few hours later, with miles behind him and his four followers, he stopped at a green highway sign.

The sign read: **INDIANA, INTERSTATE 32, NEXT EXIT, ½ MILE.**

Trying to whistle a tune, his lips dry from walking under the hot sun all day, he continued onward, knowing that every journey began with that first step.

With the sun beginning its downward descent on the horizon, slowly casting the highway into darkness, Dean smiled, his teeth flashing in the fading light.

He wasn't finished with mankind, oh, no, not by a long shot.

BOOK OF THE DEAD 2: NOT DEAD YET
A ZOMBIE ANTHOLOGY
Edited by Anthony Giangregorio

Out of the ashes of death and decay, comes the second volume filled with the walking dead.

In this tomb, there are only slow, shambling monstrosities that were once human.

No one knows why the dead walk; only that they do, and that they are hungry for human flesh.

But these aren't your neighbors, your co-workers, or your family. Now they are the living dead, and they will tear your throat out at a moment's notice.

So be warned as you delve into the pages of this book; the dead will find you, no matter where you hide.

CHRISTMAS IS DEAD: A ZOMBIE ANTHOLOGY
Edited by Anthony Giangregorio

Twas the night before Christmas and all through the house, not a creature was stirring, not even a. . . zombie?

That's right; this anthology explores what would happen at Christmas time if there was a full blown zombie outbreak.

Reanimated turkeys, zombie Santas, and demon reindeers that turn people into flesh-eating ghouls are just some of the tales you will find in this merry undead book.

So curl up under the Christmas tree with a cup of hot chocolate, and as the fireplace crackles with warmth, get ready to have your heart filled with holiday cheer.

But of course, then it will be ripped from your heaving chest and fed upon by blood-thirsty elves with a craving for human flesh!

For you see, Christmas is Dead!

And you will never look at the holiday season the same way again.

DEAD HOUSE: A ZOMBIE GHOST STORY
by Keith Adam Luethke
Welcome to Dead House

The old mansion on the edge of town, aptly named Dead House, has a history of blood, pain, and death, but what Victor Leeds knows of this past only scratches the surface of the true horrors within.

But when his girlfriend is attacked by a shadowy figure one rainy night, he soon finds himself caught up in a world where the dead walk and ghostly wraiths abound.

And to make matters worse, a pair of serial killers are fulfilling carefully made plans, and when they are done, the small town of Stormville, New York will run red. The last ingredient to open the gates of Hell, and plunge this small upstate town into madness, is rain.

And in Stormville, it pours by the gallons.

The Zombie in the Basement
by Anthony Giangregorio
Illustrated by Andrew Dawe-Collins

The spooky house at the end of the street was the one all the kids avoided. With its overgrown shrubs and weeds, the place was a modern day haunted house. Especially at night. So when Ricky sneaks into the yard to retrieve his favorite ball, he comes across something he'd only seen in movies and bad dreams. He sees a zombie in the basement window of the old house, but when he tells his friends, no one believes him. Ricky knows what he saw, that something lurks in the old house, something that isn't supposed to exist.

With his best friend Eric by his side,   Ricky will find out the truth and prove to everyone that zombies are real. And when the night is done, everyone will know about the zombie in the basement.

Note: This book is for young adults and for those who are young at heart.

DEADFREEZE
by Anthony Giangregorio
THIS IS WHAT HELL WOULD BE LIKE IF IT FROZE OVER!

When an experimental serum for hypothermia goes horribly wrong, a small research station in the middle of Antarctica becomes overrun with an army of the frozen dead.

Now a small group of survivors must battle the arctic weather and a horde of frozen zombies as they make their way across the frozen plains of Antarctica to a neighboring research station.

What they don't realize is that they are being hunted by an entity whose sole reason for existing is vengeance; and it will find them wherever they run.

VISIONS OF THE DEAD
A ZOMBIE STORY
by Anthony & Joseph Giangregorio

Jake Roberts felt like he was the luckiest man alive.

He had a great family, a beautiful girlfriend, who was soon to be his wife, and a job, that might not have been the best, but it paid the bills.

At least until the dead began to walk.

Now Jake is fighting to survive in a dead world while searching for his lost love, Melissa, knowing she's out there somewhere.

But the past isn't dead, and as he struggles for an uncertain future, the past threatens to consume him. With the present a constant battle between the living and the dead, Jake finds himself slipping in and out of the past, the visions of how it all happened haunting him. But Jake knows Melissa is out there somewhere and he'll find her or die trying.

In a world of the living dead, you can never escape your past.

DEAD MOURNING: A ZOMBIE HORROR STORY
by Anthony Giangregorio

Carl Jenkins was having a run of bad luck. Fresh out of jail, his probation tenuous, he'd lost every job he'd taken since being released. So now was his last chance, only one more job to prevent him from going back to prison. Assigned to work in a funeral home, he accidentally loses a shipment of embalming fluid. With nothing to lose, he substitutes it with a batch of chemicals from a nearby factory.

The results don't go as planned, though. While his screw-up goes unnoticed, his machinations revive the cadavers in the funeral home, unleashing an evil on the world that it has not seen before. Not wanting to become a snack for the rampaging dead, he flees the city, joining up with other survivors. An old, dilapidated zoo becomes their haven, while the dead wait outside the walls, hungry and patient.

But Carl is optimistic, after all, he's still alive, right? Perhaps his luck has changed and help will arrive to save them all?

Unfortunately, unknown to him and the other survivors, a serial killer has fallen into their group, trapped inside the zoo with them.

With the undead army clamoring outside the walls and a murderer within, it'll be a miracle if any of them live to see the next sunrise.

On second thought, maybe Carl would've been better off if he'd just gone back to jail.

ROAD KILL: A ZOMBIE TALE
by Anthony Giangregorio
ORDER UP!

In the summer of 2008, a rogue comet entered earth's orbit for 72 hours. During this time, a strange amber glow suffused the sky.

But something else happened; something in the comet's tail had an adverse affect on dead tissue and the result was the reanimation of every dead animal carcass on the planet.

A handful of survivors hole up in a diner in the backwoods of New Hampshire while the undead creatures of the night hunt for human prey.

There's a new blue plate special at DJ's Diner and Truck Stop, and it's you!

DEAD WORLDS: Undead Stories
A Zombie Anthology Volume 2
Edited by Anthony Giangregorio

Welcome to a world where the dead walk and want nothing more than to feast on the living. The stories contained in this, the second volume of the Dead Worlds series, are filled with action, gore, and buckets and buckets of blood; plus a heaping side of entrails for those with a little extra hunger.

The stories contained within this volume are scribed by both the desiccated cadavers of seasoned veterans to the genre as well as fresh-faced corpses, each printed here for the first time; and all of them ready to dig in and please the most discerning reader.

So slap on a bib and prepare to get bloody, because you're about to read the best zombie stories this side of Hell!

THE DARK
by Anthony Giangregorio
DARKNESS FALLS

The darkness came without warning.

First New York, then the rest of United States, and then the world became enveloped in a perpetual night without end.

With no sunlight, eventually the planet will wither and die, bringing on a new Ice Age. But that isn't problem for the human race, for humanity will be dead long before that happens.

There is something in the dark, creatures only seen in nightmares, and they are on the prowl. Evolution has changed and man is no longer the dominant species. When we are children, we're told not to fear the dark, that what we believe to exist in the shadows is false.

Unfortunately, that is no longer true.

SOULEATER
by Anthony Giangregorio

Twenty years ago, Jason Lawson witnessed the brutal death of his father by something only seen in nightmares, something so horrible he'd blocked it from his mind.

Now twenty years later the creature is back, this time for his son.

Jason won't let that happen.

He'll travel to the demon's world, struggling every second to rescue his son from its clutches.

But what he doesn't know is that the portal will only be open for a finite time and if he doesn't return with his son before it closes, then he'll be trapped in the demon's dimension forever.

SEE HOW IT ALL BEGAN IN THE NEW DOUBLE-SIZED 460 PAGE SPECIAL EDITION!
DEADWATER: EXPANDED EDITION
by Anthony Giangregorio

Through a series of tragic mishaps, a small town's water supply is contaminated with a deadly bacterium that transforms the town's population into flesh eating ghouls.

Without warning, Henry Watson finds himself thrown into a living hell where the living dead walk and want nothing more than to feed on the living.

Now Henry's trying to escape the undead town before he becomes the next victim.

With the military on one side, shooting civilians on sight, and a horde of bloodthirsty zombies on the other, Henry must try to battle his way to freedom.

With a small group of survivors, including a beautiful secretary and a wise-cracking janitor to aid him, the ragtag group will do their best to stay alive and escape the city codenamed: **Deadwater**.

DEAD END: A ZOMBIE NOVEL
by Anthony Giangregorio
THE DEAD WALK!

Newspapers everywhere proclaim the dead have returned to feast on the living!

A small group of survivors hole up in a cellar, afraid to brave the masses of animated corpses, but when food runs out, they have no choice but to venture out into a world gone mad.

What they will discover, however, is that the fall of civilization has brought out the worst in their fellow man.

Cannibals, psychotic preachers and rapists are just some of the atrocities they must face.

In a world turned upside down, it is life that has hit a Dead End.

BLOOD RAGE
(The Prequel to DEAD RAGE)
by Anthony Giangregorio

The madness descended before anyone knew what was happening. Perfectly normal people suddenly became rage-fueled killers, tearing and slicing their way across the city. Within hours, Chicago was a battlefield, the dead strewn in the streets like trash.

Stacy, Chad and a few others are just a few of the immune, unaffected by the virus but not to the violence surrounding them. The *changed* are ravenous, sweeping across Chicago and perhaps the world, destroying any *normals* they come across. Fire, slaughter, and blood rule the land, and the few survivors are now an endangered species.

This is the story of the first days of the Dead Rage virus and the brave souls who struggle to live just one more day.

When the smoke clears, and the *changed* have maimed and killed all who stand in their way, only the strong will remain.

The rest will be left to rot in the sun.

FAMILY OF THE DEAD
A Zombie Anthology
by Anthony, Joseph and Domenic Giangregorio

Clawing their way out of the wet, dark earth, these tales of terror will fill you with the deep seated fear we all have of death and what comes next.

But if that wasn't bad enough to chill your soul, these undead tales are penned by an entire family of corpses. The zombie master himself, Anthony Giangregorio, leads his two young ghouls, his sons Domenic and Joseph Giangregorio, on a journey of terror inducing stories that will keep you up long into the night.

As you read these works of the undead, don't be alarmed by that bump outside the window.

After all, it's probably just a stray tree branch...or is it?

The Lazarus Culture

by Pasquale J. Morrone

Secret Service Agent Christopher Kearns had no idea what he was up against. Assigned on a temporary basis to the Center for Disease Control, he only knew that somehow it was connected to the lives of those the agency protected...namely, the President of the United States. If there were possible terrorist activities in the making, he could only guess it was at a red alert basis.

When Kearns meets and befriends Doctor Marlene Peterson of the Breezy Point Medical Center in Maryland, he soon finds that science fiction can indeed become a reality. In a solitary room walked a man with no vital signs: dead. The explanation he received came from Doctor Lee Fret, a man assigned to the case from the CDC. Something was attached to the brain stem. Something alive that was quickly spreading rapidly through Maryland and other states.

Kearns and his ragtag army of agents and medical personnel soon find themselves in a world of meaningless slaughter and mayhem. The armies of the walking dead were far more than mere zombies. Some began to change into whatever it was they ate. The government had found a way to reanimate the dead by implanting a parasite found on the tongue of the Red Snapper to the human brain.

It looked good on paper, but it was a project straight from Hell.

The dead now walked, but it wasn't a mystery.

It was The Lazarus Culture.

END OF DAYS: AN APOCALYPTIC ANTHOLOGY
VOLUMES 1 & 2

Our world is a fragile place.

Meteors, famine, floods, nuclear war, solar flares, and hundreds of other calamities can plunge our small blue planet into turmoil in an instant.

What would you do if tomorrow the sun went super nova or the world was swallowed by water, submerging the world into the cold darkness of the ocean? This anthology explores some of those scenarios and plunges you into total annihilation.

But remember, it's only a book, and tomorrow will come as it always does. Or will it?

DEADFALL

by Anthony Giangregorio

It's Halloween in the small suburban town of Wakefield, Mass.

While parents take their children trick or treating and others throw costume parties, a swarm of meteorites enter the earth's atmosphere and crash to earth.

Inside are small parasitic worms, no larger than maggots.

The worms quickly infect the corpses at a local cemetery and so begins the rise of the undead.

The walking dead soon get the upper hand, with no one believing the truth.

That the dead now walk.

Will a small group of survivors live through the zombie apocalypse?

Or will they, too, succumb to the Deadfall.

DARK PLACES

By Anthony Giangregorio

A cave-in inside the Boston subway unleashes something that should have stayed buried forever.

Three boys sneak out to a haunted junkyard after dark and find more than they gambled on.

In a world where everyone over twelve has died from a mysterious illness, one young boy tries to carry on.

A mysterious man in black tries his hand at a game of chance at a local carnival, to interesting results.

God, Allah, and Buddha play a friendly game of poker with the fate of the Earth resting in the balance.

Ever have one of those days where everything that can go wrong, does? Well, so did Byron, and no one should have a day like this!

Thad had an imaginary friend named Charlie when he was a child. Charlie would make him do bad things. Now Thad is all grown up and guess who's coming for a visit?

These and other short stories, all filled with frozen moments of dread and wonder, will keep you captivated long into the night.

Just be sure to watch out when you turn off the light!

BOOK OF THE DEAD
A ZOMBIE ANTHOLOGY
VOLUME 1
ISBN 978-1-935458-25-8

Edited by Anthony Giangregorio

This is the most faithful, truest zombie anthology ever written, and we invite you along for the ride. Every single story in this book is filled with slack-jawed, eyes glazed, slow moving, shambling zombies set in a world where the dead have risen and only want to eat the flesh of the living. In these pages, the rules are sacrosanct. There is no deviation from what a zombie should be or how they came about. The Dead Walk.

There is no reason, though rumors and suppositions fill the radio and television stations. But the only thing that is fact is that the walking dead are here and they will not go away. So prepare yourself for the ultimate homage to the master of zombie legend. And remember... Aim for the head!

DEAD TALES: SHORT STORIES TO DIE FOR

by Anthony Giangregorio

In a world much like our own, terrorists unleash a deadly dis-ease that turns people into flesh-eating ghouls.

A camping trip goes horribly wrong when forces of evil seek to dominate mankind.

After losing his life, a man returns reincarnated again and again; his soul inhabiting the bodies of animals.

In the Colorado Mountains, a woman runs for her life, stalked by a sadistic killer.

In a world where the Patriot Act has come to fruition, a man struggles to survive, despite eroding liberties.

Not able to accept his wife's death, a widower will cross into the dream realm to find her again, despite the dark forces that hold her in thrall. These and other short stories will captivate and thrill you. These are short stories to die for.

REVOLUTION OF THE DEAD
by Anthony Giangregorio
THE DEAD SHALL RISE AGAIN!

Five years ago, a deadly plague wiped out 97% of the world's population, America suffering tragically. Bodies were everywhere, far too many to bury or burn. But then, through a miracle of medical science, a way is found to reanimate the dead.

With the manpower of the United States depleted, and the remaining survivors not wanting to give up their internet and fast food restaurants, the undead are conscripted as slave labor.

Now they cut the grass, pick up the trash, and walk the dogs of the surviving humans.

But whether alive or dead, no race wants to be controlled, and sooner or later the dead will fight back, wanting the freedom they enjoyed in life.

The revolution has begun!

And when it's over, the dead will rule the land, and the remaining humans will become the slaves...or worse.

KINGDOM OF THE DEAD
by Anthony Giangregorio
THE DEAD HAVE RISEN!

In the dead city of Pittsburgh, two small enclaves struggle to survive, eking out an existence of hand to mouth.

But instead of working together, both groups battle for the last remaining fuel and supplies of a city filled with the living dead.

Six months after the initial outbreak, a lone helicopter arrives bearing two more survivors and a newborn baby. One enclave welcomes them, while the other schemes to steal their helicopter and escape the decaying city.

With no police, fire, or social services existing, the two will battle for dominance in the steel city of the walking dead. But when the dust settles, the question is: will the remaining humans be the winners, or the losers?

When the dead walk, the line between Heaven and Hell is so twisted and bent there is no line at all.

RISE OF THE DEAD
by Anthony Giangregorio
DEATH IS ONLY THE BEGINNING!

In less than forty-eight hours, more than half the globe was infected.

In another forty-eight, the rest would be enveloped.

The reason?

A science experiment gone horribly wrong which enabled the dead to walk, their flesh rotting on their bones even as they seek human prey.

Jeremy was an ordinary nineteen year old slacker. He partied too much and had done poorly in high school. After a night of drinking and drugs, he awoke to find the world a very different place from the one he'd left the night before.

The dead were walking and feeding on the living, and as Jeremy stepped out into a world gone mad, the dead spotting him alone and unarmed in the middle of the street, he had to wonder if he would live long enough to see his twentieth birthday.

ANOTHER EXCITING CHAPTER IN THE DEADWATER SERIES!

DEAD UNION
BOOK 6
by Anthony Giangregorio
BRAVE NEW WORLD

More than a year has passed since the world died not with a bang, but with a moan.

Where sprawling cities once stood, now only the dead inhabit the hollow walls of a shattered civilization; a mockery of lives once led.

But there are still survivors in this barren world, all slowly struggling to take back what was stripped from their birthright; the promise of a world free of the undead.

Fortified towns have shunned the outside world, becoming massive fortresses in their own right. These refugees of a world torn asunder are once again trying to carve out a new piece of the earth, or hold onto what little they already possess.

HOSTAGES

Henry Watson and his warrior survivalists are conscripted by a mad colonel, one of the last military leaders still functioning in the decimated United States. The colonel has settled in Fort Knox, and from there plans to rule the world with his slave army of lost souls and the last remaining soldiers of a defunct army.

But first he must take back America and mold it in his own image; and he will crush all who oppose him, including the new recruits of Henry and crew.

The battle lines are drawn with the fate of America at stake, and this time, the outcome may be unsure.

In a world where the dead walk, even the grave isn't safe.

ANOTHER EXCITING CHAPTER IN THE DEADWATER SERIES!
BOOK 2

DEADRAIN
by Anthony Giangregorio

Welcome to the New America, population: 0

When a bacterial outbreak contaminates America's lower atmosphere, the resulting rain mutates into a deadly conduit for death.

Human's all over America are exposed and within a matter of days society has crumbled and the walking dead rule the land.

The America we know is gone, replaced by a new order; where the dead walk and humans are the prey.

Henry Watson and his small group of companions travel the country, searching for someplace better, someplace where the rain is safe.

In the New America the rules have changed; survive or perish.

THE PLACE TO GO FOR ZOMBIE AND APOCALYPTIC FICTION

LIVING DEAD PRESS

WHERE THE DEAD WALK

www.livingdeadpress.com

www.ingramcontent.com/pod-product-compliance
Lightning Source LLC
Chambersburg PA
CBHW070630170726
48291CB00003B/953